Copyright James Martin 2015. All characters included are fictional, and their similiarity to any persons living or dead is purely coincidental. Kinda.

Prologue.

The clock struck midnight, and I turned thirty.

DING. That's it.

DONG. Goodbye youth.

DING. Farewell dreams

DONG. Adios, aspirations.

This is the time by which one is supposed to have put aside childish things and become a man. Understand endowment mortgages. Know what an exhaust manifold is. Play squash, cook lasagne, all that kind of stuff.

The biggy. The dreaded Three – Oh. The way I'd always looked at it, whatever you were going to do – write the book, make the album, build the cathedral - if you were going to do it, then you would have done it by this point in life. And if you haven't, well then, *tough shit pal. Reality calling – we're here for your youth. And while we're at it, we'll take those hopes and dreams. Playtime's over.*

Hmm. My fourth decade on this planet began with me reluctantly and groggily returning to consciousness on a bleak, grey January morning underneath my best friend's coffee table amongst a carpet of Rizla papers, dog ends and pizza crusts with a frankly breathtaking hangover. Truly, this was one for the record books. Not the most auspicious start, I think you'd agree.

The sofa hove fuzzily into view, an uncovered old duvet thrown haphazardly across it. Yep, pretty certain that was where I'd intended to spend the night. Above me, cheap IKEA faux beech laminate, cobwebs and dust formed a backdrop for me to project images of the previous nights indulgences onto.. Pub. Second pub, with a band. Then back here to Chris's. Bottles- many, *many* bottles- contents indeterminate. Pizza. And, judging by the splodgy thing my elbow had found, quite possibly a kebab.

As my system gradually and painfully rebooted itself, I began to take stock of my situation and prioritise. My head throbbed with a pulsating mambo performed by the very devil himself and my tongue felt the size, shape and texture of a loofah. I needed water- I needed lots of it, and I needed it NOW. Shaking some life into limbs made sluggish by God-alone-knows what alcoholic concoctions from the night before, I fought my way through the chaos of Chris's living room carpet and out into the harsh cold light of day.

Pint glass. Greasy, but sod it, this isn't the Ritz and I'm not exactly in the mood to be picky. Cold water from the tap- in the glass, on my hands, splashed on my face. Jesus, that's better. Now upstairs to the bathroom- a lengthy, steaming dark amber urination and another blast of cold water to the face brought me back to some level of coherence. I grabbed a frayed and threadbare (but thankfully stain-free) towel to wipe my face, looked up and caught sight of myself in the mirror.

Christ, man, you've got bacon in your hair. Come on.

I picked out the offending morsel – resisted the urge to eat it, you'll be glad to hear - knocked back the water left in the glass and poured some more, ruefully eyeing my own reflection. My smeary, gunk-spattered self looked mockingly back at me.

Look at the state of you, for Christ's sake. Is this really what you want to be? You're THIRTY YEARS OLD. Your dad had a career, a wife and you by this time.

All the things you said you were going to do by now... "Now" always seemed so distant. There was always more time. Always. Until today.

What have you actually accomplished? What have you actually DONE?

Where the hell did the time go?

Happy fucking birthday.

My name is Dan Wyman, and this is the story of the year when everything – and I do mean EVERYTHING – changed.

Chapter 1

Ah, welcome. You join me in the pub. Specifically, the Red Lion, just off Highgate Way - in the corner, down near the jukebox, away from the cheering masses hunkered around the widescreen.. Can you see us? We're waving... yeah, there we are - about a month after the big day. Pull up a chair, there's plenty of room at the table. Allow me to effect introductions – To my left, Miles, the guv'nor. He runs the shop that provides me with at least a degree of employment and remuneration. No mean feat, really, in this day and age.

Our place is a small, independent record shop- the last of a dying breed. In a world of iTunes and downloads and streaming media, we stand alone- flying the flag for music in a physical form, be it on CD, vinyl or cassette. In fact I'm pretty certain that there are some wax cylinders and a gramophone gathering dust in the back somewhere.

Why do I work here? Well, it's a job. Pays the rent, pays the bills- just. I made the mistake of going to university to do Media Studies along with (as I would later discover) basically every single other student of my generation, and during the holidays I wound up working there part time. As the comfy warm security blanket of university slipped way and revealed a bleak wintry Real Life that was *not* after all going to shower me with offers of jobs in journalism, media, design or indeed anything more creative than flipping burgers and data entry, part time became full time and routine settled in.

To be honest, it's not a bad old place to be- no uniform, no nametag obliging me to be "Happy To Help", little to none in the way of office politics and best of all I work in an environment where my Mastermind specialist subject of Useless Pop Music Trivia actually counts as a professional skill instead of the social equivalent of leprosy.

Not to mention one or two fringe benefits- having persuaded Miles (albeit with some difficulty) that the internet is *not* a passing fad that will disappear by being ignored and every reference made to it frowned at, I set us up a website which is now where most of our business comes from. Result, we actually do better than you might think and I get the natty title of Internet Sales Manager which I can occasionally use to fool other people (read- parents) into thinking I'm at least vaguely successful, plus a PC and broadband paid for by the boss. Gawd bless you, guv'nor.

Moving round the table, my co-worker and best mate of many years, Chris. Chris is one of those strange people for whom time seems to stand completely still- as life takes its toll on all of us, as fashions change, empires rise and fall, he stands unchanging. A constant, fixed reference point in space and time – very comforting in his own way.

Not that I'd ever call him that, of course. Like best mates the world over, we mostly call each other cunts.

We met during those balmy purposeless summer days between A-levels finishing and university starting, when for the first time you're off the education treadmill and life hasn't yet started trying to bludgeon you into submission with it's routine of bills, work and commuting, and I was trying to complete my collection of Smiths and Joy Division records (the must-have accessory for any skinny indie-themed student stereotype). After a few Saturday afternoons in the shop and subsequent evenings in the pub debating the relative merits of "The Queen

Is Dead" versus "Strangeways Here We Come" Chris suggested I come in as a spare pair of hands on a Saturday. Miles acquiesced when he realised this would mean that Chris would have somebody else to talk to/ at and might therefore let him drink tea in peace, and take care of the various grown up activities like doing the books and... whatever else it is that bosses do, I don't know, I only work here.

We also, despite our combined remarkable lack of musical talent, at some point got the idea to form a band. At present, it's just the two of us, but by my reckoning we've had about two dozen drummers, bass players, keyboardists, violinists, flautists, cellists and god-knows-what-else-ists through the ranks over the years. For reasons long lost in the mists of ancient history, we called ourselves The Formidable Ale Society, and the name has sort of stuck.

That was nine years ago, and aside from us embracing the World Wide Web with varying levels of enthusiasm, surprisingly little has changed over the time. We're just all slightly fatter, slightly saggier, and in Miles' case, slightly balder.

Oh, and there's Louise, of course. The Brunette Bombshell. Can't forget her. She's not here right now, but you'll meet her soon enough and it's only right I bring you up to speed on a few things.

Louise is... well, it's kind of easier to say what she's not. She's *not* my girlfriend. Not right *now*, anyway. In fact, her last words to me suggested I perform an act upon myself with a wine bottle so physiologically impossible it makes me wonder if she learned anything from those Grey's Anatomy episodes she made me spend the last month watching with her. She does still have a lot of her stuff in my flat though- shoes, a bewildering variety of moisturisers, conditioners and lotions all laced with herbal this and citrus that. And I've noticed one or two cushions and stuffed toys cropping up in various corners where I'm sure there were never any before.

To be honest, it's kind of hard to say exactly what we are – like celestial bodies caught in each other's gravitational pull, we've sort of been orbiting each other for years.. but it seems whenever we get too close we wind up striking sparks off each other.

Arguments. Arguments about every damn thing imaginable and then some. The last one - a week or so back - was about coasters, believe it or not. Yes, I'm serious- those little things you put under coffee cups and wine glasses.

Picture the scene – my flat, living room, sofa, TV and DVD all poised and ready, just the two of us... I do believe I'd even lit a candle. Vanilla scented, no less. Oh yes, all stops pulled out – Dan Wyman set to LOVECON 1, a sexual python coiled and ready to strike...

"Why don't you get some coasters to put those on" said she, all beguiling smile, twinkling eyes and innocence as I set wine bottles (white for her, red for me) and glasses down on the coffee table.

"Nah, it's fine, it's enamel, I can just wipe it", I said. (Stay with me, I am going somewhere with this)

"Yeah, but if you had coasters you could get a nice wooden one like I saw in.. *insert magazine title or TV program name here as I've quite forgotten what it was*"

"Why would I want to do that?"

"Oh, right, why would you want to do that? Because it's something *I* suggested.. typical, you never listen to what I want do you? It's all about you, you, you, you're so bloody *selfish*..."

And we're off. To be fair, I usually give any evening that includes Louise and wine at least a 10% chance of erupting in a mushroom cloud of volcanic rage about *something*, and it's been a while so we were probably due. Occasionally she can be deflected- on one memorable evening after a meal out gone spectacularly wrong, she paused having vented an industrial-sized quantity of spleen on me, and asked me if I had anything to say. Unfortunately I was a) slightly drunk, b) full of curry and c) hadn't really been listening, so all I could do was fart. And it was a *belter* - oily, greasy and resonant.

In spite of herself (and probably helped by the two bottles of Chardonnay sloshing around her system), Louise promptly had a massive attack of the giggles which rather defused the situation, leading to the evening concluding with some frankly *startling* sex and probably pushing our inevitable break up back by about a month.

No such luck this time around. Invective is hurled, doors are slammed, and off she storms into the night, back off round to her mum's.

Well, that's that then. Again.

On the plus side, still got the wine. Oh, and *Aliens* is on in half an hour. Director's cut and everything. Every cloud.

So there you go. And for the last five or six years, this has been pretty much the way of things. After a while, you come to accept it as pretty much inevitable, kind of like the changing of the seasons or the tides of the sea.

Don't get me wrong, we like each other. We're very similar in a lot of ways- although she never quite got into *Thundercats* as much as I did as a kid, nor *Danger Mouse* and vodka as a student- and she's very pretty in her own way. Shoulder length dark hair, big brown eyes, and although she's no skin-and-bones size zero, you couldn't call her fat.

Not without getting punched, anyway.

But that's the problem- we like each other enough that every now and again we get tempted to turn it into something more, and after six months we're at each others throats again.

You'd think we'd have learned, really, but still..

Louise works at an estate agent's, in a proper grown up job with prospects and a pension and everything, but she's not without her own woes – for instance, she struggles heroically with her shoe addiction. Seriously, I've got about a dozen pairs here that I think she's just plain forgotten about. She buys things with designer labels on them, calls shopping a hobby and eats breakfast out (although still lives with her mum, which I suppose spoils the *Sex And The City* high-flying career girl image she's aiming for). No escaping the facts though - hers *is* a career, mine is a job. Inevitably, it will take her places- mine, for all that it's comfortable and quite fun in it's own way, probably never will. But that's okay- you play the cards as they're dealt and you make the best of things, that's just the way life is.

So, right now the pair of us are in a bit of a slump, and Chris has his own inimitable words of wisdom and comfort to offer.

"Well, if you two aren't at it like rabbits every bloody evening and weekend, maybe we can finally get the demo done."

"Yeah, appreciate the support there, mate, thanks."

"Oh, stop fucking crying into your beer. This is Louise, you two do this all the time. Look, just go round with a bunch of flowers, grovel a bit, and you'll be getting your end away in no time"

"Yeah, thanks, mate..." - this is one of the worst problems with breakups, be they temporary or permanent. It's people trying to help. Other people's problems always seem so much more easily quantifiable and therefore easily solvable than your own, so when yours do rise to the surface, all of a sudden you're having to wade through a sea of (mostly) well-meaning drivel from people eager to proffer their wisdom in your direction.

"Look, sooner or later either you *will* go round, most likely grovelling with your dick in your hand, or she'll wind up back at yours flat on her back and pissed out of her head. It's what *happens*. It's what *always* happens."

The irritating thing is though, he's absolutely right.

"Well, look, maybe this time I want to break this pattern- you know, we keep coming together and then falling apart, maybe it's time to break the cycle, step back a little bit and look at things differently, you know?" I said- a touch defensively, if I'm honest.

"Hit the pause button for a little while?"

"Yeah, let the dust settle and think things over."

"Well, in that case, let's get this bloody recording done. I'll bring the beers, you get the pizza and set the kit up".

Miles grinned from his side of the table - "So you two are going to knock together the next *Sergeant Pepper,* then?"

"No, why d'you think so small? We've got a whole Saturday night and Sunday- think Hendrix and *Electric Ladyland*, mate, think *Led Zeppelin IV*- our Daniel here has been wrapping his fingers round some *nasty* guitar licks now Louise has dumped him again". Ever the sensitive one, dear old Chris.

"Playing the blues because your woman gone done you wrong?" - Miles getting in on the act with his best Morgan Freeman impression.

Chris started beating out a slow shuffle rhythm on the table with the palm of his hand - duh DUH duh duh, duh DUH duh duh.

"Woke up this morning"

"Dog pissed in my shoes" intoned Miles, joining in.

"My woman done left me, I got the Dan Wyman blues"

- fuck it, if you can't beat them, join them -

"Don't got nuthin' but whiskey, wine, women and song"

"No, fool, she dumped you, you got that last bit wrong" chimed Chris in perfect time.

"I believe I'll take my leave, gentleman, as I need to have a pee" - Miles made to stand

"Well, I believe it's your round, guv'nor, so we'll have another three" - Chris waved his pint glass in the air. Miles smiled and nodded assent, getting up and heading toward the gents as the rhythm clattered to a halt.

Chris turned to me. "Seriously though mate, are you ok?"

"I don't know – yes and no, I guess" - decisive as ever there, Daniel - "I mean, it's not like this hasn't happened before-"

"True *dat*, homeboy"

"- thanks- but maybe that's the thing, you know? It's happened *so many* bloody times before. Like you said, it's what always happens... there's got to be a way to break the cycle."

Chris turned on his serious face.

"Do you really *want* to break the cycle?"

"What do you mean?"

"I'm going to come right out and say this, me old mucker – there are other women than Louise. I've known you - " he paused, attempting some advanced mathematics in his head "-well, a fucking long time, and apart from that space case from the chemists and the redhead catastrophe who used to work behind the bar here, it's just been her. You two may as well be married."

"So what are you saying to me?"

"I'm saying, broaden your horizons. Look elsewhere. If you genuinely want to change things, then *change* them, don't just sit on your arse and whine about it. Either that or go back to Louise with a bunch of flowers in one hand, your cock in the other, buy the fucking coffee table or whatever the hell else it was she wanted and kick things up a gear. Otherwise I predict business as usual and we'll be here having this same conversation again come-" he checked his watch "- July, I reckon."

He paused to lob the final dregs of beer down his throat.

"Meantime- weekend. What's the plan, Dan?"

"Knock off at half five, cashed up and done by six... I programmed the drum loops the other night so all we need to do is the guitars, sort the bassline and add the vocals. If you get over to mine by about half 7, we'll be good to go, I've got a couple of pizzas in the freezer and a shitload of coffee, so if you take care of the booze we're sorted."

"Splendid"

Miles appeared with three fresh pints of foaming

fermented goodness. Chris took his glass and held it aloft - "To rock 'n' roll!"

"To rock 'n' roll!"

"Rock 'n' roll"

We clinked glasses, a sticky puddle of overspill forming on the table waiting to ensnare an innocent elbow.

At that moment, an idea occurred to him and I saw concern flash across his face as he turned to me.

"We *are* going to have a break for *Hollyoaks*, though, right?

Chapter 2

Saturday night. Interior shot, my flat. The camera pans around to show a TV flickering on mute, a pair of empty pizza boxes resting on an enamel coffee table (free of drink rings- HAHA, I *WIN!!*). A growing pile of empty Carling cans forms a backdrop to the two guitar wielding drunks slurring at each other.

"Sounds alright, that"

"Sounds alright like your arse. Let's do it again"

"Let me just have a go at that middle bit first"

"Dude, we wrote this song eight fucking years ago, if you don't know it by now.."

"I do know it, just let me do this one bit.."

"Seriously, mess this up and I will absolutely *piss in your eye socket*"

"Pull my finger"

To be honest, I've no idea which way round this particular conversation went, as it's more or less a carbon copy of a thousand conversations-altercations-arguments-fights that have preceded it.

"Look, let's just roll the tape and get a rough version down. We can still make the pub if we're quick and tidy it up tomorrow"

"Mate, there's a very strong possibility I'll be dead by tomorrow"

"Fuck that chorus up again and there's every bastard chance, my old friend"

A can of Carling is polished off, smacked flat against the forehead and flung in the general direction of the empty cardboard box.

"Right"- Chris punctuates this statement with a powerful and authoritative belch - "let's do this thing"

The mouse clicks, the long-suffering hard drive whirs into action, and The Formidable Ale Society take one step closer to..

...the pub, most likely.

The song that we're attempting to record is "Sunshine", a little three chord wonder written originally by Chris almost a decade ago and progressively evolved/ rearranged/ fucked around with by my good self. He does (and god *damn* him for it) have the knack of coming up with an annoyingly catchy tune every hundred years or so, but unfortunately being possibly the most clumsy, oafish, cack-handed *tool* ever to pick up a guitar in the whole history of popular music he's not exactly brilliant at doing them justice.

The last chord rings out, I click "Save" and we can content ourselves with the feeling that we've achieved something with the evening.

"Pub?"

"Pub"

It doesn't matter who said what.

An hour or so later. Exterior shot, close up on my door handle. I am stabbing the key repeatedly into the emulsion-painted wood.

"Shit, my door's broken"

Chris sizes up the situation - "Shtand ashide". He assumes an approximation of a *Karate Kid* pedal kick stance and falls into the hedge.

In the meantime, I have discovered my error and inserted my key into the bit of the door designed to have keys inserted into it.

Chris struggled to his feet. "See, told you I knew Kung Fu"

"Do you bollocks, you couldn't even spell it"

"Got your door open, didn't I?"

"That was the *key*"

"Course it was, mate, course it was... if the key was my ninja fists of fury. Hah! Hoom-cha!"

"Everybody was Kung-Fu Fighting.." we began warbling in flawless drunken disharmony.

We collapsed onto the sofa, feet up on the coffee table in perfect synchronicity. Chris felt around for his backpack and pulled out a syringe.

"I think it's that time of night"

Don't worry folks, nothing sinister here. No Class A's – Chris is diabetic, although that doesn't stop him drinking enough to quench the thirst of some ancient Dionysian god. I first encountered this particular quirk after a couple of weeks of knowing him - after a lengthy session in the Lion, we retired to Amal's Kebab Emporium next door to the shop for some essential post-pub nourishment. Chris passed out and started snoring midway through a chicken doner with extra chilli sauce, which I (ever the caring, good Samaritan) was in the middle of stealing when he suddenly erupted back into life, grabbed a needle out of his ever present backpack and plunged it into his rather ample belly, before settling back into the orange plastic chair with a beatific smile on his face.

Chris is 39. From what I understand about diabetes, he had no earthly business making it past 29. I'm pretty certain if you were to kill him, burn him, and chop him into a thousand pieces and fling those pieces to the far corners of the Earth (as, believe me, I have wanted to do *many many thousands of times),* they would gradually pull themselves together a la the bad guy from *Terminator 2* and reconstitute themselves into him, with a pint in one hand and a roll-up in the other.

If he makes 40, I'll owe him a tenner. I'm sure he's only hanging on to spite me.

Fast forward back to the present day, he pricked his

finger and pressed it to the all-singing, all-dancing blood sugar level gadget Miles and I got him a couple of birthdays back. "17.6 – time for a shot. Do me a favour and pass me a can, if we've got any left".

Happily, there were still a couple rolling around at the bottom of the multipack box. I plopped them on to the coffee table and took care of the critical business of opening while Chris took care of his insulin shot. He leant back, yawned, and ran his hands through his hair.

"Jesus, I'm bollocksed."

No argument from me there.

"Yeah, me too. I don't think we're going to get anything more done tonight. Want to have a listen back?"

"Yeah, but first"- Chris rootled around in his pack - "porn"

This is another slightly worrying habit of Chris', as well as possessing a vast (if largely mod-themed) vinyl collection, he has more than a passing interest in "adult art". I was more than slightly disconcerted when I first visited his flat and was invited to place my coffee mug not, as one might expect, on a coffee table - but on a stack of strategically placed VHS boxes, the topmost bearing the legend "Barely Legal Snatch Vol. 3".

"Oh, for the love of God, what have you got now?"

"Anal Corruption Volume 12"

"Oh, mate, you can't just drop me in at volume 12. I'll

never be able to pick up the narrative"

"Don't worry, old son, I can fill you in on the salient points"

He popped the disc in and the screen filled with some fairly lurid graphics.

"Basically he"- Chris waved a vague hand at the startlingly aged small balding lead man - "fucks all of them." waving the same hand at the parade of surgically enhanced, Botoxed leathery laydeez- "And I know what you're going to say, but it's not always in the places you might expect him too"

"What, so, like the library, or maybe Tescos?"

"Settle yourself down youngling, just sit back and enjoy"

"What's his motivation? Did one of them kill his father and then secretly turn out to *be* his father? Because I'm not lying mate, that's the kind of twist that would pull me in and keep me hooked."

Chris slurped some room temperature lager and considered the question. "It's going to be tough to explain – without seeing the first 11 volumes you haven't really got much of a frame of reference.."

"So what do you suggest?"

"Just relax and enjoy, old son, suspend your disbelief and let Long Dong Silver there entertain ya."

The rest of the night is, thankfully, a blur.

There is a vicious irony in waking up on your own sofa, in your own house, knowing that your own bed is but mere footsteps away, and this was an irony I encountered face to face at half past eight the following morning.

"Bastard!"

Briefly, I entertained the idea of fetching the biggest and sharpest knife from the kitchen, running upstairs and planting it squarely in the middle of my manipulative, drunken, pornography addicted, diabetic bed-stealing bastard of a best mate's forehead.. but then, of course, you've got to consider the paperwork. And it *would* mean washing the sheets.

Oh, sod it then. May as well get comfortable. I dozed intermittently, somewhere in between sleep and full consciousness, somewhat disrupted by a remarkably vivid dream about my phone ringing.

Which was explained about an hour later when I got up for a slash by my phone gurgling and blinking - "Missed call- voicemail".

I checked the number. Louise. No, I wasn't going to deal with this on a full bladder and *sans* caffeine. First things first. I headed upstairs, performed some cursory ablutions and started to feel vaguely human again, then checked in on Sleeping Bed-Stealing Fucking Bastard Beauty if only to make sure that he hadn't swallowed his tongue. The baritone, resonant, phlegmy cacophony of snoring that confronted me when I opened the door confirmed that against all medical logic, sense and reason Chris was still, *still,* alive and well. I decided against actual murder or bodily harm and settled for enhancing his forehead with a quick doodle before heading back down to the kitchen.

I grabbed a mug from the washing up bowl, gave it a cursory rinse and dumped a couple of spoonfuls of the finest own-brand instant coffee that not-much-money can buy, and as the kettle boiled I mulled over what I was likely to encounter in Louise's message.

If she just wanted to call me a cunt, I reasoned, *she would just have texted that to me.* Precedent was definitely on my side on this one. Same went for if she wanted to arrange picking up her stuff- I had a couple of boxes in the wardrobe labelled "Louise" for just this eventuality.

She *might* be calling to apologise, tell me how sorry she is, how wrong she was to have a go at me and storm out, and to tearfully beg forgiveness – in a way, that's the most terrifying option of all- but no, she only does that when she's VERY drunk, and it's rare (although not unknown) for that to be the case at half eight in the morning.

So that must mean she wants to talk. Well, that's not necessarily a bad thing, I mused- recalling the other night's conversation with Chris and Miles in the Lion. Maybe she wants to break the cycle too, maybe she's been having the same thoughts as I have.

I dialled voicemail, which helpfully informed me that I was called February 2nd (today) at 8.43am (which I knew full well, I had been snoozing at the time mere feet away), whilst all the while billing me for the trouble.

She began by sighing. Oh, this was never going to signify good news.

"Hi, Dan... it's Louise. Look, I think. *(second sigh)*.... I think we need to talk.. Do you want to go and grab a coffee somewhere? There's some things we need to discuss."

Click. Buzz. *"To hear the message again, press 1"*

Alright, so this is an interesting turn of events. I couldn't help but smile a little at the phrasing though- "go and grab a coffee"? This illustrates a crucial difference between Louise and I- when Louise wants a coffee, she goes to Starbucks. When I want one, I go into my kitchen.

Technically speaking though, I had plans for the day. The Formidable Ale Society still had a record to produce – 48 cans of Carling had *not* been sacrificed in vain. The battered, tea- stained PC thrummed into life and went through it's pre- flight checks while I slurped coffee and wondered if there was a ever a situation in the whole sphere of human history where the phrase "we need to talk" had signified anything good. Especially when it was accompanied by not one, but *two* sighs.

Well, one thing at a time. First, to review the fruits of last nights labours now the alcohol was largely removed from my bloodstream. I clicked the Play icon, and prepared to be disappointed.

Surprisingly though – not half bad. A little hit and miss in places – Chris being blessed with the knack of being able to make any guitar a quarter tone out of tune meant that I was going to have to sneakily wipe his rhythm part and redo it myself- but for the most part, a pretty accomplished effort. In fact, so good, I thought I'd have another listen.

"*You don't bring me sunshine anymore...*" I found myself humming the irritatingly catchy refrain while clearing away some of last night's wreckage. A loud and resounding belch told me I was no longer alone, as what appeared to be Chris' reanimated corpse shambled it's way into the living room.

He cocked an ear toward the speakers. "Who're these cunts then?"

"No idea mate, some pair of tramps"

"Catchy tune though. Shame that guitarist can't play for shit."

"Oh, my old friend. You know what I like about you?"

"What?"

"Fuck all. Want a coffee?"

"Yeah, cheers. How'd you sleep?"

I glared at him. Shameless bastard.

"Fitful, cold, shivering... In fact some wolves came by and molested me."

Chris got slightly defensive.

"Ah, well, if you will fall asleep during the latest adult art instalment, what do you expect? You looked so pretty, it seemed a shame to wake you"

"I've drawn a penis on you"

"Splendid, splendid, always good to have a spare". Chris nodded towards the PC - "What do you reckon then, is she a keeper?"

I busied myself in the kitchen with the vital task of caffeine. "Yeah, I reckon we might have cracked it this time. We should take note of *exactly* how drunk we were- it's obvious we'd hit just the right level, not too nervous and stiff, not too slapdash and sloppy"

"The microphone didn't pick up the fart I did? That fucker was pretty sloppy."

"No mate, no, sorry to say that one's lost to posterity."

I came back in with two steaming hot mugs of dark brown goodness.
"I've put four hundred and twelve sugars in yours, is that enough to finally kill you?"

"Should be-" Chris pulled out his gadget and went through the blood sugar rigmarole - "7.2... Yeah, pass her over. And a Crème Egg too, if you've got one"

"Breakfast of champions"

"Oh yes."

We slumped back onto the sofa.

"So what now?"

"Well, I'm going to double up the backing vocals, redo your sloppy arse-about-face rhythm guitar and then it should be ready to go"

"Anything from Louise?"

"Yeah, she left me a message- wants to meet up, talk things over"

"Fair enough, probably not a bad idea. You reckon she's been thinking the same things as you?"

"It's possible. To be honest, I've been trying to avoid thinking about it".

This was true. Louise could be lovely when she wanted to be, but she also represented an emotional Gordian knot of hideous complexity, and I was in no state to try and untangle it at the moment.

"Well, old son, think about you must, unless all this 'making a change' and 'breaking the cycle' stuff was just your regular load of bollocks" - Chris slipped a sweetener into his coffee - "don't get me wrong, I like the old girl, but if you two can't get it together after what, five years? Six? Maybe there's a reason for that."

He's right. I fucking *hate* it when that happens.

"So that being the case, unless you need me for anything more on our masterwork"- he nods towards the PC, "I shall finish this most excellent coffee, befoul your toilet and toddle off home to let you think things through. Give us a shout later and let me know how it goes"

"Will do mate"

He stretches, belches and heads towards the door before hesitating -

"You were going to wash those sheets anyway, right?"

Chapter 3

An hour or so later, the flat is clean (well, *ish*), the washing up is done, a shower has brought me back to something resembling humanity and I really can't put this off any longer. I reached for the phone. Deep breath. Here we go again.

"Hi"

"Hiya. You alright?"

It's always odd hearing her voice after a couple of weeks off. The fact that the last time I heard it it was several hundred decibels louder and busily engaged in calling me a bastard probably has something do with that.

"Yeah, you know, ticking over.. So.. you said we had some things to discuss?"

"Yeah- look, I'm just out with my mum right now, you want to get some lunch and talk things over?"

I quickly checked my wallet. Yep, there was some proper paper money in there along with the jangling chorus of loose change – should be enough to cover things.

"Yeah, sure. Lion, about an hour?"

"OK, sure. See you in a bit"

"Yeah, see you"

Well, that could have gone plenty worse. Right, time to sit down, focus, and work out exactly what to do about this...

...or just quickly check my emails....

...or just quickly look up a couple of BBC articles..

..or just quickly look on Ebay or the shop's site, see if we've sold anything..

..or just quickly FUCKING ANYTHING because thinking too hard about the Louise Situation can often elicit the same emotional response as hearing an air raid siren go off.

With one eye on the clock, I opened up my emails and perused them, telling myself that really, this was me putting overtime and helping to spin the wheels of commerce, showing initiative and all that other good stuff.

Spam, spam, spam... with my inbox resembling Monty Python's finest hour, I deleted my way through the plethora of offers from Nigerian royalty and can't-miss offers on Viagra and Cialis (always with the lurking fear that maybe they know something I don't..)

Hang on a mo...

From: Kate Gardner – Subject: Hi Dan, Long Time No See!

Bloody hell.... no, couldn't be, surely?

Kate Gardner. *The* Kate Gardner.

What, have I not mentioned her? Well, let's press pause once again – put your feet up, get yourself comfortable and I shall tell you a tale.

Kate Gardner was the Year 9 siren of Vale Mount High School, back when I was but a waify young thing of 13 or 14. Everyone, *everyone*, fancied her rotten, myself included. Of course, I was never going to have a shot – the laws of high school status dictated that the really pretty girls would never be seen dead going out with someone from their own year or (God forbid) younger, and sure enough Kate was hooked up with some rugby playing giant from the year above who, judging from his towering height and bulk, had probably entered puberty aged 8 and spent the intervening years slinging steroids down his throat like they were Monster Munch.

My early teenage self had spent many a maudlin evening moping over her unattainability, replaying old Nirvana tracks over and over again because no one but Kurt Cobain could ever possibly have understood the emotional torment I was in – because in the entire history of the human race, no other teenage boy had ever had a crush on a girl who didn't fancy him back. In a roundabout way that experience had led to my lifelong involvement and interest – some (Louise amongst them) would say obsession - with music. Certainly, my first experience with a guitar had involved painstakingly and ploddingly plucking out the riff to "Come As You Are" which had gradually mutated into a hideously embarrassing attempt at songwriting dedicated to her called "If I Had A Car". Thankfully I'd had the good sense to keep that little gem to myself and it had never left the sanctity of my bedroom, mournfully strumming it and mumbling the lyrics to myself.

She'd actually wound up as my science partner on more than one occasion and proven herself to be pretty tedious company, but teenage me hadn't been about to let the reality of Kate impinge upon the *ideal* of her and the mooning over her continued until we left to do GCSEs at different schools.. whereupon I promptly found somebody else to have an unrequited crush on.

We probably never exchanged more than a few dozen words on the occasions we were in each other's company, but it's a sobering thought to realise that a large part of your personality, of *who you are*, was formed in reaction to a girl who barely seemed to register you as a human being.

So it's a bit bloody odd, frankly, when said girl messages you out of the blue after 16 years.

Still, I had half an hour to kill before I met Louise and as Lord alone knew what might be going to happen there, I thought I may as well sate my curiosity and see what she's got to say for herself.

Hi Dan – wow, this feels awkward even typing it! - don't know if you remember me but we were at Vale Mount together years back. We were lab partners a few times – do you remember when we lit the periodic table wall chart on fire that time? - Jesus, yes, I'd forgotten about that, that little incident with an over-enthusiastic Bunsen burner had bought me the bollocking of a lifetime and a week in detention – *And I saw your band play the sports hall at the end of term* – I'd tried pretty hard to forget that débâcle as well, a hoped-for *Breakfast Club-s*tyle style moment of geek-turned-hero triumph that in reality had turned into a mess of feedback, broken guitar strings, and a hideously out of tune singer who - after spending the three weeks of rehearsals suffocating the rest of us with his carefully honed faux Ian Brown/ Liam Gallagher style arrogance - was struck dumb with stage fright as soon as the curtain came up.

Just wondered how you were and what you were up to – we moved house recently and I found a load of old school photos, got me thinking, and then I found you on the internet at the record shop.

Drop me a line if you fancy meeting up for a coffee, now I'm back in the area it'd be nice to see you again.

Kate xox

Well, blow me down with a feather, roll me over a barrel and then fuck me sideways violently with a rusty railing. Exhaling, eyebrows practically disappearing into my hairline with surprise, I slumped back into my chair. Jesus, *that* I was not expecting.

So.. what to do next? Well, the obvious thing would be to respond, arrange to go for a coffee and then... well, and then most likely nothing. She was a notorious flake back then- forgiven her every sin by her simpering entourage of idolising gawping orbiters (of which I'd been a leading member, naturally) – the odds were she'd still be a complete flake now. We'd make a date and then at the last moment she'd text with some sort of flimsy excuse and presumably never hear from each other again.

There again... maybe I should just hit delete and forget the whole thing. I mean, when the girl who... well, for want of a better and less dramatic way of putting it, *broke your heart* sixteen years ago shows up out of the blue, you sort of what to present yourself as something of a success, don't you? Have the satisfaction of saying "yep, dahlin, look at what you passed up" while nonchalantly dropping the keys to your E-type Jag and swanky Mayfair apartment - and having your manservant hurry over to pick them up for you, put them back in your designer gold-plated trousers while you whip out your triple platinum American Express, pick up the tab for coffee and then buy the entire restaurant on a whim before flashing your chiselled washboard abs, turning on your heel and stalking out.

I looked around my little flat. Second hand dusty furniture, ancient faux wood panelled TV in the corner. Tiny kitchen overflowing with washing up. A couple of guitars piled up in the corner, along with a stereo system that may have been state of the art - in 1994. A few books and magazine strewn about the place. CDs, cassettes and records *everywhere.*

Not the habitat of the ultra-successful young professional replete with purpose, achievement, drive, all that other good stuff. Not the habitat of most thirty year old grown men who have their shit even *remotely* together, if we're being brutally honest.

I heard a sigh, and realised that it came from me. Come the fuck on man, get it together. Back to the present, we have a job to do. In fact – shit, is that the time? Right, I'd better get going.

Before I powered down the computer, I typed a quick reply - "*Hi Kate- yeah, that was a surprise! Nice to hear from you again, coffee sounds great, we'll sort something out. Take care, Dan*"

...aaaaaaaand "Send".

Nice and inoffensive - and crucially *non-committal*. And I'm out the door, pulling my jacket on with my keys on my mouth, off to meet Louise and sort this whole situation out once and for all – or not, as the case was much more likely to be.

And that was my mistake, you see. If I'd just clicked "Delete" and left it at that, then maybe none of the events that followed would have happened.

But, of course, I didn't. And so they did.

Chapter 4

The Red Lion is a different place in the daylight hours. Sunlight, or some vague approximation thereof, sidles in through the cracks in the blinds and gaps in the drapes playing across motes of dust floating in the still air. Bill, the resident toothless drunk, is still able to form vaguely coherent sentences. There are different bar staff, ones who haven't witnessed me attempting to write my own name in urine (*usually* my own) in the car park or had to physically restrain me from pissing in the kitchen sink after I got lost trying to find my way into the gents.

I mean, you just wouldn't recognise the place.

Happily, though, they do cook up a mean burger, and right now that's exactly what my system was craving as I wrapped myself around a pint of cider whilst I waited for Her Ladyship to arrive.

She gets five more minutes, I thought to myself, *and then it's the Double-Scream-Bacon-Super-Mega-Whopper-Cheeseburger with extra onion rings and the rest of the world can go fuck itself*

A shadow fell across the table. I looked up, and there she was – my nemesis.

Looking rather fetching, it had to be said- dark hair falling about her shoulders, scarf wrapped loosely around her neck, something shimmery and low cut floating down to form fitted jeans and those furry suede boot things. Louise has always had the knack of looking... I don't know how best to put it – *expensive*. Whereas I have the knack of looking like I'm being given away free with this month's copy of The Big Issue.

"Hey you"

"Hi"

I stood to greet her and was rewarded with a hug and a peck on the cheek. Okay, so that's how we're playing this. Not going to protest too much.

"You want a drink?" I offered.

"No, it's okay, I'll get these. You want another?" she asked, indicating vaguely towards my cider.

"I'm okay for the moment, cheers".

She wandered over to the bar and came back with a couple of menus and something fruity with an umbrella in it. *Alright, let's see where this is going, then.*

"So how've you been?" she asked.

"Ah, you know, so so. Keeping busy." *Keep it neutral for now, let's hear what she has to say,* I thought. "How about you, how's work?"

"Bit tough at the minute. They've laid a couple off. You remember I told you about Kathy?"

"Yeah, I think so" - getting Louise onto talking about

work was something of a double-edged sword, as whilst it always seemed to relax her, got her chatty and helped break the ice, she did have a tendency to go into detail about her office politics and forget that I'd never, in all the time we'd known each other, actually met any of her workmates.

"Well, you know her and Paul were getting married - ", this rang a vague bell, something about dresses and rings and tantrums, "- and then she found out he'd been having this fling with a girl he met while he was out clubbing with his mates from work, but now the venues all booked and everything, she'd picked out a dress - her dad's spent thousands on it, so she just doesn't know what to do about it all..."

"Uh-huh" I slurped cider and tried to radiate concern for this woman I'd never met and knew next to nothing about.

"And I think maybe that was why I was a bit stressed and emotional the other night.."

I tried to work this one out. Shook my head. No, sorry - does not compute.

"Sorry, so, let me try and get this straight – you went off on one at me about a coffee table because your mate's fiancé cheated on her? I mean, you can see why I might not immediately make the connection, right?"

"Well, it's just you know that's always been one of my hangups, and-"

No. Nuh-uh. No deal. For all my faults- and, yes, there are many - I've always been a one-woman guy. To be honest, yes, I messed around a little (although less than I would have liked) at university. But as I've got older, polygamy has progressively lost its appeal – although I've known a few guys who would brag about having three or four girls on the go, to me that seems like absolute purgatory. I mean, moral considerations aside - Christ, I can barely cope with Louise on her own, trying to duplicate that experience seems like a one way ticket to hell.

And she *knows* that, she knows full well. So I'm not buying this one.

"-and what, because Paul cheated on Kathy, I'm obviously going to cheat on you? Because there's precedent for that, isn't there? Oh, wait, no, that's right- there's absolutely no fucking precedent for it. No, Louise, no – pull the other one, it's got *fucking* sleigh bells on it".

She seemed a bit taken aback by that outburst- to be fair, I was as well. Maybe it was the cider reigniting the residual alcohol in my bloodstream from last night, maybe this was me starting to follow through on my decision to try and break the cycle, but for whatever reason today I wasn't inclined to sit and trot out the usual platitudes.

"Well, no, I know- I just thought it was such a shitty thing to do-"

Yes, yes it was. Shitty, and *incredibly* stupid. Given Louise's description of Kathy turning into a ferocious Bridezilla over the past couple of months, it would have made far more sense for Paul to catch the next flight to Nepal, shave his head and enter the most isolated, far-flung Buddhist monastery he could find. *That*, I could have understood.

Filling himself full of WKD and grabbing the nearest nineteen year old in a boob tube and miniskirt – no, frankly, as far as I was concerned the fucking idiot deserved exactly whatever the hell he got. The more so if his roving dick had given fuel to the flames of Louise's neuroses and helped caused me to get it in the neck over a case of domestic furnishings.

"-and it just got me so shaken up that men can do that."

"*Paul* did that. Paul's not men, he's one man. And from what you've told me, he's a complete fucking tool. You going to lump me in with that?"

"Look, I'm trying to say sorry here."

"Really? You are? What are you sorry for, Louise, what exactly? Starting an argument over fucking drinks coasters? Telling me yet again how much you hate me, telling me yet again that I'm a selfish prick who never listens? Sorry because you did the exact same fucking thing last summer when we went away for the weekend? Sorry because you did the same thing at the Christmas party before that?"

"Look, why are you being like this? You know me, it's just how I get sometimes-"

"No- no, I don't, I just, I can't do this any more. It's the same fucking cycle, over and over again. You can't just keep saying *oh that's just who I am, how I get*, you're fucking twenty eight. If you know – and you *do* know, you must- that you're doing something stupid, if you *know* you're being a bitch, then *just fucking stop doing it!*"

To be honest, I'd probably taken myself more by

surprise than her. I hadn't really planned that little tirade, but for all that- it actually felt pretty good.

I took a sip of my drink, sat back and looked her in the eye.

If looks could kill, at that moment I would have been skinned alive and buggered. Then nailed to a cross before being hung, drawn, quartered and set on fire.

"You know what, Dan, I came here to try and change things, I wanted to try and make things work between us for a change- but if that's your attitude then you can fuck right off. I'll be round for my stuff."

She stood - "Oh, and I stand by everything I said the other night. Except that this time I'm sober."

And she's gone.

And for a moment, all is quiet on the Wyman front.

I'll be honest with you, never been a big fan of rows and drama. That's probably why I'd quite genuinely startled myself with giving Louise both barrels. I hadn't meant to upset her, I really hadn't – for all the rows and drama, I really did care about her, but for fuck's sake, her mate's fiancé cheats on her and because of that I get it in the neck over a coffee table? Fuck that for a game of soldiers. Louise could be so lovely, sweet, kind and giving but her alter ego was a vicious, unaccountable, unreasoning bitch - and there comes a point where you just think, *fuck it, just give me a quiet life.*

That's it then, I told myself, staring dully into the cider, as a cold hollow feeling started to take over my insides, crushing my appetite. *No more Louise. After what, six years? Finally, over. Done.*

I felt a wave of sadness break over me - no, not sadness. Not regret, even. *Disappointment*. That summed things up better. Bitter, deep, soul-crushing disappointment that there was no way to work things through. That after all this time, it couldn't end any better than this.

And always the little voice in my head, the one who just loves the status quo, telling me I've just thrown away something fantastic, that my one chance of happiness has just grabbed her coat and stormed out of my life...

But no, there was nothing I'd said that wasn't true. And for fuck's sake, what was I supposed to do, walk on eggshells around her for the rest of my life because she couldn't control her impulses? Her need to lash out? Spend my life trying to placate her and apologising for imagined slights against her? No, fuck that. *Fuck that*. I'd rather be on my own.

This realisation sprang into my head fully formed and sat there for a few minutes while I examined it from every angle I could. Really? This was where the last few days had been leading me?

I felt the fog clearing. I didn't *have* to be with Louise. I didn't *have* to be with *anyone*. Mentally, I replayed some of our happiest times together – our weekend away in the Rutland countryside which was basically non-stop sex, her showing up at a rare Formidable Ale Society gig clad in knee length boots, a leather coat and underwear, the time strolling along the beach arms wrapped around each other feeling like everything was finally right with the world... every last one came with a price, every last was tainted with underlying worry of *when would the storm break*? When would she turn from the sweet, kind, funny girl into the shrieking vengeful she-demon that caused fights like the one from the other week, or like the one that ruined our last weekend away, or like that one that ruined the shop's Christmas booze-up...

Because it always happened. *Always*. Not if, but when. Every *single* time, without fail. I consoled myself with the though that although I may have lost her, I'd also lost all the conflict, the fights, the drama that she came with.

I might be alone, but I was free.

I drained the last of my cider. Fuck it, I think I will have that burger.

Chapter 5

"Fucking *seriously?*"

We are at work. Monday morning and reality has come around again with it's usual lack of consideration. Chris had made the fatal error of asking me how the meeting went, and I had made the fatal error of telling him.

Weekday mornings, Mondays especially, are usually pretty quiet, and this one was no exception. Chris was on counter duty, I was taking care of a couple of internet orders and Miles was out, doing whatever bosses do when they're not running their own shop.

"Yep. Didn't quite go the way I planned, I must admit, but.. I don't know, man, there's a bit of me that's almost relieved. Like the sword's finally dropped but I'm still standing, you know?"

Chris raised his eyebrows and exhaled, pushing himself up onto the counter giving him the appearance of a particularly mischievous garden gnome.

"Well, I've got to admit I'm a bit surprised, old son – I thought you two would patch things up again, if I'm honest"

"If I'm honest, I did too. But then, you know, you get to thinking, what's going to happen? We're going to ride off into the sunset on a white horse and live happily ever after? Or six moths down the line we'll be doing exactly the same thing, you know, right back to square fucking one again."

"Well, shit, I can't fault your logic, mate- nice to see you learning from precedent, I suppose".

He launched himself off the counter and propelled himself toward the kitchen. "You want caffeine?"

"Yeah, yeah – cheers. Never say no."

"So, do you think that's really it, then? No way back?"

"I don't know mate, I really don't, but like I said the other day, I can't just sit in this holding pattern forever... Do me a favour, while you're up, this guy wants to know what Stiff Little Fingers and Yardbirds we've got on vinyl."

"Bollocks off, what did your last slave die of?"

"Syphilis."

"Might want to wash your hands then" he grinned, making his way into the Neverland that lurked at the rear of the shop – an uncharted kingdom overflowing with carrier bags full of paperwork, loose CDs, cassettes, cases, empty milk cartons, used tea bags.... legend has it there's a fire exit back there, but in nine years I've never seen it. Lovely chap, Miles, but he never really got the hang of this "organising" business. I vividly remember, back in the early days when I was but a fresh-faced sorcerer's apprentice, coming upon an impressive pile of receipts and cash stacked both hither and thither about the toilet floor. I offered to gather it up, but Miles declined, telling me to leave it there because, and I quote, "I know where they are, when they're there".

There are moments when I get more than a little worried about the man I rely upon for my bread and butter.

I fumbled through the stacks of unsorted vinyl, trying to use the everyday tedium of work to blot out the memory of yesterday's summit gone wrong. No use though – I couldn't help myself mentally replaying every word, every inflection, every look, every gesture... no doubt about it, this time it really was *It*.

But still, I couldn't decide whether that was really a bad thing. For all the empty, slightly shaky feeling that would periodically creep up on me, catch me by surprise and leave me almost winded, there was a small flickering candle of relief that this was finally behind me and that I wasn't trapped, locked into a script any more.

In a sense, like I mentioned earlier - I really was free.

Free to do what, fuck alone knew, but I guessed I'd find out as I went along, right?

Aha. Stiff Little Fingers, *Inflammable Material,* Rough Trade Records 1979 – a few nicks and a slightly dog-eared cover, but basically pretty much mint condition. Cue one rather satisfied customer, I think. Yep, and top it off with a rather dusty but still definitely playable copy of *Over, Under, Sideways, Down* by the Yardbirds featuring the astonishing Jeff Beck on lead guitar – a personal hero of mine, whose demented genius on the guitar exactly mirrored my own, and even *Chris'*, clanging, cack-handed ineptitude.

Small successes like these kept me grounded through the day, and during the lulls I filled Chris in on the details of yesterday.

Chris exhaled slowly... "Well... sounds pretty final then. I guess you really have managed to break the cycle. You OK about it?"

"I- yeah, I kind of am, weirdly enough. I mean, there's a part of me that's going *what the fuck have you done, you tit, you've just let the love of your life walk out the door* – and then there's another little voice that keeps playing back all the rows, the drama.."

"Like my birthday"

"Like your birthday"- shit, yeah, almost forgotten that one. Chris's 35th a few years back- Louise and I hadn't been getting along too well for a week or so beforehand, and on the way into town an argument gained momentum to the point of becoming a full-blown row by the time we'd made it down to the pub where the party was being held. After delivering a particularly vicious salvo of abuse in my direction, she'd then decided to do her *Roadrunner* act – not a brilliant idea when in high heels – and plonked herself, sobbing, down on the car park wall a couple of hundred yards down. So of course, when I caught up with her, my first thoughts (after catching my breath and commending my soul to all manner of gods while so doing... yeah, I really could do with getting a little more in shape) were to try and calm her down, comfort her, talk to her...

So I spent the entirety of my best mate's 35th birthday, one that I'd spent ages organising, on a car park wall while Louise sobbed and called me a *bastard,* and a *fucking bastard,* and a *fucking cunting son of a whore.* Next morning, she's right as rain, didn't even mention it. Thanks honey, that's one more evening I'll never get back.

Closing time came, and I was so deep in thought I missed it – normally I had to be physically restrained from hurling myself over the counter to flip the sign and lock the door. Frankly, if I had my way, anyone who was still in the shop when it shut should be prepared to spend the night there.

"Swift half?" suggested Chris.

I pondered. "Nah- appreciate the thought but I reckon I could do with a quiet night. Do a little thinking, you know?"

"Sure? We can't have you getting all broody now.."

Bless him. For Chris, there is no problem that cannot be cured with the sufficient application of alcohol. He may be a one-trick pony, but he turns that trick with style.

"Yeah, mate, I'll be fine. See you tomorrow"

Twenty minutes later and I'm through my front door. Kettle on, cooker on, feet up.. oh, that's better.

You know you're leaving your youth behind when neither sitting down nor standing up can be accomplished without sighing or grunting noises of some kind. I made an interesting variety of both as I got up to get dinner on.

As tonight's pizza bubbled and spat contentedly under the grill, I fired up the PC and glanced over my emails. There'd been nothing from Louise – no call, no text. Part of me was relieved to find there was no email either. I knew that some contact was inevitable sooner or later – apart from anything, she still had a load of her stuff here - but right now I simply didn't feel like I had the strength to cope with another instalment of *Louise – The Musical.*

Oh- hello though, this was interesting. And more than a little unexpected:

From: Kate Gardner – Re: Re: Re: Hi Dan, Long Time No See!

Alrighty then, let's see what this is all about...

Hi Dan, really nice to hear back from you, I was worried you might not remember me and this would get pretty awkward! Like I said, I've recently moved back to the area and it got me thinking about the old days – when I discovered your shop I thought I'd drop you a line. It looks so much fun, just being around music the whole time, it's always been such an important part of my life –

Blimey, really? As far as I can remember, she was quite happy shaking her teenage booty to whatever Messrs Stock, Aitken & Waterman had happened to place in the charts on a given week -

...and I love all that old vinyl stuff, so retro! If you fancy it, there's a nice little coffee place near the station we could meet at, you know the Cafe Italiano? -

I didn't. Coffee shops were much more a Louise thing. That said, I knew where the station was, so it couldn't be too tricky to find, even for someone suffering from a severe case of High Street Blindness... Locations saved into my brain basically consisted of my flat, work, and the Lion. Coffee shops, restaurants and boutiques all sort of blurred into one for me – shopping was something I endured in order to eat and drink for the week, there wasn't generally much in the way of "consumer goods" I wanted (and even less I could afford..) so finding new and esoteric places to spend time and money while looking for them was a fairly low priority.

– *let me know, really forward to seeing you again, bye! Kate xox*

Well, this was an interesting new development – still, almost bound to come to naught bearing in mind the near-legendary unreliability Kate had been famous for at school. I sent her a quick reply, much in the vein of my first - *Hi, yes, sounds great, maybe Friday morning?* (I had to be in town that morning anyway, so if she were to flake out on me would be no big deal) *looking forward to seeing you too, be good to catch up* - and made a sly bet with myself: five quid says I never see that girl again.

And possibly for the best. The next couple of days passed quietly, albeit with the Louise Situation hanging over my head like a thundercloud. I fished out the boxes marked with her name and gathered up the shoes, cosmetics and occasional bits of underwear that had made their way into my wardrobe. The boxes, their contents peeking out over the cardboard flaps as if to cast a disapproving stare on behalf of their absent mistress, stood stacked in my living room like a totem to failure.

So, Friday morning rolled around. There'd been no word from Louise all week and while I was quite glad of the reprieve, it was starting to get irritating now – just come and pick your bloody pants up, woman, I've got the message now.

We're done and that's it, fine. Well, not *fine*, I suppose, but still.

Kate and I had arranged to meet at 11, and having found the place a little more easily than I'd anticipated, I sauntered in about ten minutes early. A few minutes study of the menu revealed that I could understand only about half the things on offer, and could afford fewer still, so I got myself a large black coffee and scuttled off to a corner to observe the world from behind a copy of the Observer (nice and intellectual looking without taking too obvious a political stance – or at least that was the idea..).

She's not going to show. There's no way this is going to come to anything.

That said, life had been taking rather a surreal turn recently. Louise and I seemed to have broken our holding pattern and Kate, half-forgotten for over a half a lifetime, resurfacing out of nowhere, even Chris and I seemed to have finally cracked getting "Sunshine" right.. who the hell knew what was going to happen?

On a more practical note, I suddenly realised I had no idea who the hell I was looking out for. It had been sixteen years, was she fat, thin, blonde, brunette? She'd told me in her email she'd be carrying a Prada bag, but unless it actually *said* "Prada" down the side in large print there was not a chance in hell I'd be able to recognise one.

Of course, there's always the off-chance that it's that frighteningly well-dressed and made up blonde waving frantically in my direction.

I looked over my shoulder, in true Rodney Trotter

fashion, to see who she might be waving at- nope , no one there. Either she's dropped a lot of acid and is waving at a crowd of little people she thinks she can see coming out of the wall behind me, or I'm the intended recipient of the wave and *that's* Kate.

I flash my warmest smile and get up to greet her, and am almost knocked sideways by her hug. There's a peck on the cheek and a "God, it's great to see you!" and I respond in kind as best I can.

She looked... well, to be honest - *astonishing*. Louise, as I mentioned before, has the knack of looking expensive, but Kate looked like you'd need to take out a mortgage to get within twenty yards of her. Designer clothes, *ALL* the make up, not to mention the highlights in her hair that caught her eyes and had me blind, after sixteen years, just for a second I was fourteen again at the school disco dancing cheek to cheek....

..in the middle of a coffee shop, on a cold wet Friday morning. Abruptly, Chris de Burgh stopped playing in my head. We sat. She put her coffee – well, it wasn't a coffee, it had ice cream and a straw in it, fuck alone knows what it was, but I'm trying to tell a story here, let's not get too hung up on the details – dead centre on the mat, top of the range iPhone replete with fancy pink case bedecked with Hello Kitty characters slightly to its left.

She flashed a wide and unnervingly white grin at me. "God, sixteen years! Can't believe you're really here!"

I was, if I'm honest, more than a little startled. She'd never been this arsed about me when we first knew each other, and although I can't claim to be an expert, nestling in there amongst the jewellery... was that a wedding ring? I never could remember what finger they were supposed to be on.

"Err, yeah- to be honest I'm a little surprised myself. Talk about a blast from the past – I mean, after we left Vale Mount and you moved away I never expected to hear from you again, so this is all a bit.. unexpected. So... I guess, what have you been up to the last sixteen years?"

"Well, nothing too exciting, college, university – that was where I met Martin, we got married a year or so after graduating-"she proffered a finely manicured and scented hand replete with what I assumed to be a wedding ring on it. Simple, elegant, tasteful... but you can bet it probably cost more than my flat.

"- and I know what you're thinking, kept the surname.. I'm not some militant feminist type, but I'd already set up my business and didn't want to confuse people! Martin was fine with it in any case.."

"Oh, right, what sort of business do you run?" I figured it was a grown up thing to ask.

"Oh, I'm a consultant.. promotions work, that kind of thing. Takes me all over!" She gave a quick, high-pitched laugh before continuing. I remembered that laugh- the same one she gave all those years ago when we almost set the chemistry lab on fire.

"Then a couple of years after that we had Rebecca, our daughter..." She fiddled with her phone for a moment and showed me a picture of a fair haired, freckled, toothsome young girl clad in an all-pink jumpsuit, grinning gleefully while an oversized Minnie Mouse stooped and waved at the camera, "That's her at Disneyland last year"

"She's the blonde, right?"

She punched me on the arm playfully, "Yes, got her mum's hair! And then a couple of years ago we decided it might be nice to have a little brother or sister for her and I had Jacob, and of course I didn't want to leave it too late because I wanted a chance to get my figure back"

She dropped a pause into the conversation with the same subtlety that the crew of the *Enola Gay* used to introduce the good people of Hiroshima to the power of the atom.

I really wasn't sure what to do with that last comment, but a compliment seemed like the best way forward.

"Er, well, yeah, mission accomplished there, I'd say" - although it did feel vaguely uncomfortable essentially telling someone's wife, *yes, don't worry love, you're still definitely worth a jump.*

The playful punch on the arm came out again "Still the charmer then, Dan!"

Err... yeah, okay.

"So-" she turned her eyes downward to focus on her iced-frappe-mocha-latte-with-extra-squid-and-turpentine-double-shot or whatever the hell it was, "-what about you, are you married, or seeing anyone?"

Oh Lord. I played safe and assumed she didn't want a blow-by-blow account of the last few weeks and the Louise Situation.

"No, not married., no.. and not seeing anyone actually, either, not at the moment. Just come out of... something.. and I'm letting the dust settle for now."

"Oh, I see" she grinned at me "love 'em and leave 'em, right? I suppose with you being in music and everything, it'll be a different girl every night!"

*Okay honey, I don't know what the fuck planet you inhabit, or what the fuck planet you think I inhabit, but the one I actually **do** inhabit is not filled with nubile young groupies who fling themselves at record shop assistants on being shown a guitar and played a half arsed cover of "Wild Horses".*

More's the pity. It sounds like a damn sight more fun place to be than the one I've been in the last week or so.

I smiled weakly "Er, yeah, not quite like that, sad to say-", I thought of the pile of boxes full of Louise's bits and pieces stacked in my living room, The Leaning Tower Of Break-Up, "- it's been a while coming but I think it's just reached the end of the line."

The Sid James grin turned to a doe-eyed expression of sympathy and she placed her hand over mine.

"Oh, poor you! Were you very close? Had you been together long?"

"Kind of on and off for a few years but it's never really

worked out. We just keep drifting back into one another and at first everything's fine, but it never seems to last. I think this time it's over for good though."

In an odd way, putting the Louise Situation into words, quantifying it to try and help a stranger (which, sentiment aside, is exactly what Kate was at this point) to make sense of it all helped me as well. Putting it all into a snapshot and framing it, as it were – the next step was putting onto the mantlepiece, if I may stretch a metaphor to breaking point and beyond, and from there chucking it into a binliner and moving on.

"Oh, I see..."..she was into serious Princess Di/ Martin Bashir territory now, peeking out at me from underneath fluttering impeccably-made-up eyelashes. "Well, I'm sorry to hear that, I guess.. still I'm sure you won't have a problem moving on, plenty more fish in the sea."

And the lashes again.

I was starting to get seriously confused by now. Was this- was she *flirting* with me?

Kate Gardner? Mrs Kate Gardner, indeed? **Mrs Kate fucking Gardner**, flirting with *me*?

Okay, time to keep an eye out for flying pigs.

"Well, you know, I'm just seeing it as a time out... time to do a bit of reflection, think about things a little. There's no sense just repeating the cycle and hoping that for some reason things might work out better this trillionth time around"

"Well, that's true.. and of course, you never know what's

just around the corner"

I realised she hadn't taken her hand off mine. The hand bedecked with a wedding ring she'd just proudly been flashing before my eyes not thirty seconds previously. Time to steer the conversation back to more neutral ground.

"So tell me about your kids, how old are they?"

"Oh, well, Becca's four and Jacob's just coming up to two.. that's one of the reasons we moved, actually, with Becs coming up to school age, there were no good primaries where we were and there's a really good pre-school for Jakey near where we wanted to send her..."

This went on for several minutes- Kate had clearly done her homework, and all credit to her for that, but the more she talked the more I started to feel fourteen again, and this time not in a good way. I mean, look at us – she'd come out of education, started a business, got herself married and a family – and judging from her appearance, whatever she did for a living, she clearly did it well and was paid handsomely for it. And now she's talking about school fees, Miriam Stoppard and Doctor Spock, skiing in Gstaad... good God, it was more like talking to my Mum than a woman who was (I kept having to remind myself) only three months my senior.

..and what the hell had I done with this time? My greatest accomplishment was learning to play the guitar solo in *Stairway To Heaven*, and I couldn't even do that particularly well. How had she done all this? What had I missed?

The hollow feeling I'd first experienced looking at my reflection in Chris' bathroom the morning after my birthday was back with a vengeance.

This is what you should have been doing, Danny-boy.

But you didn't, did you? You pissed it all up against the wall... and now look at you. Dead end job, no prospects, perpetually semi-skint.. and now Louise has gone too. And no wonder. You've got fuck all, you're going to get fuck all, and you know what, you deserve fuck all. Well played, sunshine, nice game plan.

As Kate talked on, leaving me feeling progressively more out of my depth with each sentence, a further realisation began to dawn on me – Kate is what Louise wants to be. Successful career, high status, no doubt a nice big detached house in a leafy suburb and there's bound to be Range Rover or something similar parked in the drive. All the trimmings.

And that's why she starts these rows. Because I don't fit this template, and I never have. I'm never going to provide any of this. I've spent my twenties bumping along the bottom of the sea bed, I haven't built a career or anything she can see a future with. So she gets scared, she gets frustrated, and out come the neuroses, because she feels like she's missing out. And I guess, yes – she is.

Kate stopped in the middle of explaining the intricacies of her new fitted kitchen with real granite work surfaces – so much more hard-wearing than vinyl, apparently they pay for themselves.... (I briefly pictured said work surfaces doing a paper round or on the till of a clothes shop on a Saturday) – as her phone sprang to life, chirping dulcet triplet of designer Apple-approved tones.

"Sorry, very rude, I know- "

"No, no, go right ahead"

She scrutinised the screen.

" Oh, Dan, I'm really sorry but I'm going to have to shoot off – childcare have just texted to me, apparently Becs is throwing a wobbly.. I'm going to have to go down and pick her up. Really sorry to dash out on you like this, I know it's rude!"

She was a pastel whirlwind of designer scarves and handbags collecting her things from the table. Pausing briefly, she turned to me and smiled a slightly rueful smile - "It's been great seeing you again, Dan, maybe we can do it again soon? Here's my number."

She slid a business card across the table to me.

"Yeah, it's been.."

I was cut off by a peck on the cheek- polite, but firm – and off she bustled. Watching her cross the street and into her car – Mercedes. Well, I was close. More to the point, large, expensive and shiny.

Absolutely everything that I wasn't.

Alone again, I abandoned the Observer and examined the business card while slurping the rapidly cooling dregs of my coffee.

Kate Gardener – Promotions Consultant

Snazzy but simple designer logo, website address, email and mobile phone number. I fished out my phone (a generation or two behind Kate's) and fiddled around with it trying to make the internet work.

Fast forward a few minutes, the remnants of my coffee now stone cold and coagulating into a gloopy grainy mess at the bottom of the mug, and the website fuzzed into focus.

Sure enough, there it was, all pastels and clean bright graphics, with Kate's gleaming white-toothed smile dazzling in ultra-high resolution from every photograph as she met with dignitaries and businessmen from around the globe, or partied in designer nightclubs with glow sticks and elaborate cocktails.

Yes, this was definitely the stuff Louise aspired to. No wonder she got wound up- this kind of high-status, jet set lifestyle was about as far removed from the mundane, humble world of the record shop and the Lion as it was possible to be. I leant back in my seat, feeling so flat as to almost be two-dimensional.

I mean, bloody hell, where are you supposed to start? I had the same building blocks as everyone else – the same number of limbs, the same Media Studies degree as a million others, I flattered myself at least a comparable degree of intelligence (well, until after the first few pints). The raw materials were all there.

I thought back to the end of my university days. Lord knew I'd tried playing the game, applied for everything I could find, wearing my fingers to the bone compiling and sending out CV's, covering letters, application forms, you name it. And all that effort had got me effectively... well, nowhere.

Things had to change. No one was going to give me this stuff- if I wanted it, I was going to have to go and get it myself. But how?

Well fate, as it would turn out, had other plans.

Chapter 6

"So this is where you've been hiding all week?"

Saturday morning. Soon the shop will be a-hustling and a-bustling with connoisseurs of the very finest popular music in all of it's forms and the till will be ring-a-ding-dinging like Big Ben on speed, but in these early hours all is calm, all is potential waiting to be tapped. Miles, Chris and I stood with steaming mugs of early morning tea in hand staring at half a dozen brightly coloured plastic boxes overflowing with every form of media the twentieth century bequeathed us. CD's – check. Vinyl – 78's, 33's and 45's, sir, all present and correct. Cassettes – oh yes. Eight track reel-to-reel cartridges – you betcha.

Oh, and dust. Lots of dust. I sneezed violently, raising great clouds of the stuff.

Miles smiled rather smugly in answer to Chris's question.

"Oh yes.. job lot here. Friend of mine was doing a house clearance, offered them to me for a song, I reckon there'll be some real gems hidden in there."

I wondered what the song in question might have been. Not "White Christmas", that was for certain. Chris and I eyed the tiny stockroom, filled to bursting point and beyond with junk as it was.

"Err, yeah.. skipper, if I might voice a note of concern.." I tried to be tactful "- we do have quite a bit of stuff in already, I mean.. where's it supposed to go?"

"Well, you boys are going to catalogue and sell it for me. Don't look like that, it'll take your mind off Louise- it'll be good for you, stop you feeling sorry for yourself."

Well, he'd got a point. Frankly, the Leaning Tower Of Break-Up was starting to piss me off royally now, casting a malign and evil shadow over my living room. Stephen King could probably have got a novel out of it, if he'd bothered to pop round. Missed out there, Stevey-boy – it's mine now. There'd been still no word from Louise and I was beginning to seriously consider carting the whole lot off to the tip if only to get my flat back.

I mean, I suppose I could always ring her, but the way we left things... something tells me that's just going to cause another bust-up, and make things even worse.

Oh, and alright, because I'm a great big no-bollocks cowardly cowardly custard, OK? Happy now?

I drew a deep breath, fetched pen, paper and clipboard, and set myself to the task ahead.

Ever the soul of tact, Chris piped up - "I don't really give a fuck about Louise, can I pass on this?"

"You can clean the bog?" offered Miles.

By lunchtime, the shop is throbbing with customers and we are all rushing around like flies with variously-coloured arses. This is peak time, from office workers looking for a present for their mums or girlfriends to oh-so-serious student indie types looking for just *the* right piece of vinyl to complete their elaborately constructed personas to the odd older chap or lady looking for a tape or record that harked them back to an anniversary or a special time of their youth. We probably pull in more cash during these couple of hours than we do during the whole rest of the week, but of course that involves us all working harder in those couple of hours than we do the whole rest of the week.

It's a brutal shock to a fairly slovenly system. Thankfully, as the afternoon wears on, Miles has treated us to a pizza, and the smell of rich cheese-and-tomato meat-feasty deep-fried deliciousness coming from the back room has got everyone's mouths watering. With the shop now largely emptied, Chris and I dove into the back to avail ourselves.

"Mmmgh hrrgllgh fllurglh grrghhly?" he asked.

"Oh, good God, you're speaking in tongues...." I grabbed two biros and jammed them together to formidable a makeshift crucifix.

"The power of Christ compels you! The power of Christ compels you!"

Chris swallowed the slice of pizza he'd crammed into his face.

"Shut up, you tit. I said, are you coming down the Lion after?"

Daft question. It was Saturday. They'd have saved us a

seat. And a few slabs of pizza would serve as a solid wedge of ballast to absorb the evening's libations.

"Yeah, course. Wouldn't want to set tongues wagging"

"Any word from Louise?"

"Nope, not a peep."

"Why don't you just grow a pair and ring her?"

"Right, yeah, and right after I've done that I'll stick my head in a lion's jaws while poking it in the bollocks with a stick.. Look, I know what she's like in these moods, the best thing to do is let her cool off and take the initiative herself. To be quite honest it's been nice to have a bit of a break and focus on other things."

"Like our recording, perchance?"

"Ooh, now, funny you should mention that-" I pulled out my phone, quickly checking that I hadn't missed a call or text from Louise... nope, nothing... plugged the connector end of the earbuds into the socket and the earbuds themselves into Chris. Which was a rather more greasy and unpleasant experience than I'd hoped for.

"Take a listen to that bad boy..." Over the week I'd busied myself redoing Chris' woeful rhythm guitar playing and generally mixing the whole thing down to what I felt was a rather decent finished product.

Judging from the broad grin slowly spreading across Chris' face as the tinny fuzzy reflections of sound filled the room, it wasn't just me either.

"I'll give you credit there, Danny boy, that ain't half bad"

"Amazing the difference a decent rhythm track makes, isn't it?"

"I just write 'em, old sport, never claimed to be much of a player"

"Bloody good thing too, you ten thumbed talentless arse bandit"

There was a polite but firm cough at the entrance to the back room.

"If you gentlemen have quite finished your erudite discourse... how's that inventory coming along?"

"Right on it boss" Chris and I chorused, a pair of naughty schoolboys caught smoking behind the bike sheds.

Laboriously we began to pick up where we left off, sorting the many, many, many and varied contents by media type, then artist, then album...

A mere five to ten years later Miles finished hustling the last customer out of the shop and popped his head around the door to check on his minions.

"Home time boys, how are we doing?"

Chris put his hand up to shield his face "The light... it

burns"

"Please, Master, not the lash again" I croaked.

Miles arched an eyebrow.

"Well, you two can sit there and take the piss if you want, but I'm going for a pint, you joining me?"

Silly bloody question.

Half an hour later we're in our usual spot, but something seems amiss, an unusual smell that keeps catching the back of my throat and making me cough.

"Ah, that might be me, I'm afraid," Chris ventured by way of an explanation, "I was a bit whiffy after all that cataloguing so nipped to the bog to give myself a quick squirt"

"What, aftershave? You?"

"Er, not quite. I had to improvise – used the air freshener"

"Yes, I thought you seemed like you had a good 30% more Citrus Zest than usual. Why don't you do what normal people do and have a bath?"

"Nah, mate, wrong time of year for that."

"I could take you down to the carwash, run you through that?" offered Miles "High gloss rinse, get the bugs off you with a nice soapy brush, even get you a waxing"

"Not enough wax in the world to deal with Pete and Roger, skipper, but I appreciate the thought all the same."

Pete and Roger - I should probably explain – you know how some guys name their penises?

Yes, you do. Don't look at me like that.

Well, Chris – a very committed fan of The Who – simply took the process one stage further, naming each of his genitals after the.... members (sorry) of his favourite band. Keith Moon had the honour of having the penis named after him, Pete Townshend and Roger Daltrey got a testicle each and John Entwhistle was unfortunately relegated to the anus, because in Chris's (very drunken) words, - "fuck bass players, they're not drummers, they're not guitarists, they're nothing... just standing there going fucking *plonk*".

This was an opinion in no way biased by the fact that the last bass player to come through the ranks of the Formidable Ale Society had run off while owing him fifty quid, of course.

To be honest, I can't say I'm any better. Louise claims she never got over one evening when I drunkenly introduced my bespectacled and bewigged testicles to her as a tribute to the legendary acoustic duo Hall & Oates. But we're not talking about her right now, that's right - keeping the mind on other things. I edged her out of my mind and returned my attention to the conversation, evidently choosing just the right time as Miles waved his glass around to ask if we needed another drink.

"Oh, please, guv'nor, thirsty work in them thar dark and

dusty forgotten corners"

"Never let it be said I don't do right by the serfs" Miles grinned and disappeared off to the bar.

Chris turned to me. "So d'you reckon we're going to shift any of that crap he's gone and bought?"

I puffed my cheeks and exhaled "Probably some.. there's all sorts of stuff in there. DATs and Minidiscs, Laserdiscs, eight track cartridges, reel-to-reels... there's a hell of a lot of unlabelled 78s too, at least I think they're 78s. The easy stuff, the LPs, there are a few decent ones, but it's going to take a while."

"Laserdiscs... sweet Jesus, he probably thinks they're state of the art." He exhaled. "Hell of a haul, isn't it?"

"Amen to *that*, my brother". We clinked glasses.

I could feel the mood changing though. Chris obviously had something troubling him.

"Do you think he's getting worse?"

"What?"

"You know what I mean. Do you think he's getting worse? More distracted, around less.... making fewer decisions and buying more crap like that load from this morning."

I was a bit taken aback.

"Well, no, not really – I hadn't really thought about it

that much though, to be honest."

"No, I guess not, you've been a bit away with it yourself, haven't you?" He grinned. "I have though- noticing it more and more. "

He looked around furtively.

"I checked out the books the other day"

"I thought he kept them in the safe?"

"He does, but he never locks it. I think he's forgotten the combination"

This I could well believe. Miles had certainly forgotten the combination for the burglar alarm before now, leading to one or two awkward conversations with the police.

"And? What did you find?"

Chris craned his head closer to me. "Mate, we've been losing money. And I don't just mean a few quid here or there. I mean close to a grand every month. And it's been like that for a year and a half"

I was aghast.

"You're shitting me? How?"

"Well, sales aren't brilliant, are they? Even over the website"

This was true. I had noticed a bit of a downturn. To be

honest, a part of me was amazed we'd kept going as long as we had.

"And instead of doing something about it, he's out buying up more and more crap while we have fewer and fewer customers interested."

"Well, I guess, but I mean, what can he realistically do about it? We can't turn things back to the nineties, and he can't force people to buy Walkman's and Discman's so they need to buy stuff from us to play on them."

"Advertising? Trade shows? Record fairs?"

"He goes to those.." *I think.*

"Yeah, and he *buys* stuff. We should all be going down to sell. Or better yet, just you and me, set up a stall and shift some of this stuff, get the name around." Chris slurped his Carling . "And to be honest, I don't think the money is in records and CDs any more. Everyone just downloads stuff these days, that's not going to change."

"So what do you reckon?"

He grinned at me. "Merch."
"Merch?"

"Merchandise. T-shirts, posters, DVDs - that sort of stuff. We need to diversify or we're going under, two years tops. And this way, we'll still be appealing to the customers we have now, and maybe get a few new ones."

I was impressed. "You've been doing your homework,

haven't you?"

He tapped his nose and gave me an Artful Dodger smirk. "More than just a pretty face, my old son.. Listen, how does he pay you?"

"Standing order , every week. Why?"

"See, I get cheques. Always have done. A couple of weeks ago, one of them bounced. Left me right up the shitter."

"You're joking?"

"Nope. Just after Christmas, right when no-one's got a pot to piss in. I mean, don't get me wrong, I talked to him about it and he made good, gave me it all in cash, but still... It's got me worried, Danny old son, I don't mind telling you."

He turned and took a sip of his drink. "Aye-aye. Look alive. Here comes El Capitano"

Miles returned, three fresh pints jammed together precariously in two hands. Catastrophe threatened at every bump and turn, but sure-footed, swift and nimble as a mountain goat, he navigated the route flawlessly.

"Here we go gentlemen.." He dished out the refreshments "..what have you little scamps been talking about while I'm away?"

"Nothing much, skipper, just trying to convince young Daniel here that there are plenty more fish in the sea, not to be downhearted... all the usual bollocks your friends tell you when you've just been chucked."

"Actually, he seemed to be doing a pretty good job of taking care of that himself" Miles grinned.

"Huh?" we chorused, Chris and I taken equally by surprise on this one.

"That blonde lady I saw you with on Friday, in the coffee shop. I don't believe I've seen her before – credit to you, Dan, you don't hang around."

Ah. Hadn't realised I'd had an audience.

Chris turned to me slowly, relishing the moment, a grin about a mile wide splitting his face like two tectonic plates moving apart. "REALLY?????"

Mm-hmm. I hadn't actually mentioned anything about Kate to either Chris or Miles, and given Chris being Chris, he was inevitably going to put two and two together and make seven hundred and nine.

I did a pretty good impression of a goldfish for a moment – mouth flapping aimlessly, halting monosyllables coming out Hugh Grant-style.

The two of them beamed mischievously at me. #

"WELL?"

"Well, nothing really.. I mean, it's.."

"Is she fit?" enquired Chris.

"As all holy fuck." answered Miles.

"Hang on, hang on, look you're really getting the wrong end of the stick on this one. We're just friends, she's an old friend from school, it's just..."

What? What is it just? Coffee? Flirting? The resumption of a teenage crush long buried? The plot of Brief Encounter (Which I'll admit now I've never seen, so I'm just guessing on that one.)

"Bollocks is she just an old friend." Chris was not to be put off the scent so easily. "I've known you since you were practically a sperm. If you've had a smoking hot blonde hidden away all this time, I'd have at least heard about her."

"Well, it's not quite like that. I know her from school, but I'd not actually seen her for a while."

"How long a while?"

"Sixteen years"

"Bloody Nora"

"Indeed"

"So, what, she's just turned up here out of the blue? How'd she find you? I mean, no offence mate, but you're not exactly on the cover of NME."

"At least I'm not on Crimewatch... No, she found the website. Said she was moving back to the area, was doing a little research- you know, what's around, places to go, things to do - "

"And people to do"

"Yes, yes, very good" I gave him a little light applause "found the shop, found that picture we took of us all and recognised me from that."

"Well, damn, Danny-boy, so am I right in thinking this internet business can be used for things other than porn, then?"

"So it would seem, yes"

"And as well as letting us flog records to far flung Aberdeen and Plymouth, it might play a strong supporting role in helping you get a bit of how's-your-father?"

"Oh, come on, give it a rest. I mean, for one thing, she's married"

"Did you meet him, too? It could be that they're looking for an innocent pawn in their twisted sexual games..."

"If she offers you a coffee and it's fizzing, for the love of God don't drink it" chipped in Miles.

"I've heard about stuff like this... I reckon she wants your kidneys. Sell them on the black market. I saw a documentary about this." Chris asserted confidently, the voice of all reason. "She'll lure you round to her place, slip you a Rohypnol and then open you up and hoover out your insides. Next thing you know, your spleen'll be up on Ebay."

"I wouldn't want that turning up at my door in an

envelope... let's hope they wrap it up in a carrier bag or two" Miles, ever-conscious of the logistical details.

And so the evening progressed, becoming increasingly louder and more blurry, and the conversation ever more surreal and slurred.

To be honest though, this was exactly what I needed. An element of normality. Louise and the worrying things Chris had said about the shop's finances took a back seat for a couple of hours. Eventually though, the time came. As befitted the elder statesman of the group, Miles was the first to leave.

"Right then gentlemen, I think it's time for me to bid you adieu"

Chris and I bade him a fond farewell. "Night skipper, a pleasure as always"

"Yep, night mon Capitan, look after yourself"

We settled back to finish our drinks before the inevitable trudge home. Chris was suddenly serious again.

"Remember mate, keep schtum about what I told you earlier, I'm not supposed to know about this. But we can't go on losing money hand over fist like we are. If things don't turn around, and fairly sharpish, I give it a year before we fold."

"Jesus, seriously?" This was a blow – I mean, admittedly I'd never envisaged myself still working there aged thirty, but frankly I was fond of the old place. It felt like home.

"Yeah- I mean, I just don't know where the money's

coming from to keep this place afloat. He must have either got a loan, or remortgaged, or something."

"The Mafia."

"Don't jest there, young Daniel, there's a dodgy element in every town.. I can't imagine he'd be that fucking stupid though..."

"Bet your thumbs?"

This was met with a derisive snort. We both sank back to finish our pints.

Time to leave. Chris and I grabbed our coats and sidled through the now almost empty pub to the doors, waving a cheery "Night!" to our bartending friends, before heading out into the chill night air.

"Right, I'm going to head home mate, look after yourself"

"Yeah, you too, youngling, take it easy"

A brief hug and we went our separate ways, breath condensing in the cold.

Turning into my street, fishing around in my pocket for the keys, I almost didn't notice the figure sat on the wall outside my building until I almost ran into it.

A soft voice – a little shaky, a little slurred, but all too familiar nonetheless.

"Hi Dan"

Bathed in the orange glow of a street light, and still managing to look expensive despite a good deal of smudged mascara, Louise rose to greet me.

Chapter 7

Sunday morning. The sunlight pushes it's way past the curtains to wake me up and gradually my room comes into focus... IKEA wardrobe (with duff hinge), scuffed bedside table, pile of dog eared Q, NME and Empire magazines, battered bedside lamp... all present and correct.

Sheaf of dark hair across the pillow next to me....

Oh, *shit*.

I seem to be wearing rather less than the T-shirt and boxers I usually sleep in...

Double SHIT.

Look, don't start. I'm not going to bother with the "*I was pissed, your honour*" line of defence, but you need to understand a couple of things. Firstly, despite everything that had changed between us in the last couple of weeks, Louise and I had been an enormous part of each other's lives for the last six years. That's a full fifth of my time on this planet – an even higher proportion for her. We both had too much time invested in the other to simply draw a line under things and forever part ways without at least a backward glance.

Secondly, for all that I'd been focusing on her demonic crazy side recently, she could be remarkably sweet.. and to give her due credit, there's no escaping the fact that she's a very attractive girl. And, well, not to be crude, but it'd been a while.

Oh, alright. Thirdly, we were both pissed as arseholes.

I got up, quietly so as not to wake her, and tiptoed downstairs to make some coffee and try and reconstruct the previous night's events.

What Chris said was very troubling. I mean, I knew the vinyl trade was never going to make any of us rich, but I'd had no idea things were so bad. We had bad days and good days – same as any other shop, I imagine – and although I'd noticed a slight decline in what we were selling over the website, it was nothing so bad as to make me think we were in genuine danger of going under.

This was a biggie. This needed thought, and it needed action. Decisive action.

Thought and action required coffee. I boiled the kettle.

Taking a fortifying slurp of Nescafe knock-off, I decided to file *that* problem away till later, and focus on the task at hand.

Louise had come round to pick up her stuff, or so she'd claimed. God knows why she thought it would be a good idea to do it in the middle of the night without ringing me first, but from the sweet vinegary scent of her breath when I met her I'm guessing her ol' partners in crime Pinot and Grigio had been involved somewhere along the line.

I'd let her in – by now dog-tired and at least two sheets to the wind myself, I really hadn't been in the mood for another conflagration. I showed her the Leaning Tower Of Break-Up and suggested that *perhaps this might want to wait till morning?* She seemed to agree and we sat down on the sofa.

She rubbed the coffee table ruefully – and not a little seductively, to my eyes.

"I suppose it's not so bad, is it?"

"Hmm?"

"The table... it's alright. I'm sorry I yelled at you about it."

Note the time and place, ladies and gentlemen. *Louise* has just apologised to *me*. 12.03am, February 16th. Damn, but the times, they truly *are* a changin'.

"Yeah, I'm sorry you yelled at me too" - only half sarcastically.

She smiled. I'd forgotten how pretty she is when she does that.

She put her hand on my thigh. Somewhere in between playful matey banter and sexual tension, we lurked uncertainly in the middle but definitely enjoying the flow. I'd missed this.

"I miss this" she said.

Somewhere in the recesses of my mind, alarm bells were ringing – *Danger, Dan Wyman, Danger* – but right now they were getting no attention. Right now we were both bathing in the warm waters of Lake We-Know-We-Really-Shouldn't-Be-Doing-This-But-What-The-Hell, and we were both enjoying it. Major decisions could wait till the morning, right now we were both happy.

"Yeah, I do, too."

"What you said in the pub... you really upset me."

"I'm sorry." I was. It had needed saying, but I'd taken no pleasure in hurting her.

"It got me thinking though.. maybe we should call it quits. Maybe we've both outgrown this whole situation."

I was hugely relieved to hear her say this – although, I must confess, there was a part of me that was rather annoyed at the prospect of getting my end away tonight receding into the distance.

"I've been thinking the same thing. You and me... we've had some great times, and you know I'll always care about you, but it always ends up the same way, doesn't it? Maybe we're just not right for each other after all. Maybe we just keep running back to each other because it's easy."

"*Easy?*" She arched an eyebrow. Whoops, poor choice of words there. No woman wants to be thought of as the easy option.

"Well, not *easy*. Familiar is more what I meant."

The eyebrow fell back to its natural resting place.

"Yeah... I mean, six years, you know? That's a hell of a long time. If we were going to make it... We'd have done it by now. Most couples who are serious, they'd be married, at least moved in together by now. But we always seem to stall, don't we?"

That's one very fucking diplomatic way of putting it.

"Yeah, I know what you mean.. and then back to square one."

"Could you ever see us living together?"

It's probably not a good sign when your bowels freeze up when a woman asks you this question. I'd had flatmates when I was at uni, and had fled back to the ancestral home after finishing my degree and discovering that no one out in the big wide world of industry gave a flying arse about it.. but since finding my flat I'd always lived on my own and relished the space and freedom it gave me. Admittedly, it wasn't exactly a Mayfair penthouse, but it was *mine*. Much as I loved (*Woah, did I just say that??*) Louise, it was just too big a leap of imagination to conceive of sharing it with her.

I mean, apart from anything, the girl has about eighty pairs of shoes. There just isn't room.

My legendary goldfish impression came out to play again.

"Wuh... I......"

"No, you can't, can you? Look, Dan, I'm not trying to have a dig at you, I'm really not- you like your space and that's fine. What I'm saying is, if we were going to work, we'd be doing all that stuff by now. I guess..." She seemed to deflate for a moment. ".. I guess I just need more."

I thought back to Kate. The house in the suburbs, the Range Rover, the glamorous, jet- setting, high-status lifestyle.. that was what she wanted. What she'd always wanted. And at last, Louise was realising the truth, that I was never, ever, going to be able to provide any of that.

So this really was **It**. The very last, the absolutely final, The Ultimate Break Up. *Come on Danny boy, it's not like you weren't expecting this.*

And it's not like she didn't have a point, either. This had been a long time coming, but in an odd, bittersweet way it was kind of refreshing to hear my own thoughts voiced by someone else, my words given form by another.

"Okay... so, what now? Where do we go from here?"

"I think...", she looked away for a second. "I think this is it for us."

Even now, I couldn't resist the temptation. Before my brain could stop it, my mouth had already said - "Again?"

Give her her due, she smiled. "Yeah, again. But this time... this time I think it's for keeps. "

I nodded. It was inevitable. I'd prepared myself for this, made my peace with the idea... but the reality was something different again. What do you know, turns out it's not that easy to say goodbye to six years of your life without getting just a little emotional. I felt a prickling sensation behind the eyes, the same sensation I remember as a kid watching Bambi's mum die.

At the same time, though, I knew she was right - we both did. We were a bad habit. An addiction both of us had been too lazy, or too scared, to crack.

I looked her in the eyes and managed half a smile. "Yeah.. it's about time, isn't it?"

"I'll always.. well, you know I'll always care about you. We've had good times."

"I know. And I'll always care about you too."

This was all starting to get far too Hollywood for either of us.

"Goodbye hug?" she asked – a tiny crack in her voice.

"C'mere." I pulled her close to me and we wrapped around each other. Her hair felt soft and silky, and I could smell hints of peachy-coconuty expensive shampoo underneath the wine and cigarette smoke. The skin of her cheek felt like velvet against mine. Instinct and habit, ingrained deeply over the last six years, kicked in, and I kissed her. Just on the cheek – a kind of consolation prize. *Well, you didn't win the speedboat, but at least you had a good time, thanks for playing. Give them a big hand, everyone. After the break, James & Charlotte from Leicestershire who'll be playing for the chance to win a break in sunny Tenerife!*

A sob. Don't know if it was from her or me. She turned her face to mine, foreheads pushed together, and we looked into each other's eyes for what seemed like an eternity. Gently,

I stroked her cheek with the back of my hand.

Her lips found mine, and all the rationality I'd so carefully armoured myself with over the last couple of weeks just dissolved. Our bodies, grown so accustomed to each other over the last six years, began to intertwine almost on autopilot.

"*This is still goodbye*" she whispered to me, between feverish kisses.

"*I know. It's okay. It's okay*" I whispered back, my hands running through her hair, kissing her lips, her neck, her throat.

She stood, took my hand. Placed a finger on my lips. Wordlessly, she led us up to the bedroom.

Still silent, she slipped out of her clothes effortlessly as I fumbled socks, T-shirt, jeans into a hastily discarded pile on the carpet. We both took refuge from the cold of the winter night underneath the duvet. Normally at this point Louise would be bollocking me for not getting the radiator fixed, but not this time. This time she was silent and serene as I joined her under the covers and we folded into each other, our bodies melding together.

I kissed her again. Lips, neck, breasts, stomach. I wanted to consume her. If this was goodbye – and this time around I knew it most assuredly was – I wanted to store as many good memories as possible. She kissed me back, hungry and passionate, and as my hands caressed her she guided me into her.

Louise and I must have had sex a thousand times over

the years. But this time, this final time... it felt just like the first. And afterwards, as she nestled back into me as she'd done so many times before, she said one final word to me before drifting off to sleep in my arms.

"Goodbye".

.…................

"Hey you."

Her voice broke my reverie, and I was back in the kitchen, holding a mug of now slightly tepid instant black coffee.

Bit of a comedown, really.

"Hey" I smiled. "Morning. You sleep alright?"

"Yeah.. head's pounding though. Vodka shots and white wine... not a good idea." She smiled weakly and waved a hand towards my coffee. "Got another one of those?"

"Yeah, no problem." I turned away from her to boil the kettle and do the necessary. Louise addressed the back of my head.

"Look, last night.. I.."

"I know. It's okay. We've both known this was going to happen sooner or later." Mug, teaspoon, coffee powder. Stir.

"I know it's so corny to ask this.. but I'd like to think we could still be friends?"

Milk. Fridge. Sugar. Cupboard. I turned back to her, mission complete.

"Course we can. I don't think there's any way we couldn't, after all this time." I passed her the mug.

"I don't know, maybe it's what we should have been all along."

"Maybe so"

We faced each other across my tiny kitchen, each waiting for the other to break the tension. A Mexican stand-off over the washing-up bowl.

"Look, I should probably get my stuff.." her voice tailed off as she looked into the living room, mentally calculating the hassle involved in carting the boxes back to her mums. While in heels. With a hangover.

Where x = hungover 28 year old intermediate size woman and y = three boxes of shoes, bath salts, shampoos, conditioners, moisturiser and other cosmetics too varied and numerous to quantify, divided by half an hour's walk across town, and factoring in the inherent instability of a pair of leopard print kitten heels which have been known to break at inopportune moments in the past, the inescapable conclusion must therefore equal "fuck it, I'm calling a cab"

"D'you mind me calling a taxi?" she asked.

"No, go ahead- I've got to tidy up a bit"

Louise pulled out her phone and went into the living room wile I moved things around the kitchen and prepared to launch an assault on the menacing pile of unwashed crockery that was colonising the sink and threatening to annexe the windowsill.

"It'll be about ten minutes" she called, coming back in and catching me pulling on the Marigolds. She started to laugh. "Dear God, are you doing what I think you're doing?"

"Yes, yes, very funny... about ten minutes? You can help me then." I squeezed in detergent and set off the hot tap.

"Alright.. you know, I don't think I've ever seen you in pink rubber before. It's a good look for you, you should wear it more often."

Detergent foamed up over the plates. I swiped some bubbles and placed them deftly on Louise's chin.

"So speaks the Bearded Lady"

She returned the favour, smearing suds all over my face.

"Ooh, Santa! Where was my bike this Christmas, I was a good girl all year."

"No you bloody weren't" I grinned and before I knew it, my arm was round her waist, pulling her to me...

She stopped. I stopped. The momentum and the laughter stopped. The rom-com gloss fell away.

I let go of her, more than a little reluctantly. "This... this is going to take some getting used to, isn't it?"

She nodded. "Yeah. Going to be weird for a while. It doesn't make any difference though, this is still best for both of us."

We stood for a moment, eyes locked. A thousand thoughts tried to force their way thorough to my larynx at once – none of them made it.

The tension, back once again with a vengeance, was broken by the sound of a car horn. Looking out of the window, I saw a silver Ford Mondeo with a yellow and black phone number garishly emblazoned across its side.

"Taxi's here. C'mon, I'll give you a hand out".

We loaded her boxes into the boot. As the driver slammed it shut, Louise turned and hugged me fiercely. I wanted to lighten the mood, to joke that it wasn't like she was moving to the ends of the earth, I was still going to be where I'd always been... but none of the words would form. I pulled her to me and hugged her just as hard as I could.

"*Take care*" she whispered.

"*Yeah, and you*".

With a couple of sniffs, we disengaged and she disappeared into the front seat.

"Cavendish Close, please"

And she was gone.

Walking back into my living room, the emptiness hit me like a punch to the stomach.

Chapter 8

Monday morning. My head throbbed mercilessly. The previous evening, I'd gone and done exactly what I'd promised myself I wasn't going to do – cracked open the wine and drunk myself into an idiotic, pointless stupor till I wept. Horrible, bitter, mean, miserable tears, as much for myself as for her. Pathetic. Cringeworthy. Ridiculous.

This morning though, despite the brutal hangover, I felt surprisingly positive. However, as I wiggled and jiggled the key into the worn old Yale and did battle with the sticking handle, Chris' words about the parlous state of the shop's finances came to mind. This was serious, adult stuff, not teenage adolescent girlfriend problems. The idea of the place closing and having to go out into the real cold, unfriendly, grown-up world to try and make my fortune filled me with a cold dread.

I got inside, lights on, flip the sign, kettle on, PC on. First coffee of the day – and sure enough, drawn in like a moth to a flame, next to appear was Chris.

"Make us one of those while you're back there" he grinned in his best shit-eating way.

"Yeah, sure, there's a full pack of sugar here, I'll put the lot in." I returned from the backroom, two mugs of steaming caffeiney goodness in hand. Gingerly, Chris reached over and took his.

"Cheers – Jesus mate, you look like shit. What happened to you last night? Get all teary watching *Titanic* or something?"

I caught a glimpse of my reflection in the window. Not great – not that it was ever exactly fantastic – but even more not great than usual. Red eyed, puffy, bags under my eyes that were more bin liner than carrier bag. I stretched and yawned.

"No, just a bit of a rough night. Actually..." I gave him an abridged version of the weekends events. Leaving out the bit about me filling myself with cheap red wine and crying myself to sleep, obviously- there's some things a chap keeps to himself.

"Well, here's to you then Danny-" we clinked mugs "It's been a long time coming but I think you two have done the right thing for each other. So on to pastures new.."

"Yep", I agreed.

"..aaand blonde?" He grinned.

Here we go again. This was starting to get old.

"Oh, for fuck's sake, no. Look, she's married for a start, and for another thing, I'm not going to just jump on the first woman who says hello to me... Louise and me, it's a big deal, you know? I want a bit of time off - think about things a little bit, get my breath back, not just go hurling headlong into something because a woman gives me her number."

"She's given you her number?"

"Yes, and what of it? She gave me a business card, not like she tore my shirt off and wrote it on my chest with lipstick."

"Hmm... I think the lad doth protest too much" he smirked at me "Anyway, listen, is the skipper in yet?"

"No, not seen him"

"Right then Daniel-san, you're on look out duty, I need to use the computer"

Blimey. "Alright, fire extinguisher at the ready"

"Yes, yes, fuck you very much, I'm not a complete technophobe."

All was deathly quite for a few minutes. I kept one eye on the door and the other on Chris' face, bathed in light from the monitor and wearing an expression of intense concentration...

Which within five minutes gave way to frustration...

Which in its turn gave way but a few short minutes later to..

"Oh, FUCK YOU THEN!"

Chris doesn't get on well with technology. I recognised the symptoms – shortness of breath, clenching of fists, sweat glistening on the brow - the options were either a) watch him attempt to beat the works PC to death with a shoe or b) do whatever it was he was trying to do for him. Although option a) scored far higher in terms of sheer entertainment value, I was at least nominally responsible for the computer side of things and I was pretty sure Miles wouldn't see the funny side. I sighed and chose option b), the noble high road.

"Oh, come on then. Whatcha doing?"

"Trying to get my bank statement. I rang them first thing this morning and they said I need to check it online"

"Okay, well that's the credit card bit you're trying to log into"

"Oh right... where does it tell you that then?"

"Right there where it says CREDIT CARD in great big letters in the centre of the screen...."

I waited a beat.

"... you utter tool."

I navigated him back to the HSBC login screen. "Look, password there, account number there, alright? What's the emergency anyway?"

"Hang on" Chris painstakingly copied his password and account number, typing one fingered while reading from a scrunched up yellow Post-It note.

"Yes! Danny, you're a genius. Right...."

"So go on, what's the problem?"

"Ask me what I did yesterday."

I shrugged. "What did you do yesterday?"

"Fuck all. You know why?"

"Why?"

"No money. Hang on... there, look, I bloody knew it."

I looked. Sure enough, right there on his statement, it showed cheque paid in.. and then promptly removed again. It had bounced.

Which meant Miles himself didn't have any money to pay him.

Which meant that we must all in rather deeper shit than I'd first thought.

Chris stood and ran an exasperated hand through thinning and equally exasperated hair. "Fucking hell, I'm going to have to have words with him on this one. This is the third time now."

"Third? I thought it was just after Christmas and now?" This wasn't good. Not just for Chris, for all of us.

"Nope, happened last month as well. You were in a tizzy over Louise, I didn't want to worry you. Plus, it's not like you could have done anything, is it?"

I felt hugely guilty all of a sudden. Whining away about girlfriend trouble like a spoilt bloody teenager when my best mate was struggling to keep a roof over his head. *Way to go, Danny boy.*

He sighed, a hard, worried, angry exhalation of breath. "No sign of him yet then?"

"Nope, nothing"

"Right, fuck it, I'm taking a look at the books. Hold the fort for us mate, give me a shout if you see him coming."

Chris disappeared off into the Forbidden Zone of the back room. The few customers who drifted in during his absence didn't seem too perturbed to have their browsing accompanied by muffled grunts and crashes coming from the back - all part of the retail experience at your friendly neighbourhood indie record shop.

He emerged a few minutes later carrying a ledger. Yes, a ledger – Miles hadn't really embraced the twenty-first century. I wouldn't have been surprised if there was a quill strapped to it.

Miles' handwriting was frankly appalling, but even that couldn't disguise the magnitude of the problems we were facing. I'm no accountant, but even to an untrained eye like mine it's not difficult to see that when outgoings exceed income by progressively more each month, then you're in the shit.

"God almighty, we really are in trouble" I breathed, scanning the last few months tallies.

"Told you. And yet he still goes out buying crap like that last haul" Chris nodded his head towards the back room where the latest multiformat mass of media lurked, waiting to be organised, catalogued and hope-to-fucking-God sold.

"Christ, yes, I'm supposed to be cataloguing that. Right, you keep an eye on things, I'll get in there and see if I can find anything that might make us a few quid."

"If not, we can always pimp you to a Russian businessman," Chris grinned "Actually, give me a sec – let me use the bog and do a blood test."

I sensed a trap. This was a common manoeuvre of Chris's - "using the bog and doing a blood test" could mean that the idle sod was going to be gone for upwards of half an hour.

Acutely aware of customers browsing the racks, I couldn't make my point in my usual manner, so I grabbed a scrap of paper from the counter and a marker, and scribbled NO MASTURBATING in very large letters on it. Jabbed the paper very firmly just to make the point, with my sternest headmaster expression brought out for the occasion.

Chris dabbed the coffee he'd spat out all over the counter and nodded agreement. "Okay"

"Promise?"

"Promise. I couldn't anyway, I can't see you from in there." He beamed and scuttled off.

I chose not to dwell on that and went back to the ledger. A thought occurred – what date had Miles bought the last haul of miscellany? Keeping one eye on the door and another on the customers, I began to trace back through the accounts to find out how much that little lot had cost us.

Which was a neat trick, if you think about it.

Chris reappeared after a couple of minutes – obviously being true to his word this time - and joined me behind the counter.

"It was the 10^h, wasn't it, when he bought that last load?"

Chris paused, mentally working through the days. "Err... yeah, yeah, sounds about right."

I traced down the dates. Bloody hell.

I grabbed the pen and paper again.

FUCKING HELL FIRE, I wrote, passing the paper to Chris.

WHAT?, he scrawled, passing it back

FIVE GRAND. Chris' eyebrows almost flew off the top of his head.

SERIOUSLY???

"Let me have a look.. Bloody hell, you're right," he exclaimed, drawing a raised eyebrow from a elderly lady browsing Country & Western M through to Z, "No wonder my pay cheque bounced. What in the hell is he doing throwing money around like that when we haven't got any to spare?

Jesus Christ, I've been working here twelve years, he should be worrying about paying me, not buying junk! "

"Mate, he's... he's losing the plot. He must be. I mean how in the hell else can you explain this?" I shook my head – I really didn't believe what I was reading, but what other conclusions could you draw?

"I think he must be desperate – buying in any old crap just to find some sort of golden egg.." - it was all I could think of to frame the situation in any sort of rational terms.

"Yeah, well, he may as well be blowing his money on magic fucking beans" snapped Chris. "This bollocks has gone far enough, I'm not having this."

Again, a few glances were thrown in our direction. But by this point, both of us were too worried by our discoveries to pay too much attention.

"Right, tea. And then we're making an action plan." Chris disappeared back into the back, leaving me alone with the Ledger of Doom – before reappearing a second or so later.

"There's no milk, mate, and no bog roll, you ok for five while I nip up the road and get us some?"

"Yeah, yeah, no worries.."

The door banged shut as Chris scuttled out. Scanning the pages, I could feel my stomach dissolving into an icy vapour... we were losing money hand over fist. This couldn't go on.

"Good read?"

I looked up.

Oh, SHIT.

Yes, you guessed it – El Capitano himself, Miles stood over me, a tower of cold fury, as frosty and unsmiling as I'd ever seen him.

Say something. Say anything.

"Uhh, skip.." - *yes, genius, Dan, that's the way to handle the situation.*

"Don't, Dan. Don't even try."

Both customers had decided there was nothing they fancied and hustled themselves out.

"Look, Miles, we're all involved in this place, we all.."

"You KNOW full well the ledgers are confidential. You KNOW I deal with those, not you, not Chris."

"Yeah, but come on, we're in trouble here, we all need to be taking action-"

"Then you ASK me, you do NOT go snooping around behind my back, break into the safe and get them yourself, you understand? This is MY shop, my business, and I run it for the benefit of all of us, you understand me?"

This I didn't like. Arbitrarily pulling rank. Christ, we

were all on the same side here, couldn't he see that?

"Look, we're in trouble here, anyone can see that, all I'm trying to do is help- Chris's cheque bounced again, I'm just-"

"Oh, has he put you up to this?"

"No, no, I'm just trying to get a handle on what's going on here, I'm just worried that-"

"If you're not happy with the way I run this shop, Dan, you're welcome to seek employment elsewhere."

I was stunned.

"What the fuck?"

"In fact I think that might well be the better option. I think you should go home."

"Are you serious? You're firing me? Jesus Christ, Miles, I've worked for you for nine years!"

"Yes, and you repay me by snooping around behind me back, betraying my trust and betraying my confidence. I can't employ anyone I don't trust, Dan, if you're happy to go into the safe behind my back, how do I know you're not happy to steal from the till?"

"Are you fucking kidding me? So you think I'm a thief now?" I was aghast. What the hell was going on? I wasn't – he couldn't fire me, for God's sake, I'd worked there forever. The three of us were a team. This just didn't make any sense.

"What I'm saying is I clearly can't trust you, and I can't employ anyone I don't trust. You knew the rules, Dan, and you broke them. You went behind my back instead of coming to me. You brought this on yourself. Go home. Get your stuff and just get out of my shop."

I was absolutely staggered. This just... it couldn't be happening. Any minute I would wake up and it would be a normal Monday morning, arguing and swapping fart jokes with Chris. I couldn't take it in.

Miles was unmoving.

"Get your stuff together, Dan, and go home."

"But I mean... none of this makes sense. Who's going to do the website, for one thing?"

"Not your problem."

"But you can't... you can't just fire me, I mean there are rules and things.." I was fairly certain you couldn't just snap your fingers and tell someone they were fired, there were dismissal hearings, tribunals and... well, all sorts of stuff that I'd vaguely heard about but never really assumed I would need to read up on.

"Yes, Dan, yes, there are rules, not many of them but they matter, and you broke them. Go *home*."

He was serious. He was actually, genuinely, really serious. I just couldn't believe what was happening. Anger like you would not believe flashed over me.

"Right, fine, I was trying to HELP, Miles, to fucking HELP you and all of us. This place was everything to me, you want to throw that away, then FUCK YOU, damn it!"

I stormed into the back to grab my coat. Coming in this morning, I'd thrown it over the latest box of goodies – as I grabbed it, a couple of the more intriguing white labelled 78s fell onto the floor.

Fuck it, I thought, *if he's going to call me a thief I may as well fucking be one*. I picked them up, shoved them in my coat pocket before heading back out into the front. He stood silent and impassive behind the counter. I glared at him as I pushed my way angrily past out to the door. Grabbing the handle, noticing the intricacies of the brass finish caked in nine years of grime from my hand, I turned for one last salvo. One last appeal to sanity.

"Look, Miles- mate, I'm sorry, I just-"

"Go *home*, Dan"

And that- ridiculously, ludicrously, unbelievably - was that.

I walked out, blinking back the tears into the cold morning air. Nine years. I just couldn't wrap my head around what had just happened. In twenty four hours, first Louise, now this. What the fuck was going on?

That shop had been my home for basically my entire adult life. I simply could not imagine getting up to go to work there ever day. We'd been a team, our little gang, through thick and thin. This couldn't simply be the end?

Could it?

Chapter 9

You find me in something of a state of shock.

Having walked home with emotions oscillating wildly between astonishment, hurt and flat out murderous rage, I'd found it necessary to stack up a tower of cushions, pillows and other squishy things against the wall, and then punch seven, eight, nine shades of fuck out of them. Nine bastard years, almost a third of my time on this planet I'd spent in that pokey little shithole and he kicks me out for, what? Trying to help him? Giving a damn about trying to keep his business afloat? Caring about the place that had been my livelihood? It was – and here comes my inner teenager – just so *unfair*.

Come on, man. Get it together. This has happened, this is real, and you need to deal with it. I retrieved my coat and battered old rucksack from the floor they'd been hurled to, retrieving from the rucksack a cracked Tupperware box containing the sandwiches I'd taken with me for lunch (usually eaten while sat on the toilet, in the absence of our place – whoops, come on now, my *former* place – having any kind of break room), and from my coat three white label 78's.

I munched the sandwiches and looked at the 78s, feeling grateful I was at least compus mentis enough to get those actions the right way round.

I ought to give those back. I have basically just nicked them – there isn't really any sort of mitigating circumstance I can put it down to, said the angel on my shoulder.

On the other shoulder, a little red fellow with a trident popped up – *Fuck him, he fired you for no good reason, after nine years good service, with no redundancy pay off, no warning, no nothing. Fuck that guy. Fuck him right in his fucking ear, till it bleeds and falls off his bastard head.*

They both made excellent cases.

I thrust moral considerations aside for the moment and contemplated the practical. Thankfully, I had some savings I could fall back on, but they sure as hell weren't going to last long. I was going to need income, and fast.

I needed a plan.

A brief hunt around the detritus on my coffee table (still drink-ring free, I might add) yielded some scrap paper and a Biro that despite having the end chewed off it at some stage in its existence, still showed some signs of life. I sucked on the biro, stared at the paper, and began trying to make a plan.

Money – I was going to need a new source of this quickly. *Redundancy*, I wrote, and then added a question mark. I really didn't know a damned thing about employment law. I was going to need to find somebody who lived out in that big wide scary grown-up world to help me on this one. I was fairly certain however, that outside of Hollywood or *The Apprentice* you couldn't just point a forefinger at somebody, tell them they were fired and that was it. There must be rules and... things.

I thought of Chris – and then just as quickly dismissed the idea. He'd know sod all about this sort of stuff, he'd been down our weird little rabbit warren even longer than I had. Louise might – but I found myself, to my shame, reluctant to tell her the news. The idea that on the Sunday we could be breaking up and saying goodbyes, and then ringing her up less than twenty four hours later to tell her I'd lost my job and could she help? No, that just reeked of desperation.

New Job – well, I was going to have to sort that out and sharpish. It had been a long, long time since I'd been jobhunting, but I still remembered the soul-crushing misery of ejection after rejection, that feeling of being forced to bash your head against an unyielding and uncaring brick wall. I groaned inwardly at the thought of going through all that again.

Still, maybe this was a chance to do something new, to find that elusive career I'd always wanted.... *yeah, of course it is, Dan, that's exactly how the world works. You'll be lucky if you're not sucking off Turkish businessmen in a phone booth this time next month.*

Qualifications – 9 GCSEs (no one cares) 3 A-Levels (no one cares), Media Studies degree (no one cares, to the extent that everyone just assumes you have one without asking).

References... I vaguely recalled telling Miles, in the heat of the moment, to go and fuck himself. References could be something of an issue.

Shit, this was going to be harder than I thought. And I'd thought it was going to be pretty fucking difficult to start with.

Experience – well, nine years in a record shop. Again, can't imagine that sounds particularly enticing to the Alan

Sugars out there.

I tapped the biro against my lip reflectively. Hmm.

Tea. Tea would make everything better.

While the kettle boiled, I paced. Like a caged mountain lion, or like a freshly unemployed former record shop employee.

I almost jumped as my phone rang. Checked the number – Kate. Odd, I was pretty certain I hadn't given her my number. Still, I pressed "answer" on the grimy old Nokia's keypad - let's see what happens here.

"Hello?"

"Hi Dan!"

Even through an ancient tiny speaker, her voice had an unnerving girlish quality – there was still the girl I'd been smitten with all those years ago in there, underneath the highlights and the foundation and the designer labels.

"Hi Kate, how are you?"

"Oh, great, thanks, how are you? I hope you don't mind me calling you, I rang the shop but a guy called Chris said that you weren't there? He gave me your mobile number and said to try you on it."

I choked back a laugh. "Erm, yeah, this is kind of strange but... I don't work there anymore."

A tiny pause as she registered surprise. "Oh.. right... wow, since when?"

God, this was making my toes curl. I laughed, half nervous, half bitter. "Haha, well, oddly enough, since about three hours ago, since you ask."

"Oh God, Dan, really? God, I'm so... what happened? Are you ok?"

"Uhm, well, I've had better days."

"God, that's awful.. listen, I just, I wanted to... tell you what, you sound like you could use cheering up."

Well, yes. Yes, I could, as it goes.

"Yeah, I don't suppose you know if Google are looking for a new CEO, do you?"

She laughed. "I'll ask around."

There was a brief pause. "So what are you up to tomorrow?"

Well, fuck all, obviously, I didn't have a job anymore. I struggled to think of a way of putting that more diplomatically.

"I was thinking about standing by the main road with a sign saying WILL CATALOGUE RECORDS FOR FOOD, but I don't know how much take up there'll be" I smirked bitterly to myself, "So, no, nothing much really."

"Tell you what then, do you want to pop over

tomorrow? Have a bit of lunch?"

Hmm. This could get a bit awkward. Still, I was unemployed now - a free lunch was nothing to be sniffed at.

"Yeah, sounds good – but I'm just thinking, I mean, Martin, the kids.. are you not working tomorrow?"

"No, no, I'm between contracts right now – Martin's away on business, the kids will both be at pre-school, we'll have the place to ourselves. We can crack open the wine and you can tell me all about it, we can actually have a proper catch up, I felt really bad about having to rush off the other morning."

Between contracts. I liked that. Kind of implies a certainty that there'll be another one. I decided I would steal that phrase and apply it to myself to boost morale.

"Yeah, yeah, that sounds great."

It did – with everything else going suddenly and absolutely to shit, I needed something positive to cling on to, and perhaps Kate's reappearance in my life might yet prove to be just that.

"Okay then, pop over about half twelve? Let me give you the address.."

I grabbed a pen and scrap of paper and jotted it down. As I'd expected, it was in a very upmarket part of town, about half an hour's walk from my place.

"Okay.. brilliant, yeah, I should be able to find that, I'll see you tomorrow."

"Great! I'll get the wine in- you like red or white?"

"Er, red, I guess, but I-"

"No problem, I'll make sure I've got some in. See you tomorrow!"

This was going to be interesting.

It certainly beat the Herculean task of trying to make my CV seem impressive. That said, with Kate's PR expertise, maybe she could find a way to sell me?

There was a local paper sitting amidst a pile of magazines on the coffee table – I picked it up and scanned through the unpromisingly small Vacancies section.

It made for some pretty depressing reading. Virtually the only things I seemed to have the qualifications or experience for seemed to involve stacking shelves or flipping burgers. I cursed myself for not having had the foresight to do something more practical – if I'd trained as a plumber, I'd be raking it in. I could have had my own van and everything. Name down the side – I'd practically be a celebrity.

I took my last swig of tea and mulled things over. Kate had a career. She had her shit together. Maybe she could explain to me where I'd been going wrong all this time. I tried to put a positive spin on the events of the past few days – why shouldn't I see this as a chance for a fresh start? Stripping away the things that had been holding me back, stopping me from growing.. Why shouldn't this, in fact, be the best thing that could have happened to me?

Why, because, of course, *life doesn't work like that.*

Next morning, I treated myself to a lie-in. Every situation had an upside, and if the only one this had to offer was the opportunity to lie around in my pants till ten in the morning, then you'd better bet I was going to make the most of it. Thankfully, I'd paid my rent and bills a few days beforehand, so I had the best part of a month before I became in imminent danger of being homeless and relegated to the Dark Ages. I'd determined not to panic about the situation, but to go about dealing with it in a calm, mature, detached state of mind, approaching things methodically.

Which apparently included getting drunk in the middle of the day with a former high-school crush.

I had a couple of hours, so I showered, shaved and dressed (best jeans and T-shirt combo), doing my best to make myself look presentable, before moseying down to the kitchen for some coffee and another look over the CV. Settling myself down on the sofa, I scanned through it again, sucking on the biro in the hope that it might somehow yield some inspiration.

It didn't. Did wind up with a disconcerting dark blue stain on my tongue, though.

I decided to take the CV with me and see what magic Kate might be able to work on it. Careers guidance and a boozy free lunch, that was something to look forward to.

Settling back into the sofa with my coffee, I contemplated the rest of the day – and the day after that, and the day after that. I could feel an unusual sensation creep over me, and it took a moment or two before I could work out what it was.

I was *bored*.

I hadn't been bored in years – I never had the time, for one thing. But now, well... I had nothing *but* time.

Potentially for ever.

No, I shook that thought from my mind. This whole situation was a slump, a trough, a bump in the road – nothing more. *You're only thirty, for Christ's sake, there's plenty you can do. You just need time to figure it out.*

My battered old acoustic guitar, a faithful companion since the age of fourteen, stood propped against the sofa. I picked it up, gave it a contemplative strum and tune, and reflected that it was this very instrument I'd composed my original paean to Year 9 Kate all those years ago. Before I realised it, I was playing the thing again, fingers moving almost by themselves over the notes poached from a Nirvana album. I couldn't help but smile as I remembered the painful, awful title.

If I Had A Car..., well, shit, Dan, you're thirty and you still don't have one. Or a job. Or a girlfriend, now. Bloody hell, what a week.

I played a little more, just glad to be doing something, anything rather than sitting waiting for whatever the next blow the world was going to inflict on me. I meandered through some old blues riffs and eventually found myself strumming "Sunshine", the song Chris and I had recorded back in that other life. Only a couple of weeks had passed, but sweet Jesus things had changed. It was hard to believe.

I finished the coffee – cold, now – and checked my watch. Time to head on over to Kate's, especially with my propensity for getting lost in any part of town without pubs to navigate by.

As it turned out, the world must have been feeling sympathetic, and I stepped out into a crisp, clear, and unusually warm and sunny day. I took this to be a good omen, for the simple reason of *why the fuck not?*, and headed off Kate-wards. Sure enough, as I crossed town towards her street, I noticed the houses getting gradually bigger, the trees greener and more frequent, the cars shinier, larger and more expensive.

Here we go, Kingfisher Avenue. Number 12 – yep, there was Kate's Mercedes parked on a wide gravel drive in front of an impressive detached house with an impeccably trimmed, strimmed and mowed garden.

I wound my way up the drive, suddenly feeling a bit naked. I hadn't brought a present, or a bottle, or anything. Looking up at the door, immaculately styled wood panelling and brass numbers, I felt again completely out of my depth. She was only three months older than me, for Christ's sake. Where'd she get all this stuff? I mean, it didn't just grow on trees.

Well, okay, the wood did, sort of, but... oh, you know what I mean. Let's not get pedantic here.

As I rang the bell I almost hoped she wouldn't answer.

"Dan!"

There she was, a luminous presence in Gucci... or Armani... or something, I don't know. Expensive and floaty, anyway. She flung her arms around me and gave me an enthusiastic and aromatic hug, followed by an immaculately lipglossed kiss on the cheek.

"Great to see you, come through, come through"

She ushered me through into a gleaming kitchen lifted straight from an advert. It must have been – nowhere that didn't have heart surgery regularly performed in it was this dust free. A haven of perfectly co-ordinated pine, granite, chrome and glass. A glass of white wine sat on a sun-dappled worktop that snaked off into the middle distance.

"Can I get you a drink?" She twinkled.

"Yeah, please, I - "

She dangled a variety of bottles in front of me "Shiraz or Merlot?"

Christ, I don't know, the only criteria I ever chose wine on was what would let me get three bottles for a tenner or less. I plumped for the Shiraz, on the grounds that it sounded vaguely more sophisticated. She smiled and reached for the corkscrew.

"So you know your wines, Dan?"

Yes, yes, I know there are red ones, there are white ones, and some weird hybrid pink ones. I know if I get pissed on red I sleep like a baby, but doing the same with white means that the next morning it feels like someone's trying to take the top off my head with a buzzsaw. I know that when Louise drank Chardonnay she would either get incredibly horny or incredibly angry with me (or both- quite often both, actually), but beyond that, well, I was as out of my depth as a toddler trying to swim the Channel.

"Uhm, well, I'm usually pretty good with what's on special offer at the corner shop.." I offered.

She laughed and sipped her wine. "Listen, I don't know if you fancy it, but I was thinking – it's such a nice day, you want to head to the park? I can wrap some things up, take some wine, we can have ourselves a little picnic?"

Picnic? Well, this was a little unexpected, but.. shit, why not? It was a remarkably nice day, there was free food and wine.. *never look a gift horse in the mouth, Danny boy.*

"You know what, that sounds great, really nice idea. Can I give you a hand?"

"No, no, it's fine – I know where everything is. You can talk to me while I'm doing this though?" She smiled again, finishing her drink as she turned to open the top-of-the-range, brushed aluminium fridge and began unloading foodstuffs from Harrods, Fortnum & Mason... this picnic represented an investment of over a week's wages for me. Clearly, PR was a very lucrative field to be in.

"You don't have any allergies, do you?", asked Kate as she hunted through cupboards.

Strange question, I thought. "Uhm, pollen, I get hay fever in the summer, but.."

"No, Dan, no, *food* allergies. Are you alright with peanuts?"

"Love 'em – the peanut that can take me down hasn't been invented yet"

"Great, what about gluten?"

What the fuck was gluten?

"Sorry, are we onto religion now? Is that a thing like Scientology?"

"You know what, I'm just going to assume you're fine with it", she smiled.

I cast my eye over the range of goodies – as well as a delightful variety of wines, there were cheeses (plural), crackers and bread with.. *stuff* baked into them. Oats and things. Fantastic, this was going to be a veritable feast. I decided to have a go at upholding my end of the conversational side of things.

"So what's this new contract all about? I saw your website, it all looks very glamorous."

"Oh, just some promotional stuff for a drinks company. I'm organising an ad campaign, it's another of these alcopop jobs..."

I sipped at my wine while Kate loaded a couple of

woven tote bags to overflowing with goodies and talked about sales projections, target demographics and marketing strategies. After a few minutes, the bags were loaded and I was thoroughly bewildered.

"Okay" she beamed "grab a bag and let's go and get pissed in the park"

If only she could have said that to me sixteen years ago...

"The park", thankfully, was only a couple of hundred yards away as I struggled under a hundredweight of wine and luxury foodstuffs. A smooth grassy slope dotted with trees tentatively experimenting with the idea of blooming, bordered by woods and orbited by joggers. By the looks of it quite a few people had had the same idea as we had, so we picked our way through families having an unexpected day out and found ourselves a relatively secluded spot under an oak.

Kate unfolded the groundsheet and enthusiastically unpacked the wine, pouring us a glass each.

"Chin chin" she giggled and we clinked glasses. "This is lovely, isn't it?"

It... it really was. I reflected on the events of the past few days- this was definitely the high point.
"It's gorgeous" I agreed "And very unexpected – I mean, talk about a blast from the past, who'd have thought we'd be out picnicking together?"

"Life is unexpected at times." She leaned back and stretched herself out, enjoying the sensation of being warm and alive, and I had to do a quick rush job slapping down my inner adolescent. *She's a married woman, Danny, and this isn't a Jilly Cooper novel.*

"Truth can be stranger than fiction sometimes" she continued, eyeing the world through the prism of her wine glass, "I've found the best thing is just to run with it, see where it takes you"

"Seems to have taken you to some very good places- you've done really well"

"How d'you mean?" She took another sip and went back to contemplating the mysteries of her wine.

"Well, you know, the job, the house, marriage,, kids- you did it, you aced it, got the lot"

"Hmm" For a moment Kate was changed, suddenly more distant, more thoughtful. An ironic half smile played at the edge of her mouth.

She snapped back into focus, beaming smile back in place "Anyway, The Enigmatic Mr. Wyman, you owe me – I've told you all about me, it's time for your end of the catch up!"

"Okay, but you should know there are some facts that are highly classified, when I was working undercover for MI6"

"Right, yeah, absolutely" She nodded seriously, playing along.

"And obviously you know about the time I was

launched into space to punch an asteroid that was going to impact on New York and kill millions?"

"Well, yes, we all know about that"

"I tell you, it was a damn good thing Miles let me get the day off work, otherwise those girls from Sex & The City would have been toast."

"In that case, I owe you- all women owe you – a huge debt" She smirked at me. "Now if we could cut the bullshit please..."

"If we cut the bullshit, it's a pretty boring story to be honest. " I looked down into my glass.

"After we were at school, it was GCSEs, A-levels, University.."

"Oh, right, where did you go?"

"Leeds. Media Studies"

"Oh, right – what did you want to do when you left?"

"No idea – that's why I did Media Studies" I half smiled. "Anyway, while I was back here I met Chris at the shop and worked there part time over the summer, and when I graduated Miles offered me a full time post. It was going to be just a temporary thing while I found something else, but that was nine years ago and as it turns out, finding something else is a lot easier said than done."

I paused, took another sip of wine. "So I guess like you

said, you just run with it and try and make the best of things."

"Do you still play? Do any of your own music?"

"Uhm, yeah, yeah, just a sideline really... I didn't think you..."

"My friend Natalie told me you'd written a song for me when we were at Vale Mount, she thought it was really sweet."

DANGER. DANGER. EMBARRASSMENT LEVEL CRITICAL.

"Oh, fuck, no..."

She grinned hugely at me. "Don't worry, I'm not going to ask you for a rendition now. I just thought it was really sweet, no one's ever done that for me."

"Well, to be fair, it's a bloody awful song, I mean, it's not really me at my artistic peak.."

"Well, even so, it'd be nice to hear it one day." She put her hand over mine and squeezed briefly. "So you mentioned this girl you'd just split up with, what happened there? Was it a long term thing?"

Ooh, crikey. Where do I start with this one. "Erm, well.." I entirely failed to begin.

Kate squeezed my hand again. "Don't worry, you don't have to tell me if you don't want to, you can tell me to mind my own business."

"No, no, it's fine – we met about six years ago, and it's been on and off since then. We have times where we get on great and everything's roses, and then all of a sudden, I don't know how to explain, *things just go wrong*. We have a fight and then it's all just arguments and bitterness and recrimination... and it seems to be an endless cycle. So after the last one, we agreed to call it quits, just to be friends."

"Do you love her?" Kate looked me straight in the eye.

Fuck, you don't mess around.

"You know, I... I hear this trotted out as a cliché so many times, but I think maybe just this once it's applicable. I do, but not... not in the right way, you know? In some ways she's my best friend, in some ways she knows me even better than Chris does, but there's always been.... I don't know, something missing, something holding us back. Does that make sense, or am I just rambling here?"

Kate looked down at her glass, a little sadly. "No. No, it makes perfect sense. So you never married, never got engaged or anything?"

"No, no – never even lived together, she once stayed over at mine for a week and we were at each other's throats by the end of it."

Christ, what a week *that* had been. We'd never even gone on a proper holiday together – apart from the fact that I never had the money, the memory of that week had kept us from spending more than three or four days away together.

"Seems a little odd... I mean, Martin and I had been

together just over a year when he proposed. We got married just after we graduated, he landed this great job in his final year, I was able to start the business, it all seemed... I don't know, just so *right*, so *obvious*. And I knew that we could have such a great life together. And we did – we do." she corrected herself hurriedly. "And there's never been anyone else?"

"Well, there's been a few."

Kate gave lecherous Sid James-style grin. "I bet there have."

"Not as many as you seem to think – hate to disappoint you, but I really do just mean a *few*."

"None of them lasted?"

"No." And they hadn't – it had usually only taken a couple of weeks to discover that when the alcohol wore off, we had absolutely nothing in common. God, she really was painting quite a depressing picture of my personal life here.

"And so you always came back to... what was her name?"

"Louise."

"And so you always came back to Louise? Or she came back to you?"

"Yeah, I guess... I mean, I probably wouldn't put it as dramatically as that. We just drifted back together. We have a lot of the same friends, we go to a lot of the same places.. inevitably we'd find ourselves chatting, and then the wine would flow and then one or other of us would make a move and the other one would think *what the hell,* and then off we'd go for another round."

Put like that, it sounded pretty tawdry, to be honest.

Kate sipped her wine. "It sounds like you two have always had some chemistry though?"

"Well, yes, but that's been good and bad. I mean we both have the gift of pissing the other one off quite monumentally."

She smiled ruefully. "Yeah, I know how that goes."

"But it's just got to the point where.. I don't know, I think we had to break the cycle. It was holding us both back. We were each other's safety net, I suppose you could think of it that way."

Except that instead of supporting each other, we'd somehow wound up strangling each other.

"So it's over for good this time then?"

"I think so, yes. Yes." *No more equivocating, Dan, no more wooliness. You've made your decision, now stand by it.* I finished my wine.

"Yes. Definitely over. We had to make the break otherwise we'll just spend forever in a holding pattern."

"And this was Sunday? And the next day you lose your job? Jesus, Dan, that's a rotten weekend."

"I've had better, that's for damn sure." I agreed.

"So what are you going to do now?"

Well, ain't THAT the sixty-four million dollar question.

"Well, that's the tricky part. I've been looking over the Wanted ads and there's sod all out there – and my CV's not exactly impressive. In fact, I was wondering, I know it seems a bit cheeky to ask but.."

Kate leapt into action. "Oh, don't you worry about that – you wrote me a song, the least I can do to thank you is help spruce up your CV. You've got email, haven't you?"

Awkward. Technically it was Miles who had provided the antiquated PC and broadband connection so that I could monitor the shop's website from home – so I was probably going to have to kiss that little luxury goodbye. That said, a man who filed credit card receipts on the toilet floor was probably a man who let certain details fall by the wayside, so I probably had a few weeks grace.

"Yes, for now."

"Well, email me a copy, I'll pick through it for you. How much notice did he give you?"

"Erm, well, none." I told her the story, omitting some of the swearing and the purloined records- I still wasn't sure what to do about them.

Kate was aghast. "So no disciplinaries, no warnings,

nothing like that?"

"Nope – I mean, apparently I was in breach of my contract, but to be honest, I've never *had* a contract." This was true, if you don't count the blank one I'd got Miles to sign and then filled in the conditions and salary myself - £50,000 per annum, fifty weeks paid vacation per year, a company Ferrari and a human clone... oh, and a lightsabre.

Sometimes it paid to be the only employee who could use a computer.

"So you knew these accounts were confidential?" Kate asked, all business now.

"Well, yeah, but thinking about it it was Chris who told me that when I started, not Miles. And it wasn't in any strict professional sense, it was *just leave the accounts to the boss, he's a bit funny about anyone knowing what he's up to.*"

"Right, so, he could have been money laundering, or gambling, or anything. I'd say you had every right to ensure that you weren't inadvertently part of some illegal activity that you could end up potentially being prosecuted for."

Bloody hell, this girl was *good*.

"Tell you what," she said refilling our glasses, "I know a fair few people in Human Resources and some of them owe me a favour or two. When you send me your CV, put down everything relevant about how he fired you, bullet point by bullet point. We'll get his sorted out, okay?" Kate raised her glass in a toast.

"I'll drink to that!" I felt a surge of positivity. I wasn't simply going to take this one lying down, this time the world could bloody well bend around me for once.

The rest of the afternoon was one of the most pleasant I can remember, sitting back sipping wine and stuffing ourselves with fancy snacks while we relived old school days (which were infinitely more enjoyable the second time around, from the perspective of a couple of decades distance). Around five, we packed up and headed back, as Martin would be home fairly soon and was presumably expecting to find his wife more or less where he'd left her, not pissed as a rat in the park with an old school friend who used to have the hots for her.

We wobbled up the path to Kate's front door, me with the now mostly empty bags in one hand and a giggly, slightly drunk Kate in the other steadying herself against me. She propped herself up against the door and fumbled her key out of her bag and into the lock.

"Thanks for today, Dan, I haven't had such a nice time in ages" She smiled blurrily at me.

"Thank *you*, Kate, for everything, this has been great."

"Don't forget to email me, and we'll get this job thing sorted out."

"Sure thing. Really appreciate this, Kate, thanks again."

"S'alright" she grinned a little dopily at me – and then reached in and kissed me full on the lips.

To say I was startled would be a massive

understatement.

Kate grinned again and giggled, raising a finger to her lips "Sssshhh" she whispered, "Mummy doesn't want to get in trouble"

Neither does Danny. "Okay, hun, you alright?"

She straightened. "Yeah, yeah -you'd better go, Dan. Thanks for a lovely day- email me, remember?"

"Will do. Okay, take care"

She smiled at me again, gave me a five-finger-wiggly wave goodbye, blew me a kiss and closed the door.

As I made my way back home to my flat – narrowly avoiding being knocked down by a large, gleaming angry-looking BMW driven by an equally large, gleaming, angry-looking man with a couple of very preened and starched kids in the back - all I could think of (and this was starting to seem like a running theme over the last few days) was-

What the fuck just happened?

Chapter 10

Hello again. You join me about a week and a half later. Pull up a chair, make yourself at home and I'll fill you in on the details. The kettle's on.

It seems to be a full time gig, this being unemployed business – as per Kate's instructions, I'd sent her all the gory details of my termination and attached my excuse for a CV to see what she could do with it. I'd also taken my first few bewildering steps to the job centre, and looked up the local temp agencies. The result – well, no actual job, nothing that netted me any actual money but holy *shit* would you look at that pile of forms I've got to fill in.

So between paperwork, general moping, and cursing Miles' name to the pits of hell, it had been a fairly busy and intense few days. I'll never forget my National Insurance number again, that's for damned sure.

Kate had been in touch, helping me out with the elements of paperwork that seemed to be written in Klingon – and to give credit where it was due, she'd been extremely patient with her idiot new student. I deliberately hadn't brought up the kiss, deciding to write it off as drunken flirtatiousness. People probably did this all the time – people who moved in more interesting circles than I - no point making a big deal out of it.

I was deliberately avoiding Louise, trying to put some distance between us since the split. If we were going to resist the temptation to go back to old habits, it made sense to spend a little bit of time establishing ourselves away from one another. I fervently hoped things were going better for her than they were for me right now.

Chris and I had exchanged a few texts, proposing meeting up for drinks and chats which mysteriously had yet to happen. I don't quite know what I'd been expecting – for him to hurl himself onto Miles' sword and offer himself up instead of me, to threaten resignation unless Miles hired me back – but I'd expected something. Between us, we'd kept that place going for the last nine years. I had a very strong feeling that all was not well, but for the moment, more immediate concerns took priority.

Sipping the first coffee of the day, I sat back and contemplated the towering pile of forms – the Leaning Tower Of Unemployment, if I may stretch a metaphor from earlier – that threatened to engulf the living room. It was a depressing prospect, especially it was almost certain that none of these would get me any closer to a job. The job market clearly hadn't changed much over the past decade – it was still a case of throwing as much mud at the wall as you possibly could, in the vain hope that some of it might end up sticking. Still, what options did I have?

a) Feel sorry for self. Fill in forms while drinking coffee.

b) Feel sorry for self. Watch daytime TV, considering

taking own life.

    c) Answer text message from Kate that's just arrived.

And the correct answer, as everyone should have guessed by now, is c).

Hi Dan, how r u doing? Hope the paperwork isn't getting u down...Had chat with HR colleague and might have sum gd news, cum 2 mine 4 lunch & i'll tell u all about it!! Kxx

Ah, that was more like it. Good news and a free lunch. I was on it like Wallace and Grommit. I prodded the ancient Nokia's grimy keypad (you have to be extra firm with the space bar, you see, really push it in like *that*... yeah, you've got it.).

Hi Kate, don't worry, takes more than a few forms to break me ;-) That sounds fantastic – what time do you want me there? And then after a moment's embarrassment - *D xx*

Oh, come on now, don't start. If someone puts kisses in a text to you, aren't you supposed to put some in your response?

The phone gurgled again.

About 1? Kxx

It's a datf (delete) *diet* (delete) *date ;-) Dxx*

It's amazing how minor successes like that can buoy you up, even when 99% of your life has moved absolutely, completely and irrevocably into the toilet. I spent a couple of hours trawling through benefit forms and making the most of Miles' internet uploading my CV (now fitter, trendier, looking half a stone lighter and five years younger courtesy of Ms Katherine Jane Gardener) onto as many job sites as I could find before hitting the shower, scraping the embarrassing remains of two days stubble growth off my chin and toddling off towards the posher end of town.

Kate greeted me at the door, a whirlwind of blonde cheeriness and expensive shimmery clothing, topped off with immaculately couiffeured hair and lipgloss.

"Dan!" - an enthusiastic peck on the cheek - "How have you been, you look great!"

I didn't look great. I'd just had a wash. But I suppose all things are relative – If you put a mouldy old dog turd under a gentle shower and wash the cobwebs off, it'll look marginally better than it did.

"I'm ok thanks," I smiled, "Been keeping myself busy – you look pretty fantastic yourself"

Well, she'd brought the subject up, it would have been rude not to mention it. Besides, my compliment at least had the benefit of being true- Kate did look fantastic, in the way that the rest of us can only manage with the aid of Photoshop, a dedicated makeup artist, or in my case, a head transplant.

"Thanks – I've been trying this new diet, cutting down on carbs, trying to lose the love handles."

Actually, this one didn't throw me as much as you might think - Louise had had fads of hopping from one diet plan to the other, so this stuff was pretty familiar territory.

Don't get me wrong, I still didn't actually understand what the fuck half this stuff meant, but I had learned what encouraging noises to make and what times to make them.

"Uh-huh, well, yeah, looking good, very svelte" - whoops, need to rein in some of the encouragement... there's a thin line between complimenting a woman on her appearance and actually trying to talk her into fucking you, and what with Kate being someone else's wife and all, probably best to play safe and try very hard to stay on the right side of that line.

We made our way through to the kitchen, which I could swear blind had managed to grow in size since I last saw it. Or maybe I'd just got reacclimatised to mine, where you got out a frying pan and that was all the available work surface gone.

"Right, first things first..." She poured us a glass of wine each, red for me and white for her, setting them down next to each other on the spotless granite counter. Knows how to treat a guest, our Kate.

She turned back from putting the white back in the fridge with a beaming toothsome grin splashed across her face and picked up her glass.

"To good news!" she proclaimed, holding her glass aloft. Hell, I'll drink to that, especially when someone else has been generous enough to provide the plonk - I followed suit, bringing the glasses together with a musical *clink*.

"Yeah, you mentioned in your text, what's the deal there?" I asked.

"Well, a company I did some work for a couple of years back.. I got to be good friends with the girl who runs the HR department there. She knows her employment law – they were downsizing, needed to let some people go, and basically it was her job to ensure that there was no nastiness, it was all above board and there'd be no comebacks."

I nodded and sipped "Okay, so what did.. I mean, how...

"Well, basically, your old boss really dropped the ball. If you had no contract or anything in writing after nine years, if there was no disciplinary structure in place... really, you should have had a verbal warning, then a written warning, *then* he can start threatening you with the sack. She reckons you might have a case to sue him for unfair dismissal."

Suing someone? Bloody hell, that seemed a bit drastic. And difficult. And expensive. I mean, we've all heard (and scoffed at) the stories of silly fat Americans who've sued McDonalds for not warning them that their coffee might be a bit hot, but actually doing it for real? I just didn't have the faintest idea where to even start.

"Wow, right... so how would I go about that? I mean, I've never really had cause to.."

Kate shook her head. "Don't worry about that. I know some people."

This was starting to sound a bit *Sopranos* all of a sudden. Would it involve having anyone killed? Pissed off as I may have been at Miles, that was taking things a little far.

She took a sip of wine. "First thing you should do is actually tell him you're going to pursue this. To be honest, that might be enough on its own to get him to climb down, I've seen that happen before."

"Okay, great, I can do that. Kate – you're a star, thanks so much for doing all this, I'm really grateful."

She twinkled at me. "You can write me a new song then."

I returned her twinkling with my best shit-eating grin. "Deal."

"Do you still have the band together? I remember that gig you did in the assembly hall at the end of Year 9.."

"Oh Jesus." I buried my face in my hands. "I still have nightmares about that."

She punched my arm playfully. "It wasn't that bad."

"No, it was bloody worse."

A thought occurred to me, and I began rummaging around in my jeans.

Oh, come on now. Credit me with just a little self-restraint. I pulled out my phone and the little earbud – headphone things that came with it.

Menu – Music- scroll down a bit – Aha! *Sunshine - The Formidable Ale Society.*

I passed Kate the phone. "Here you go, have a listen to this."

"Ooh..." She popped the earbuds in (thankfully I'd had the presence of mind to give them a brief wipe earlier) and hit Play. I could hear the tinny, trebley sibilant strains of Chris's masterpiece filter out into the kitchen.

Kate bobbed away happily. "So this is you and..."

"Chris, my mate from the shop." *Who I haven't seen since I got fucking fired while trying to help*, I thought sourly.

"Did you write it?"

I shook my head. "No, he wrote it years ago, I've just tweaked it, tarted it up here and there."

She nodded approvingly "It's very good – really catchy."

"Yeah, he does knock out a good tune every once in a while. It's like that old saying about monkeys and Shakespeare – give Chris enough time and lager, and sooner or later he comes up with a good 'un." I smiled, thinking of the good times we'd had in our little band.

Lunch blurred into afternoon as we relaxed into each other's company, picking up where we'd left off in the park the previous week. And gradually, almost inevitably, the conversation gradually worked its way back round to relationships.

"How are things with you and that girl you were telling

me about?" Kate asked, almost shyly.

"Louise? Not heard from her actually – I wanted to let the dust settle a bit first before we spoke, plus I've been a bit busy with this little lot." I motioned a hand towards the pile of forms and notes on Kate's kitchen counter.

Unfortunately, it was the hand with a wine glass in it.

"Oh, bollocks, sorry about that, let me.." I looked about for something to wipe up the mess.

"Here, don't worry, I've got it" Kate conjured up a couple of cloths from somewhere.

"No, no, let me – it's bad enough I've just sploshed about twelve quids worth of wine all over your floor"

"Go Dutch then" she grinned, chucking me a cloth. We padded up the small lake of wine I'd managed to throw all over her expensive kitchen, and then I noticed a dark puddle on the floor. Kate had seen it at exactly the same point and as we both bent down together we were suddenly incredibly close to one another. Abruptly, the atmosphere was charged with tension.

I ought to do something, I thought.

The fuck you should, I thought, *she's -*

This last thought was interrupted by Kate grabbing my head, pulling my face to hers and kissing me with an urgent, almost desperate passion.

Casanova that I am, I fell over.

Enthusiastic and presumably drunk as she was, Kate came with me.

"Sorry, I.." - oh, come on. I'm English, apologetic is my default setting.

Not so Kate, as it turns out, who told me to shut up and kiss her.

Now, normally, this type of situation is the kind of thing I would welcome with open arms (I assume, anyway, as it had never happened to me before – but it always looked fun when I saw it on the telly), but there was a fairly big red flag attached to this situation in the form of Kate's tastefully understated but almost certainly ruinously expensive wedding ring.

"I want you" she breathed in my ear.

Well, that was pretty bloody obvious. I just couldn't for the life of me see why.

"Yeah, but, come on – Martin? I mean, you're married to the guy, what the hell?" Nothing about this situation made any sense to me.

"Don't worry about him."

Right. Well, that's my mind at ease.

"No, come on, how.."

"Trust me" she said, nibbling on my ear, "There are things you don't know."

Clearly.

"Come on, Dan, I know you were crazy about me back then. Now you can have me."

Now here's a surprising discovery. Turns out, it's actually really difficult to persuade a very attractive woman not to have sex with you when she's apparently *determined* to. That was something I hadn't expected to learn today.

Still, this couldn't be right. There's no way this could be a good idea – she'd regret it and I would too. Kate had only just reappeared in my life and had proved to be a very good friend right at the moment when I really, *really* needed one.

"Look, Kate, believe me, I'd love too.." - and this was emphatically not flannel, as I may have mentioned before, Kate was as stunning now as she was back then - "..but this is wrong, you've got a husband, kids, I just don't see...."

She stood up, sniffed, ran her hands through her hair.

"Yes. You're right. Sorry Dan, I didn't mean to make you feel uncomfortable, I just.."

I hauled myself up.

"Look, no, don't be sorry, I.."

She shook her head. "You should probably go"

Nice one Danny, you managed to fuck up with the only person you've got in your corner right now. Somehow. Just what the hell is going on here?

I pulled her to me and hugged her.

"Look, Kate, I'm sorry, I don't... I didn't expect this. I don't want things to get weird between us, it's great having you back in my life, I don't want you to do anything you'd end up regretting."

Is that patronising? Fuck, I don't know, I don't think I've ever turned a woman down before. This is totally unfamiliar territory. I may as well be initiating first contact with a Martian.

She shook her head. "No, no, it's fine – it's fine. Let's just forget about it."

"Friends?"

"Friends." She smiled. "Oh, I think your phone's going"

She reached over to where I'd left it on the counter, unplugged the earpieces and passed it over.

Louise.

I pressed "Answer". Pressed it again (that button's a bit wonky too). "Hiya hun, you ok?"

An avalanche of sniffing greeted me. "Dan..."

"Jesus, Louise, you alright?"

In between sniffles, I caught the words *late* and *test*.

"Sorry, say that again?"

The tears stopped. I heard her draw breath.

"I'm *late*, Dan, I've just taken another test."

Driving? Maths?

"I'm *pregnant*, Dan."

Chapter 11

Silence.

Nothing moved.

I stared at the phone in mute horror, frozen in place like a statue. A slow thud as my heart attempted to push the blood through my veins. Dizziness overcame me. I saw Kate, concern on her face, lips moving, but no sound.

I looked down at my phone, but it wasn't in my hand any more. And the floor wasn't the floor any more either, somehow it had become the wall. Through the roaring in my ears, I could just make out the word ".....alright?"

I staggered to my feet. "What.. what just happened?"

Kate propped me up against the counter.

"You blacked out, or something. Here -" she turned to the sink and got me a glass of water.

"Drink this."

"Thanks" I slopped some into my mouth, a fair bit finding it's way onto my t-shirt.

"Here". Kate passed me my phone. "Whoever it was, I think you need to ring them back pronto. You OK?"

"Yeah – yeah, thanks." I dialled Louise's number. A disembodied calm female voice told me that the number I was dialling was unavailable and invited me to leave a message after the beep.

Shit.

SHIT.

I turned to Kate, all colour drained from my face. "I've got to go."

She nodded. "Yeah, sure – are you sure you're okay?"

"Yeah, yeah, fine – I'll explain later."

Fumbling the Nokia, I texted Louise that I was *on ny way ovr niw* – fuck it, she'd get the gist – and *ran*.

Yeah, that didn't last. With the best of intentions, Louise's place was a good four miles away across town. I pulled up, a breathless, wheezing, hacking mess after about ten minutes, and made my way along the last few streets at a slightly more sedate pace.

The drive was empty – not necessarily a problem, Louise didn't have a car. Probably just meant her mum was out, and frankly that was a relief. Trying to navigate the most difficult and important conversation of both our lives to date was not going to be made any easier by constant interruptions for tea and digestive biscuits, and having to keep our voices down while she watched *Countdown*.

I banged on the door the way countless Hollywood movies had told me I should in this situation. Just as I was wondering if I should start to yell her name, Louise opened the door.

Red eyed from crying, hair matted, cheeks stained with mascara – she looked utterly terrified.

I couldn't say anything – what was there to say? I just wrapped my arms around her and pulled her to me as hard as I could. A fresh batch of sobs erupted from her into my shoulder. I pressed her to me, stroking the back of her hair, *ssshhing* and *don't-worry-it'll-be-OKing* for all I was worth.

The time – a few minutes later. The place – Louise's mum's kitchen. The supporting cast – two steaming hot mugs of tea.

"So... how.."

Louise looked balefully at me.

"D'you want me to draw you a FUCKING DIAGRAM?"

Okay, bad opening gambit.

Her head dropped and she took a sip of tea.

"I worked it out - it was that last night – when I came round for my stuff, remember?"

I remembered. Normally, we were both pretty careful, but you could never be 100% sure. Condoms split, birth control pills get forgotten about, or made inactive by antibiotics. Sometimes a chap gets over-excited.. without getting too graphic, you get the general idea.

"I'm nearly a week late, Dan. And I'm never late. Ever. So I took a test, and then I took another, and another... they all came up positive."

I nodded, numb. I couldn't take this in, it was just too much.

"I've got another pack, I thought.. we could take them together? Just to be sure."

"Yeah.. yeah, can't exactly hurt, can it?"

We trotted up to the bathroom. Louise foraged around in the mirror fronted cabinet.

"I had to hide them" she explained, "Mum would have gone nuts."

I was going to make some crack about her turning up at my door with a wedding suit and a shotgun, but this wasn't really the moment. I felt sick with fear - and whatever terror I was feeling, Louise was surely feeling amplified a thousand times.

She found the box and pulled out the two plastic tester strips. I watched apprehensively.

Louise looked at me oddly. "Erm, Dan, are you just going to stand there?"

"Hmm?" I was perplexed.

"Well, I mean.. I have to pee on them."

"Oh, right. Yeah, obviously. Sorry." I excused myself and hustled out of the bathroom.

Out on the landing, I tried to steady myself, breathing deep and slowly. Hands – shaky. Skin – cold and clammy. Heart – having palpitations. I made a concerted effort to think straight, but any attempt at forming a cohesive mental sentence got about three syllables in before it was interrupted by one simple phrase, blaring in my mind like a klaxon.

OH FUCK. OH FUCK. OH FUCK. OH FUCK.

Calm down man, for God's sake. She's scared enough as it is.

I heard a flush, and moments later the door unlocked. Louise beckoned me in.

I didn't quite know what I was looking at at first.

"There, look-" she pointed towards the little quartz-crystal display. Three little lines blurred themselves into existence. I checked the instruction manual.

In a positive result, within two minutes two lines should form around the display centreline forming the image / / /.

Yep, there it was alright - / / /, clear as day. The klaxon in my brain started over again, faster and louder than ever.

OHFUCKOHFUCKOHFUCKOHFUCKOHFUCKOHFUCK

"Yeah, yeah... three lines, it's definitely positive." I heard myself say.

"Okay... now what?"

I don't know. I don't know. I was pressed up against a wall, a gun against my head - terrified beyond belief. There was no way I could think rationally.

I mean, seriously – a baby? A baby in my flat? Or at Louise's mum's? Just.. *how*, the fuck? What was I supposed to do in this situation? *The right thing, of course, but just what in all holy fucking shitting cocking hell* was *the right thing?*

I gazed mute at the little plastic stick. Goodbye hopes and dreams. Goodbye aspirations. Goodbye... everything.

There was a sob. I looked around to see Louise crumple.

I wrapped myself around her. "Hey, hey.. come on, it'll be ok, whatever happens we can do it together... it'll be alright honey, I promise, please don't cry"

What's going to be alright, Dan? How is ANY FUCKING THING going to be alright?

EVER FUCKING AGAIN?

"Oh God, Dan, what are we going to do?"

I didn't know. I had know idea. Each passing second dragged us both – Jesus, dragged all three of us – deeper into the petrifying abyss of the unknown, and whatever action or inaction I made was only going to make things worse. I had never been more scared in my life. My bowels had turned to liquid nitrogen.

"We'll figure it out honey, I promise, we'll figure it out." I tried to make the best soothing noises I could, while inside my head all hell broke loose. I couldn't be a father. I couldn't look after a child. I couldn't look after Louise. Christ all-fucking-mighty, I could barely look after myself, what in God's name was I supposed to do with a baby? Where was I going to put it?

As Louise sobbed into my shoulder, I tried my hardest not to throw up as I saw my future dissolve into a ruin of poverty, rows, guilt, worry and frustration. This was a catastrophe. The worst thing that could have happened. My inner teenager came hurtling back into the frame.

IT'S NOT FAIR. IT'S NOT FAIR. IT'S NOT FAIR. IT'S NOT FAIR.

Chapter 12

It was late, very late. Louise had eventually fallen asleep, exhausted after hours of sobbing onto my shoulder. I, meanwhile – there was a very strong possibility I would never sleep again. I just couldn't believe it. This was all so wrong – I couldn't be a father, I had absolutely no idea what to do.

I paced the bathroom, tracing figure panicky eights on the linoleum while my guts twisted with fear, trying like hell to think straight. On one level, there was a simple solution. The easy thing, the obvious thing was to abort – she could only be a couple of weeks gone. We hadn't planned this, we were in no position to look after it, we'd just been very, very unlucky. We could just get rid of it and that would be it, back to our lives, never speak of it again – it would be like nothing had happened.

But... could I? Could I really ask her to do that? To put herself through that trauma?

And yet what choice was there? I had no job, no particularly promising prospects of getting one in the near future. Our relationship was a farce – for all the affection we held for one another, it basically did consist of wine, sex and arguments. We couldn't even go a week without trying to kill each other, we'd proved that a few years back when we'd briefly flirted with the idea of Louise moving in with me. Big,

big mistake.

And most importantly – how the fuck was I supposed to be a dad? What did you do? Mine had always had a steady job, always been in control and unflappable, it was hard to believe he'd ever been the trembling, nail-biting, terrified wreck that I saw when I looked in the bathroom mirror.

Calm down, Dan. Just breathe. Just breathe.

I grabbed hold of the sides of the sink and held on for dear life as waves of hot and cold flooded through me. There was a black cloud at the edge of my peripheral vision, threatening to engulf me. I tightened my grip till my knuckles were white as the room started to spin around me and my knees buckled. The black cloud lurking just out of sight now had its hands around my throat, suffocating me, I couldn't breathe, I couldn't think, I couldn't – I convulsed, and deposited a chunk of half digested Marks & Spencers Finest snackfoods in the sink before my legs gave way and I collapsed to the floor in a heap.

Louise must have heard me, as the next thing I knew the bathroom light was on and her hands were pillowing my head.

"Hey you.. come on, try not to worry, come and let's get some sleep."

I nodded dumbly, struggled to my feet and rinsed out the basin before splashing cold water on my hands and face.

Louise took my hand and led me back into the bedroom. Numbly, I followed her stripping down to T-shirt and boxers before clambering in next to her.

"Louise, I..."

She put a finger to my lips to shush me.

"I know. We'll talk about this tomorrow. We both need to be calm to do this, okay?"

"Okay"

She snuggled backwards into me, and I wrapped my arms round her.

She looked like an angel.

Sleep must have eventually come, because the next thing I remember is Louise stood over me with tea in hand.

"Morning" she smiled "You sleep okay?"

"Yeah, yeah, good, thanks." I sat myself up in Louise's bed. Which was no mean feat, actually, as as well as being a refuge for sleeping, it was also a repository of throw pillows and stuffed animals. I offered a mute apology to Mr. Huggy Badger as I realised he'd spent the night with his face in my crotch and took the tea gratefully.

"How about you?"

"Yeah, okay... we need to talk though."

Oh yes. Boy do we ever.

"The thing is, Dan... I know we didn't plan this, and I know there's like a million reasons why this is a bad idea.. but I can't, I just can't get rid of it, I couldn't face the idea. Every time I thought about it I just felt sick. I mean, I know I've always gone on and on about being pro-choice and everything, but this.... this is different, this isn't the theory, this is real."

She paused, biting her lip.

"I know this isn't your fault, and I'm not trying to ruin your life over it... but I think I have to have this baby."

I tried to croak something reassuring and failed abysmally.

"You don't have to be involved, Dan, you really don't, and I won't resent you for just doing a runner, I promise you. But I *have to do this*. I have to. I just couldn't live with myself otherwise."

I nodded dumbly. "Are you – are you sure you know what you're doing though?"

She almost laughed. "No, Dan, no – I don't know what I'm doing, I don't have a fucking clue. But Mum does, and I've got nearly nine months to learn from her. I know it's not ideal, and Christ, I never thought I'd be one of those women who's a single mother before she's thirty, it's one step away from being on Jeremy Kyle.."

She paused briefly, running her hands through her hair.

"I always thought I'd know what to do in this situation.

Grit my teeth and have an abortion because I know I'm not ready for it. But now I've got to make that decision for real and I can't, Dan, I just can't, I'm so sorry.." She started to sob.

"Hey, hey..." I hoiked myself out of the the clutches of a stuffed Winnie The Poo and onto my feet, gathering her into my arms. "It's okay, it really is."

It really isn't. I always thought I knew what I'd do in this situation – run to the fucking hills. But that wasn't an option.

The way I saw it, three things could happen.

I could persuade Louise to have an abortion – well, I could try, anyway - and she'd probably never speak to me again, and I'd always have the awful knowledge that I'd have pressured her into it. It was the easiest, and logically speaking the best choice to make – we weren't together, neither of us had the resources to raise a child, and how we could give it any kind of a future was beyond me at the moment. But I understood what Louise was saying, that she couldn't do it, and I couldn't make her, that would be inhuman.

She could keep it, and as she put it, I could do a runner - absent myself completely and have no ties to it or her. Again, easier for me – but could she look after it alone, here at her mum's surrounded by nappies? And again, could I live with myself knowing I'd just abandoned my infant son or daughter?

Or... we go for it. Try and raise this kid together, try and be a proper grown up couple.

So, then, Danny-boy, will you look behind door number

1, 2, or 3... clock's a-ticking, sunshine.

Chapter 13

Home again, some hours later. A much-needed shower and a sandwich had helped calm my nerves. I'd left Louise after trying to reassure her as much as possible that everything was going to be okay, but back in the familiar surroundings of my little hovel, I couldn't for the life of me see how.

Under the circumstances, I felt the best thing I could do was call on the two most vital skills I'd developed in the workplace – making lists, and making tea.

Sitting down at the coffee table, note pad and pen (both pinched from the shop in happier times, I realised) and crucially *tea*, in hand, I perched myself on the edge of the sofa and started to figure out what the fuck I was going to do about the rest of our lives.

Right. First off, JOB. I wrote this down and underlined it several times over. This was now of critical importance. If Louise was dead set on having this baby – and I had to assume that she was – there was no way I could just leave her to deal with it on her own. I just couldn't – I knew that as surely as I knew my own name. So I was going to have to get myself to the position where I could support myself, and us.

I was going to have to scour every paper, every website, and apply for absolutely everything. Unfortunately, I didn't have a great deal (on paper at least) to offer a potential employer, so whatever I wound up doing, it was going to be at the absolute lowest level, at least to start with. But I had to find *something*, and fast.

I resolved the next step after list-making was to hit the internet and the local paper with a vengeance, anything that I'd rejected out of hand would now be applied for anyway.

Next step – LOUISE. This one was a little trickier and more ambiguous. After all these years, after all the ups and downs, the fights and the make-ups... just what did we have between us? Could we make it, could we actually pull it together and raise this kid with a mum and a dad, like I'd been raised? Louise had lost her dad when she was very young, so she'd always been the product of a single mum – maybe this was why she felt more confident about doing it, she was firsthand evidence that this was possible. Me- I'd been raised about as traditionally as it was possible to be raised. Honestly, if it had been actually possible to produce precisely .4 of a child to bring us into line with government national averages, my mum and dad would have found a way to do it. So, I really had rather less confidence in my abilities.

I thought about my dad (making a brief, and guilty, mental note that I was waaaaay overdue to give my parents a call) – he'd been twenty-eight when they'd had me, younger than I was now. Reflecting on that, reflecting on my state of mind when I'd been that age, I found it hard to believe anyone could ever have thought themselves ready for this kind of decision.

But there again, they'd got married two years before that. Pledged their *entire lives* to each other aged just twenty-six and twenty-four. The more I thought about it, the more that absolutely staggered me. To make a decision of that magnitude so very young... me at twenty-six, fuck, me *now* – I was just a kid, I couldn't take that decision. Louise and I had had so many false starts, so many fights, so many breakups, it was insane to think that what we had was anything similar...

...And yet.

And yet, I realised, we'd always wound up back again together. And when we'd tried to say goodbye, to make a clean break from each other... well, look what had happened. I was almost tempted to see the hand of a second-rate Hollywood screenwriter at work, controlling our fates.

Maybe what we had ran deeper than either one of us realised.

Maybe what we had really was strong enough to make this work.

Maybe we..... Jesus, was I even about to *think* this? Maybe there *was* a one, and just maybe, Louise was it.

In which case – and I was starting to go dizzy again here – *why don't you go and slip a ring on that girl, Danny*

This was so far through the looking glass it was ridiculous.

Your parents did it. Aged a lot younger than you, they did it. And it worked out pretty well. People do this. All the time, all over the world, every day. And I bet a hell of a lot of them are just as scared and confused as you are right now.

I tried to argue back. I mean, this was *me and Louise*. The standing joke of the decade. Six months on, six months off, for the last six years.

And what happened when she called out of the blue? You ran – well, yes, part of the way, before getting out of breath and having to have a quick sit-down – *you ran straight back to her. You were the first, and the only one she told.*

That's got to mean something.

But what?

Afternoon became evening became night as I paced my way further and further down the rabbit hole. I had told Louise if she needed anything, anything at all, to let me know, and was mildly reassured to get a text back from her telling me she was *OK 4 now thnkx xx.*

I responded letting her know *evrythng will b OK* and telling her *nt 2 wrry xx*

Looking round my little flat, I tried to imagine it full of nappies and babyclothes, cot propped up in the corner.. I mean, it wasn't ever going to be a candidate for *Better Homes And Gardens* magazine whatever happened - maybe it wouldn't be too bad.

I shook my head. This was ridiculous. I needed to get out, take a walk, clear my head. Pacing my flat like a prison yard and driving myself crazy was doing no one any good. I needed to talk to someone, get a perspective other than my own on things. Louise had enough to deal with, I didn't want to burden her any more. Kate – well, Kate was very definitely out after yesterday, the last thing I needed was any more complexity.

Jesus, that was a thought. Kate and Martin couldn't have been more than about twenty-five when they got hitched and started popping out kids. And there must be a big ol' problem with that particular relationship when one of it's chief participants starts ramming her tongue down my throat – is that what me & Louise would turn out like?

No, I couldn't talk to Kate. Damn shame though, she'd really helped me over the last week or so. It was a bitter, *bitter* irony- I'd been so absurdly hung up on her as a kid, and here she was practically throwing herself at me.. and I couldn't do anything about it. *Careful what you wish for, Danny boy.*

I resigned myself to the fact there was really only one person I could talk to at a time like this.

"Jesus Christ, you look like shit. Come on in, there's beers in the fridge- grab yourself one and tell Uncle Chris what you've gone and done."

Gratefully, I entered Chris' bombsite of a living room, a place where many a drunken evening had ended in more innocent times. I thought back to the last time I'd woken up here under the coffee table – seemed a million years ago now, another lifetime.

I should feel at home here. I didn't.

So much had changed these past couple of weeks. I felt like an imposter, like I was playing the cartoon version of myself.

I slumped back onto the sofa, popping the tab off the can of lager. Swore as a foamy geyser engulfed my thumb and forefinger, shook off the excess and slurped at the frothy goodness within. My best mate of nine years' standing plonked himself down next to me.

"So what's been happening then, not seen you for a while."

"Well, yeah – we were going to go for a drink last Thursday, remember? Pretty sure I texted you to arrange that.. pretty sure I didn't hear anything back from you either."

Give him his due, he did have the good grace to look embarrassed.

"Ah, yeah, about that... look, if I'm honest, I've just not had the time. I know that's a shitty excuse , but it's true."

"Busy then?" If any of those hours as a twelve year old in the bathroom trying to imitate Roger Moore had paid off, I would have had the necessary skill and co-ordination to arch an eyebrow in an effortlessly cool wordless put-down. Sadly, they hadn't, so Chris entirely missed the sarcasm.

"Well, yeah, believe it or not. He's not hired anyone to replace you, so at least I'm getting paid regularly now, but trying to do the website stuff when he doesn't know what he's doing is... pretty fucking trying, to be honest."

God, I could just imagine that. I felt a rush of sympathy for the poor shop PC, by now most likely as riddled with viruses as a backstreet Bangkok crack whore and probably kicked and beaten just as regularly.

"Well, he's not fucking getting away with it. I've been doing some research and you can tell him from me he should be saving his money, because I *will* be taking him to the fucking cleaners." I said with feeling.

"Mate, I... well, you've got to do what you've got to do." Chris shook his head and slurped his lager. "It was fucking stupid, what he did, I can't say I agree with it, but..." He tailed off.

"Anyway, that stuff is all between you and him. What's been happening with you, why the urgent message?"

Showtime. I took a swig of lager and a deep breath, mistimed both and had a brief coughing fit. I had another go and ordered the whole sequence rather better this time.

"Well, it's Louise. I've.... we've...." I tailed off. Shit, this was harder than I thought.

"You back together again?"

"Kind of..."

"So, what, you two are getting hitched? Moving in together?"

Once again, there wasn't much of a reply I could give. "Well......"

"Oh Christ, she's up the duff, isn't she? You've knocked

her up?"

"My old friend, you have the soul of a *fucking* poet." I smiled sourly and sipped more beer. "And yes. Yes, she is, and yes I have."

"Jesus, you serious? You've heard of condoms, right?"

I should have expected that, I suppose.

"Of course I have, you dick – look, you want the gory details, it broke, ok? Neither of us realised till after it was too late."

(I'll spare you the sloppy, sticky details of how we found this out – it's not that kind of book. Wait until Chris tries novelising the *Anal Corruption* saga.)

"Whewww..." Chris exhaled. "Shit, man. I mean, I hate to ask this, but are you sure it's yours?"

I felt irrationally annoyed by the question. "Yeah. Well, sure as I can be, anyway. Look, I'm not going to go into the details, but we tracked it back to the night me and her split up, and, well... it fits, put it that way."

Chris shook his head in apparent disbelief. "Jesus... well, I suppose – congratulations?" He extended a hand.

I looked balefully at him.

"Don't take the piss."

The hand returned to its natural resting place – wrapped

around a can of room-temperature Carling. Chris shrugged.

"Alright mate – what do you want me to tell you?"

"I don't know" - I really didn't - "Just – needed to talk some stuff through, I suppose, try and make sense of things."

It was horribly frustrating. Too many thoughts crowding each other out, stopping me from finishing any of them coherently, stopping me from asking what I wanted to ask, from *knowing* what I wanted to ask... I tried to voice something sensible.

"I just don't know what to *do*..."

I felt my voice crack theatrically at the end of that sentence. Almost, *almost*, lost it right there and then. Fear kept hitting me in waves – a realisation of the sheer unbelievable ludicrousness of the situation and my inability to deal with it. All of a sudden I was gone from standing on solid ground to teetering on the top of a precipice.

Chris squeezed my shoulder. "Easy, mate. Easy. One thing at a time. Let's figure out what you *can* do. She want to keep it?"

I nodded. "Yeah, she doesn't think she can handle getting rid of it."

"You planning on emigrating?"

In spite of everything, I couldn't help laughing. Unfortunately, this involved spraying a fine amber mist of lager over Chris' table.

"No, I don't really have the funds right now"

"Right then old son, you are going to be..."

There now began a painfully elongated sequence which I'll gloss over here as Chris rummaged through a drawer full of cassettes, pulled one out, plugged it into his massive, creaking ancient hi-fi system, rewound it to the right place (with several stops along the way), and switched on his speakers before filling the room with about a hundred decibels of Boney M's "Daddy Cool"

I applauded. "Very good"

Chris shrugged. "Well, if I'd have known I could have prepared a little better. So look, by a process of elimination then, we have sussed that she's keeping it and you're not doing what I would do in your situation, which is..."

There was another flurry of activity which a few minutes later produced an Iron Maiden album and another hundred decibels of "Run To The Hills".

"Yeah, look, mate, we're going to have to steer clear of song titles or this is going to take all night."

Chris grinned. "Yeah, I suppose this is the sort of situation you want an iPod or something for."

Frankly, trying to imagine Chris successfully negotiating his way around something that modern and sophisticated was an eventuality far more improbable, and contained far more potential for disaster, than my impending fatherhood.

"So that really only leaves one option, then, doesn't it? Stick around and see if you two can stay together for more than six months without killing each other, go find a place together and get a white picket fence and a dog and spend the rest of your lives together bickering about soft furnishings."

I nodded assent. "Well, yeah – that was pretty much my thinking."

"Well first things first mate, you need a job unless you're planning on making a living featuring in Channel 5 documentaries."

This was undeniably true, but the observation irked me.

"Yeah- I seem to remember having one, a pretty regular steady one actually, for nine solid years before getting kicked out out of it."

Chris shifted uncomfortably. "Look, I know you're pissed off about that mate, but that's really between you and Miles.."

I turned to look at him, straight in the eyes. "Well, I also seem to remember that one of the main reasons I got fired from said job was because I was poring over the accounts trying to help figure out why the fuck *you* hadn't been paid."

Chris bridled at this. "Hey, I told you to keep an eye out while I looked through those things. No one made you go and start doing your whole Sherlock Holmes investigation bit into the accounts. All you had to do was put the damn things back and he'd have been none the wiser."

"Did you tell him I only had them out because you'd taken them out of the safe?"

"Look, you know what he's like, he gets the blinkers on. Cross one of his lines and that's it, the switch flips."

"So what exactly did happen when you got back and discovered he'd canned your best mate of a decade's standing, then?"

"Honestly? Nothing. Seriously. I asked him where you'd gone, and he said 'Home' – and that was it. Said he wasn't going to talk about it, left me on the till for the day and fucked off. Next day, I get in, asked where you were and he tells me you don't work here any more, and that he's not willing to discuss it. And that was it".

I believed him. Miles had always been an odd chap – spending your life obsessed with running a small, tumbledown cartoon of a shop in an industry apparently dedicated to gradually phasing you out of existence will do that to you, I suppose. That said, I expected at least something more from Chris – at least a protest of some sort would have been in order.

"So did you even try talking to him about it?"

"Well, yeah, but, I mean.." He looked away and took another swig. "Look, I'm not Spartacus. I've got to keep a roof over my head. Can't exactly help you if I'm fired myself, can I?"

"Feeble, mate. Feeble"

Frustrated, he began gesticulating. "Well, what? What would you have me do? He'd sling me out too, you know. Fucking tapped in the head, that guy. And then what? You're fired, I'm fired, that shop goes down the pan in two months max. Who wins there?"

Rationally, it was difficult to argue. But rationality wasn't the only force at work here. On a very basic, almost primal level, I felt betrayed and stabbed in the back by the two people I considered my closest friends – and I wanted payback. If Miles wasn't within reach, I wanted to know what the bloody hell Chris had been up to on my behalf. Damn sure I'd have kicked up a stink and a half if Miles had pulled this shit with him.

Well, pretty sure, anyway.

"Look, put yourself in my shoes. I'm trying to help you out and I get shat on, royally. I'd like to think that at some point, my best mate, the same best mate I lost my job trying to help out, would at least have made some noises to the boss about getting me reinstated... or just at least tried to fight my corner to at some degree."

Chris exhaled with a long sigh and ran his hand through his hair, placing the can on the coffee table with an audible thump.

"Look, mate, that's all very well and good, but this is the real world, okay, and all that shit is going to accomplish is getting me fired too. Look, he's a cock, a complete arsehole for doing what he's done, but what do you think is going to happen? He's going to suddenly see the error of his ways, invite you back and the Three Musketeers are back together again? No, you know him – he's a stubborn stupid bastard. He'd fire me and run himself into ruin before he admits he's wrong. Pull all the heartstrings you want, but you fucking KNOW I'm right."

I do, but at the same time I know he's wrong. Chris was definitely stuck in the middle of a no-win situation, no doubt about that, but I did feel more than a little offended that he'd basically gone "oh, right, ok then" and offered no explanation to Miles about why I'd been going through those bloody ledgers in the first place. There was more than a whiff of skins being saved here, while mine was being thrown to the wolves.

"Well, did you even *try* explaining the situation to him? Explaining about you not being paid, and explain that you were worried? That I was worried? I mean, for fuck's sake, does he think I was trying to pull off some industrial espionage?"

"You've *met* Miles, right? He hears what he wants to hear when it comes to this shit. You think he's going to be honest and admit to himself he's buggering up his business, or do you think he's going to lash out and blame the first poor bastard that he sees for his woes? You know the guy, and you were unlucky enough to be the first poor bastard he saw. I can't change that, and if I try, the *only* thing I'm going to accomplish is getting myself fired. You haven't known him as long as I have – trust me on this."

"Oh, don't pull that 'you don't know him like I do' crap – you may have worked there longer but I've still known him for nearly ten years, that's plenty long enough. You could have said *something*. You could have at least have bloody tried."

Chris hurled the rest of his lager angrily down his throat.

"Right, yeah, and can I come stay on your couch after I lose my job and they foreclose on my flat? You'd love that, wouldn't you?"

This was starting to get serious. Tempers were fraying to the level of the upholstery on Chris' ancient decrepit sofa. Things were going to be said here – big, important things that couldn't be forgotten about. But it was unavoidable now, the row was reaching critical mass.

"I'd do it, because friends look out for each other, right, that's the whole fucking point. Where as you, you cunt, you were quite happy to see me thrown out on my arse and just give me a wave goodbye. And I come round here to try and talk this through and you can't even see why that's wrong?"

"No, you came here to mope about Louise and get some sympathy, just like always. Same shit, different month."

"Fuck you! I lost my job trying to help you, and now I find out she's pregnant.. My fucking world's falling in on itself here, I'm at my wit's end..."

"Me, me, me, me, me, me – always the same. And you're expecting me to risk my neck with fucking Miles, giving him ultimatums when you know damn well he'd set himself on fucking fire before he'd admit he was wrong?"

For the second time in a month, I couldn't believe what I was hearing.

"Are you fucking serious? I take a fucking fall for you and you're going to make out I'M the bad guy?"

"Don't try and play the wounded hero, Dan, I never asked you to do that for me and I never would have done. For fuck's sake mate, what was I supposed to do?"

"SOMETHING!" This was getting ridiculous, we were just going in circles. I couldn't believe that he couldn't – *wouldn't* - see why I felt so let down.

Chris looked me straight in the eye. "Dan, you're thirty years old. You're my mate, but you're not my responsibility. I'm sorry, I really am, but I just can't help you on this one."

Once again, words failed me. I stood. "Fine. Bye."

Turned on my heel and stalked out. Done.

Chapter 14

    I don't know what time it was. In fact, by now, I was struggling to keep track of what *day* it was. Watching motes of dust dancing in the grey daylight, silhouetted against the grimy once-was-white of the ceiling was fast becoming the entertainment high point of my day. Frankly, with each day seeming to have a nasty weighted sucker-punch up it's sleeve, I was finding it harder and harder to find the motivation to get out of bed in the morning.

    Things weren't good, put it that way.

    The ancient Nokia bleeped it's way through the riff to "Take On Me", startling me out of a miserable reverie.

    I debated answering it. The last month I'd lost my job, my girlfriend, a potential friend in the shape of Kate, discovered I'd accidentally got my now ex-girlfriend pregnant and lost my best mate. God alone knew what might be lurking at the other end of the phone – a Mafia don demanding £250,000, a doctor telling me I had every strain of hepatitis and that they were going to take my thumbs (and charge me £250,000 for the privilege). Maybe it was safer to hide under the duvet and ignore it.

    Old habits die hard. I checked the screen – Kate.

Fuck, that was potentially even worse.

Potentially.

I pressed the grimy green "answer" button, grinding my thumb in there until the damn thing clicked.

"Hi Dan!"

Sure enough, there it was, the dancing coquettish girlish giggle.. you could almost believe that none of the insanity of the last couple of weeks had happened. Honestly, if a voice could *sound* blonde, hers would.

I heaved myself upright and perched on the side of the bed.

"Hey Kate, how are you?"

If her voice sounded blonde, mine sounded grey and arthritic and close to death.

"Oh, great, thanks, great" - *of course you are,* I thought sourly (and a bit unfairly), *everything's great in teak-panelled, flat-screen, impeccably mowed, groomed and leather-furnished KateWorld. What have you got to worry about? What have you got to **not** feel great about?*

Stop it, Dan, this is the only person in the last catastrophic few weeks who's actually tried to HELP you... whatever else she wants or doesn't want from you, she's probably the only person right now who CAN help you.

"-are you OK, you sound awful? Everything alright?"

Nope. Everything is completely and utterly fucked and I have absolutely no idea what to do about getting my life straightened out, and oh, here's the kicker, in just under nine months I'm going to be responsible for another human life forever and I have no idea how in all holy hell I'm going to take care of them.

I forced a smile. Well, a semblance of one, anyway.

"Been better. Rough night, that's all."

"Oh, sorry – listen, though, I've got some news that might cheer you up. Are you still looking for a job?"

Yes. *Yes.* No – I didn't want a new job, I wanted my old one back. My old *life* back - it might not have been much, but it was mine and I knew how to do it.

But now I was going to be a dad. Everything had changed. What *I* wanted didn't really matter any more, and Kate was offering me a potential lifeline.

"Seriously? You're a lifesaver – what kind of thing are we talking about?"

Mining salt under the lash of an evil overlord, I thought wryly, *or perhaps something that involved dancing in a cage in fetish clubs.*

Still, if it paid – times were getting seriously hard.

She hesitated for a moment. *Yeah, it had to be fetish clubs. Probably they got to use a whip on me while I dance some twisted macabre take on the Macarena.*

"Look, I don't want to get you too excited, it's nothing that fantastic..."

"Are there whips involved?"

"What?"

"Nothing, sorry – look, if you've got anything you think I could do, I'm more than happy to give it a shot... I'm not really in a position to turn any opportunities away."

"Ok, well, great – it's a desk job, admin stuff, you ok with that?"

"Sure, sure, yeah, whereabouts?"

"Well, it's one of the recruitment places in town, my friend Rebecca runs the office there. It's in the town centre, I'll get you the address. It's just data entry stuff, I'm afraid, nothing fascinating."

"Kate, I'm reusing my teabags here – if they'll pay me, it's all good! You're a lifesaver.."

"Hey, glad I could help – there is an interview you'll need to sit though.. do you have a suit?"

Umm. Probably. I seemed to recall owning one around about the time I moved into the flat. It probably hadn't gone anywhere since then. I decided to be positive – it was bound to be somewhere, most likely buried in the bowels of the wardrobe. The graveyard for T-shirts and pants that grew too full of holes to be used in decent society. Fingers crossed.

"Yeah, sure, I'll fish it out."

"Great – they've got your CV and I've put in a good word for you.. they're honestly not that scary, it's a nice office... as long as you don't come in vomiting pea soup and speaking in tongues you should have no problems winning them over."

I smiled, beginning to see a small pinprick of hope on the black stained bedsheet of my current situation.

"Well, that rules out two of my key workplace skills, but I'll try my best."

"Brilliant! Best of luck then Dan, I'll text you over the time and place when Rebecca gets back to me – should be a little later today."

"Thanks Kate, you're a star. I won't let you down."

"You're welcome, Dan, take care"

We mutually "goodbye"-d and I leaned back onto the bed, exhaling deeply. *Fuck. I might just have a fighting chance after all. Thank Christ.*

Hang on, Danny boy. Don't get carried away. Got to pass this thing first. Got to get the look right. Got to get the suit. Got to find *the suit.*
An hour later, the wardrobe is empty, it's contents strewn all over the floor. I am excavating my way towards its core and finding clothes that I'm sure I never owned. Clothes that must have grown and fashioned themselves deep in the

bowels of the closet, where the underpants goblins made their home. For God's sake, there was a zip-up cardigan and a tracksuit in here.

Digging deeper – past the strata of porn in DVD, VHS and magazine form (nine years of birthday presents from Chris), down through the layer of mould-addled, motheaten T-shirts from the days when Oasis fought Blur for the top spot in the album charts, and the days when I knew what the hell was in the album charts, finally... there she was, the motherlode.

I'd had this suit since graduation, and I could count the number of times I'd worn it on the fingers of one hand. Forty quid well spent there.

Still, it didn't seem to have gone out of style – probably because it had never been in style in the first place – and I reckoned that so long as I did my exhaling discreetly and in private, it should still just about fit. The single shirt and tie I possessed completed the look.

I gazed at my rumpled reflection in the mirror. A podgy, smeary, badly drawn unconvincing imposter of a successful young entrepreneur stared back at me. I thought back to that morning at Chris' flat, after my birthday – two months and a lifetime ago.

You wanted to grow up, I thought. *Here we go.*

A symphony of bleeps grabbed my attentions. Kate.

Hi Dan! Just got details from Rebecca – can you get into town for 8am, the office is called TC Harveys, they're on Market Street just next to the library. Good luck! Kate xox

8am? Good god, what manner of slavery was she trying to sign me up for? *That meant getting up at half 6, was she insane?*

The pile of unpaid bills on the windowsill caught my eye.

Oh. Yeah.

Mashing my thumb into the Nokia's keypad – bloody space bar – I managed to tap out a response.
Yeah, I'll b thr – thnkx again hun x

I barely slept that night. I was as nervous as I could remember being – scared of getting the job, scared of not getting it. Once again, my life was spiralling out of my control.. If I was brutally honest, grateful though I was to Kate for arranging all this, in my heart of hearts I didn't want this job. But it wasn't about me any more, was it? That era ended when Louise got pregnant. When *I* got Louise pregnant.

Don't panic. Breathe. You're doing the right thing here. Get this job, you start getting yourself on track. And you might just have a chance at doing this right.

The last thing I remembered that night was seeing the alarm clock on my phone read 4.30 am.

So you'll understand if I was just a little less than sprightly when the bastard went off just two hours later. Fuck, this is not a good way to start the day.

Shower. Coffee. More coffee. Slap self in face and shake self vigorously.

Come on, you can DO this. You NEED to do this.

Shave.. I don't grow proper stubble, just an embarrassment of a moustache. Like a fifteen year old trying to rent a porn video. But still, not a great look for someone trying to pass a job interview. Clean teeth.

The cold air – and bloody hell, I'd forgotten how cold these early mornings were – did a number on clearing my head. At least I had a rough idea of where I was going – I knew the library even if I couldn't recall seeing any recruitment places nearby.

Step by step, the tension and worry began to solidify in my belly, turning into a hard, cold, leaden ball. *Never mind that. Think of what's in Louise's belly. That's why you're doing this.*

I turned onto Market Street – sure enough, there it was, big eye-catching sign with designer logo in red and grey. Even though it was still early – 7.45 according to my watch, stifling a yawn as I checked it – there were about half a dozen people hanging around outside, studying the noticeboard in the window intently. Peering further inside, I could make out whitewashed walls, aluminium and glass, flatscreen monitors and expensive looking leather office chairs manned by expensive looking men and women. The whole thing screamed *success* and *professionalism*.

There was no way they were going to let me in there...

Bang on the dot of 8, a glamorous mid thirties blonde woman – basically Kate, but a couple of inches taller - unlocked the front door and poked her head out.

"Mr. Wyman?"

For an idiotic moment I thought she was looking for my dad. *Head in the game, come on.*

I cleared my throat and stepped forward. "Hi"

She smiled and proffered a hand. "Hi – Rebecca Parsons. Kate's told me about you. Come on in."

I shoved the nerves right down into my colon, gave my most bestest grown-up smile, thanked her and stepped into a brave new world. A world where computer monitors were not covered with Post-It Notes, where fire exits were visible and usable, where makeup, hair and businesswear were immaculate... Jesus, I half expected to combust as I walked through the door.

"Just got a couple of things to sort out, Mr Wyman, do you mind taking a seat?"

I nodded dumbly and duly found myself perched on a plush padded leather chair clutching a plastic cup of water a couple of moments later. I tried to make sense of the framed certificates peppering the walls while trying to slow my heart rate down somewhere below "terrified hummingbird" tempo.

Easy, they're just people. They can't hurt you.
They can just shatter you emotionally and consign you to a perpetual poverty-stricken misery.

The door to "Conference Room D" opened and a friendly looking blonde head poked out.

"Mr Wyman?" - wow, think I've been called that more in the last ten minutes than the previous thirty years - "Would you like to come on through and have a seat."

I sat down. Six faces stared back at me, all looking thoroughly unimpressed at what they saw.

Rebecca coughed. "Right then, Mr Wyman, perhaps you'd like to tell us a little about yourself and why you feel you're right for the role"

The role. Fuck, I knew I should have done some homework. Desk job admin-y.... thing, that was all Kate had told me, and idiot that I am, I hadn't thought to find out anything more. Suit, desk, salary, lack of whips – that'd do me nicely.

"Well, I like to think I'm a capable, flexible person who's able to function well either on my own or as part of a team.." I tried to stifle the sweat as I desperately recalled every interview cliché in the book.

Bless her, Rebecca lent me a rope to pull myself out of the quicksand.

"So it says here you set up and ran the internet sales department at your previous employer's?"

"Yes, yes, that's true." *Technically*. In actual fact, all I'd done is register us on eBay as a seller. To a pair of chronic technophobes like Miles and Chris, this counted as the work of some techno-voodoo high priest, but I had a sense that standards were a little different here.

"Would you like to tell us a little more about that?"

No. There's fuck all to tell.

"Well, yes, I saw the way the record market was going and figured that if we were going to survive we'd need to widen our sales base and draw in a larger...." *come on, you dopey fuck,* **think***,* "catchment... demographic... sphere..."

Heads nodded, notes were taken, boxes were duly ticked – I crossed my fingers under the table that they were positive ones. *Have I passed yet? Can I go home? I really need to pee...*

One of Rebecca's cohorts spoke without looking at me, a disgustingly chiselled and designer label suited man who'd clearly dropped in on his way to a GQ fashion shoot.

"So your IT skills are current, and you have an interest in developing that area?"

"Yes, absolutely, always keen to take any opportunity to learn new skills." *After all, I think I've honed the craft of making tea to about as fine a point as it can be.*

Maybe here they'll have an espresso machine. Maybe I'll master making frothy things and putting chocolate powder on them. The sky's the limit...

Designer 5 O'Clock Shadow spoke again.

"And you're literate with the usual business packages, Power Point, Excel, that type of thing?"

"Yes, I've done that sort of thing before." *Well, there was no way in holy hell I was going to trust the others to do it. God knows where that might have led.*

Opposite him, another chap who had obviously chosen to embrace baldness as a lifestyle choice – in the process cutting a deal with the Gods Of Hair to allow him to sport an immaculately trimmed goatee beard – decided to fuck up my morning.

"So what caused you to leave your previous employment?"

That was the question I'd been dreading most. On the walk over I'd mulled that one over and decided to try and keep things as neutral and bland as possible.

Difference of opinion? No.

Trying to help out a stupid stubborn ungrateful bastard and maybe save his chaotic rickety situation comedy of a business from plunging headlong off a cliff? No.

Looking for a field of employment with more security and the prospect of career development? - yes, I'd though that one up all by myself. It sounded plausible enough – there was never much chance of going anywhere at the old place, it was always going to be a simple comforting holding pattern at best... and to be fair, those ledgers had shown that the writing was very clearly on the wall. Maybe Miles had inadvertently wound up doing me a favour, slinging me out of the ship before it sank with all hands.

I duly trotted out option c), and the Bearded One appeared to accept this.

A few more questions followed about computer skills and admin experience, but it wasn't long before Rebecca smilingly brought proceedings to a close.

"Okay, well, thank you for your time, Mr Wyman, we'll be in touch over the next few days"

I thanked the assembled gathering in return and let the grown-ups go back to the office.

On the way home, the wintery sun was poking shyly from behind the clouds.

Please. I prayed silently. *Please.*

Chapter 15

"Are you sure you should be drinking that?"

Louise looked at me balefully over the steam rising from her herbal green tea-based concoction made from eagle's tears, children's letters to Santa, and snowdrops.

"Yes, Dan, I think it'll be fine."

Well, Louise's was on the way home and I thought it couldn't hurt to see how the mother of my potential child was doing. Plus, when was the last time I got up at 6am?

Seriously – I have no idea, help me out here because I don't think it can have been in this decade.

So a little infusion of caffeine couldn't hurt.

"So.." - this was odd. Very odd. The initial hit of hysterical panic had subsided (just), but it was impossible to just try and pretend things were back to normal. Fuck, I'd pretty much forgotten what normal even *was*. I temporised.

"- how are things?"

Louise cupped her mug with both hands and blew .

"Uhmm... odd. I've not told Mum yet, but she's going to find out sooner or later anyway "

Well, yes, when there's a screaming infant at the breakfast table that she's sure wasn't there the day before.

"I mean I've done about twenty tests now and they've all come back positive. I've hidden them all in a box in my wardrobe. I still can't really wrap my head around it. "

"No, I know what you mean. I don't think it's sunk in with me yet either."

Certainly, with every other aspect of my life falling apart, I felt like someone who'd taken too many blows to the head. Dizzy and woozy and unable to think straight. And this was just such a massive idea... too massive to comprehend.

The elephant in the room began to wave it's trunk about.

"So.. " - *help me out here, woman* - "what about... I mean, where does this leave us?"

I'd never seen a pregnant 28 year old woman try and hide behind a cup of herbal tea before. Louise shielded herself with said beverage and tried to back herself into the breadbin.

"Erm, look, it's difficult.. I mean everything that happened between us... we did say we were trying to end things and move on."

God almighty, that conversation was just a couple of months back... but a lifetime ago.

"Yeah, but I mean, things have changed, haven't they? We're having.." I swallowed down a large hairy football.. "We're having a child together, surely we should..."

*Should what? Must start thinking **ahead**, Daniel.*

Louise interrupted my burgeoning goldfish impression. "When will they let you know?"

"Hmm? Oh, right – the job. Should be today, actually, maybe even lunchtime. Apparently they need someone pretty quick and there were only a couple of people so we'll see."

"Really? That's quick – fingers crossed then"
"Yeah, otherwise it's going to be cardboard box in the gutter at this rate.."

Louise touched my forearm. "Don't worry . It'll be okay."

*I HATE when people say that. It's NOT going to be okay. Best case scenario I get a minimum wage admin job and am having a child with a woman who after two bottles of wine regularly wants to fuck me and kill me and isn't too concerned about the order she does it in. Worst case scenario is all that happening **and** loan sharks coming for my thumbs after I'm forced to borrow £10 from them at one million billion trillion squillion percent interest to keep my newborn child in nappies for another week.*

Probably best to keep that to myself though. I tried to get Louise back to the original topic.

"So... like I said, what about us? We have to figure out

what we are and what we're doing, surely."

She retreated back to the breadbin.

"We're having a child, Dan. Correction, I'm having a child. Look, I can do this by myself if I have to, I know I can. You don't have to be involved. I know we didn't exactly plan this. "

Too fucking right.

"No, look, I *am* involved, like it or not – I can't just leave you to deal with all this yourself. Are we going to make a go of this or what?"

"You old romantic, you..."

"Don't take the piss, you know what I mean. We've got to think bigger than both of us."

"Look, you don't have to be all noble and *won't-somebody-please-think-of-the-children* about it – it's not exactly brilliant if the kid grows up with parents who are fighting all the time, is it? My mum raised me pretty much single handed and I turned out alright."

Bite the tongue, Dan, bite it hard.

"I just think we have to at least try and make things work between us, that's all. What's so wrong with that idea?"

"Because this isn't what you want, this is what you feel obligated to do.. you're just doing this because you feel you should, that's not what this should be about, that's not.."

Louise was interrupted by my phone going into spasms on the worktop.

"You going to get that?" she asked, pointedly.

The attitude was starting to piss me off. I ignored her and checked the Nokia. Kate – this was either going to be very good or very bad.

And as it turned out, for once it was the former. I let out a WOOHOO worthy of Homer Simpson and punched the air. Fucking finally! Something was going my way...

"So you got the job then?" asked Louise, all smiles. I Victory Danced my way around the room.

"Who'sthewhiteguyrecordshopworkerwho'sasexmachineandknowshowtoworkher – Dan!!!"

"HELL yes!" I couldn't remember the last time I'd had some good news. And god bless her, Kate really didn't fuck around.

Congrats Dan , U did it! R U Ok to start tomorrow? They need sum1 ASAP and I said u wouldn't let them down. Go 4 it! :-) Kxx

"When do they want you to start?"

"Tomorrow morning – apparently they're struggling for people, this was a bit of an emergency"

"You never did say – how did you find out about this?"

Mm. This could be tricky. Louise had a tendency toward the jealous and the dramatic. But there again, it wasn't exactly like I had anything to hide, was it?

Was it?

"Oh, just an old friend of mine from school, got in touch a while back." said my mouth.

Okay, we'll deal with this one later, said my brain, off-camera.

I couldn't help but notice Louise starting to grin.

"What are you smirking about?"

She struggled to stifle a giggle. "I just never expected to see you in a suit, that's all."

"Oh yeah?"

"Yeah, you know... like a real grown up."

"Charming! Bollocks to you then, Ms Marshall, I'll have you know I was suaveness consultant on the last three Bond films."

"Oh, the shit ones?" She beamed.

This was more like it. The old chemistry was firing itself back up again. If I squinted really, really hard, I could almost believe that the cataclysmic, life-changing events of the last few weeks hadn't happened, that the baby - *our* baby, *my* baby – wasn't growing inside her like a storm cloud brewing. *One thing at a time, Dan.*

Focus. Job equals, paycheck, and Lord alone knew that was something I sorely needed. Once I could pay the bills again, then we can start planning, figuring out how the hell we can make this work.

"There are no shit Bond films, as well you know, just a sliding scale of awesome."

"Whatever..." Louise slid off the worktop and stood up. "Anyway, Dan-Dan-the-working-man, I've got to get going, you're not the only one with a career."

"Yeah, no problem, I've got to sort out a few things before I start tomorrow".

And have a nap.

Parting, we stood close, but it was a strange closeness. As if the room were filled with a fog too dense to see through and all we could do was grope blindly, arms flailing, towards each other. *Where are you ? I'm here.*

Where are you? I'm here.

Home. The flat is a hive of near-feverish activity. I've made sandwiches, I've found and pre-tied a tie (taking no chances here), I've ironed, I've even been through the notes that Kate gave me (albeit without really understanding a good chunk of them) – cleaned my shoes, for God's sake. I don't know what this is, but it isn't me.

Although that said, being me has brought me a dead end job and a farcical relationship, followed by redundancy, loss of even that relationship and an unplanned baby, so maybe a dose of *not* being me might be exactly what the doctor ordered.

Almost midnight. I set the alarm and gradually drifted off into a fitful, dreamless sleep.

Maybe things were going to be alright after all. Maybe.

Chapter 16

Oh, the joy of gainful employment. The happiness of being part of a team. The fulfilment of seeing a bank statement with something actually going *in* to my account. The satisfaction of wrapping up the day with the knowledge of a job well done. The...

Oh, alright, I'll put my hands up. I hate this place. I thought I understood tedium, but sweet Jesus, this place takes it to a whole new level. The job seems to consist purely of copying documents no-one has read onto a computer system no one understands to file them away in a place no one will ever find while listening to my co-workers bitch about each other's choice of partner, shoes, and holiday destinations. Literally, the high point of the day is my toilet break (and no, not for the reason you're thinking... Stop sniggering at the back there. In any case, I'm pretty certain doing that is a sackable offence, and while I might not like it, I do need this job).

In other news, Louise has moved in with me.

Pick your jaw up, you've dropped it.

Let's jump back a step, shall we? Honestly, do try and keep up, 007.

It's been a month since I got this job. In the first couple

of weeks, flush with my new-found ability to pay the bills and the novelty of a job which required wearing a suit, I grabbed the cape labelled "Grown Up", tied it on enthusiastically and struck a Superman pose. A proper job, with prospects (well, allegedly). That's one leg sorted. The next thing, with nipper on the way, was to reach some level of accommodation with mommy-to-be. After some cajoling, Louise had agreed to a summit at the most select and exclusive Italian restaurant I could afford.

"You go hit the salad bar honey, I'll keep an eye on your bag"

"Thanks – never knew Pizza Hut had such a wide selection.."

Hey - I said I could pay the bills. I didn't say I was Bill Gates. Cut a brother some slack.

Which, interestingly, Louise was doing.

"It's really good to see you again, Dan – how have you been?"

"Busy". This was true. Something strange had happened to my perception of time during the few weeks of unemployment. An entire morning could be taken up with the decision of whether or not I needed to get up and go to the toilet. Now, suddenly, my day was already spoken for and the time for navel- gazing and general contemplation was drastically reduced.

"How's the job?"

"Okay thanks – very different from the shop though. Tapping away at a computer keyboard all day long.. It's a killer on your wrists."

"So no porn at the end of the day?" She grinned impishly.

I choked on a slab of gooey cheese and tomato.

"Ahem. No.. They actually seem to have rules about stuff like that. Codes of conduct and stuff. And I've got a real contract, written down."

"Ooh, who's a big boy? Let me see."

"It's at home, sorry – got it sat right next to the dictionary."

I fiddled with a pepperoni. This was all well and good, but we had important things to sort out and I was impatient to get started.

"So does your mum know yet?"

"About what?"

This was classic Louise, trying to avoid talking about the big stuff. But like it or not, we had to sort it out. Sooner or later – and most likely sooner - the tiny bump would become a larger bump, and then a larger one still, and then finally a small screaming human being we were going to have to find a way of taking care of. There just wasn't time to fuck about.

"What do you think? She's going to figure out

something's up sooner or later, and there's not that much time."

"Thanks – I'm aware the human gestation period isn't infinite."

I declined to take the bait.

"So you haven't told her?"

"Does it matter?"

"Yeah, it does, she's going to have a grandchild. Plus, isn't it a better idea not to try and do all of this alone? Wouldn't you feel better if you had some support?"

"Wouldn't *you* feel better, more like – less guilt, less to worry about."

The bait was dangling temptingly close, but I kept my nerve.

"Here's what I'm thinking-" - figured out while trying to keep my sanity at the mind-numbingly tedious administrative grindstone that was the office- "-when the youngling shows up it's going to be very tough, she's going to need a hell of a lot of attention-"

"Figured that out all by yourself, did you?" Louise carped.

In a billion parallel universes, a billion versions of me let fly with a loaf of garlic bread across the back of Louise's head. Happily, in this one, I merely gritted my teeth and kept to the plan.

"And it's going to be much, much easier for us if we're all together, under one roof. TO help each other out, you know? We're going to need each other's support.."

"You're not moving in. My Mum would go spare."

In a billion more parallel universes, a billion more loaves of garlic bread were broken over a billion immaculately glossed brunette heads.

"No, okay- that wasn't quite what I had in mind. What about you moving in with me?"

"Uhm, Dan, if you remember.. we tried that a few years ago and it didn't exactly go brilliantly, did it?"

"Yeah, but things are different now. *We're* different now – or at least we'd bloody well better start to be.."

She started to backpedal at a rate of some knots.

"No, no, no – we've been down this road before and it *doesn't work*, you know that as well as I do, I don't know what you're trying to prove to me or yourself but.."

"Shut up."

Mm, interestingly enough, it turns out I said that. I think Louise must have been almost as surprised as I was, because she actually *did* shut up.

"If we're going to have any chance, any chance at all, we need to be in this together, not bitching away and trying to score points off each other. Now knock this shit off – it may not have worked before, but we'd damn well better make it work this time. You're a fucking nightmare when you're smashed, but I'm guessing you've stopped drinking, right?"

She shrugged. "Right."

"So no more stupid rows, no more bitching, no more tantrums – I think we can do this"

I must admit, internally I was trying to figure out how many teeth I was likely to lose as a result of this little spiel.

Amazingly enough though.. she seemed to be going for it. I was starting to wonder if I'd been taking the wrong tack all these years. Maybe I should have just clubbed her over the head and had done with it. Still, no time to waste, got to keep the momentum going – in for a penny and all that. Louise sipped her spritzer, eyeing me curiously.

"Where have you borrowed all this testosterone from, then?"

"Never mind taking the piss – you in?"

More spritzer-sipping and plate-fiddling. Eventually -

"Yeah, go on. Got to be worth a try."

Ladies and gentlemen – we have a winner.

It was a good hour of free salad refills and eking drinks out as we hammered out the specifics. Frankly, I think I was getting a little carried away with the whole alpha male schtick, there was no way I was going to be able to keep this up long term... but for now, I must admit, it was kind of fun.

As we left the restaurant, poised to go our separate ways, there was a moment of dizziness – amazingly enough, for all that I'd been thinking about this in terms of baby and crisis management, I'd almost forgotten that this kind of meant we were back on. I went in for a hug and was rewarded with a tentative kiss and a softly voiced "goodbye" before she got her taxi.

Back together again. I'd got what I set out to achieve.

Why didn't I feel better about it?

Weekend. D-Day. Boxes. Shoes. Furry toys. Mountains of designer clothes. Towers of Louise's stuff have sprouted like giant redwoods throughout the flat. It's hard not to feel a little shell-shocked; harder still to silence the little voice in the back of my head asking me what the *fuck* I thought I'd done.

Holding her in bed that night, dark hair cascading over her shoulders and mine, the answer was clear.

What I had to do.

Chapter 17

Spring is definitely here. The clocks have gone forward, the evenings are lengthening out, the bitter winter chill has left the air – it's always been one of my favourite times of year. Always fills me with a sense of almost unbridled optimism.

Except this year. Louise has been living with me for almost a month now – don't get me wrong, it hasn't been a repeat of the nightmare week a few years back (her being off the booze has probably contributed there), but it's just.. *odd*. It doesn't feel like I always thought it was supposed to feel.

Did you know there's never been a formal end to the Korean War? They called an armistice, a sixty-odd year "time out", but at the border both sides stare suspiciously at the other, waiting for the first move. Waiting to pounce. For all the civility and the strained attempts at touchy-feely intimacy, that was the atmosphere I came home to.

Which goes some way towards explaining why I felt the need to dawdle on my way home from the office and share some left-over cheese sandwich with the local pigeon population. The shop and the Lion, our old watering hole, are literally a few hundred yards apart. Five minutes as the drunk staggers. I could see them both from where I was sat on a bench dedicated to the memory of Geoffrey Hollister, 1933 – 2007 (don't know if you knew him, but as benches go, it's a fine example. Well done.).

The shop was shut – no surprises there, it was after closing time. Frankly, the miracle was that the place was still there at all. I'd half expected to find a smoking crater, but I guess they were managing well enough without me. The memory of the 78s nagged at me – *must do something about them* – but it was pretty quickly drowned out by a chorus of other memories. Culminating in a shouting match with a man I'd thought of as a friend for almost ten years and the loss of the job I'd had there for nearly as many. I wondered what had happened to that insane job lot of multimedia bric-a-brac Miles had picked up "for a song".. which turned out to be five grand. I wondered if Chris was getting paid regularly now. I wondered if they'd replaced me.

I wondered if they even remembered me.

The Lion. Jesus, I hadn't been in there in months. They probably thought I was dead. I had a vision of our little corner table with a stool (*bar* stool – get your minds out of the gutter) dedicated to the memory of Dan Wyman. Or at least the memories that didn't involve me being escorted out of the kitchen for pissing in the sink.

A long sigh escaped from me. *How the fuck had it come to this?* I hated my job, but I was stuck with it because I'd somehow, in the face of all the odds, managed to knock up a girl I should have ended things with years ago - and joy of joys, I'd convinced her to live with me because how the hell else were we going to be able to look after this kid? Now the only moments of peace and quiet I was going to be able to snatch would be stolen seconds like this.

Even now, she was probably wondering where I was, and I could expect the third degree when I got home. Followed by a thrilling evening trawling catalogues for soft furnishings and trying to force small talk in front of some godawful reality TV show.

Reality. Hah. That was a bitter fucking joke. No one told me about *real* reality, that life was going to be like this. No one told me I was going to wind up caught, broken, saddled and about as free as a fucking carthorse. Work, snatch some sleep, work some more.. Hadn't seen a friend in weeks. Any spare cash went on baby stuff. Brand new cot, brand new elasticy bouncer thing... nothing was too good for our approaching offspring. Apparently even newborns need designer labels. Funny thing though – there was *Louise's* money, and there was *our* money, and there was.. well, that was it.

I shouldn't be here. None of this should be happening. I should be in the Lion after a day playing at working for a living selling the odd record and swapping fart jokes with Chris. That was my life, and God knows it wasn't much but I was *happy*. I had *freedom*. You couldn't put a price on that.

Thankfully the park was pretty much exclusively mine (well, apart from the usual smattering of unwashed alcoholics clutching underfed dogs on bits of string, circling the Lion like zombies waiting for the last living humans to be starved out of the shopping mall... a glimpse into my kid's possible future, perhaps?) - because I couldn't help the waves of self-pity breaking over me. I'd never seen life panning out this way and I just couldn't see a way out. Or any sort of way it was ever going to get any better.

I'd had happiness and hadn't even known it.

Without even realising it I found myself doubled over, rocking backwards and forwards, trying to keep the tears from flowing. Hands clenched into fists, pushing against my temples, trying to push against the pulse of sheer blood-boiling frustration that was overwhelming me. I couldn't ever remember feeling so lost, so lonely.

"Easy there tiger, it might never happen."

A familiar voice snapped me out of my reverie. Blonde hair and gleaming smile. Kate.

You made it work, I thought, glancing up at her.

Hang on, no you bloody didn't. With everything you've got, I still found myself on your kitchen floor with your tongue down my throat.

Hmm. Let's keep that thought quiet.

I cleared my throat and did my best to pull myself back to some semblance of normality.

"Kate. Hi – sorry, didn't see you there. You ok?"

"Yeah, yeah, I'm fine." She nodded towards the bench. "Room for one more on there?"

"Yeah, course... good to see you again."

It was. The last month, the only people I'd seen were either Louise or my fellow cubicle drones. Don't get me wrong, everyone at the office (God, that still seemed weird to say) was nice enough, but it wasn't the same. These people had husbands, wives, mortgages and cars, I had nothing whatsoever in common with them. How the hell could I explain the simple joy of watching *Withnail & I* for the 702nd time with your best mate, quoting each and every line over a 48 pack of room temperature lager cans? Or the value of an in depth slurred debate over differing interpretations of the lyrics to *Heaven Knows I'm Miserable Now*?

They'd think I was a lunatic.

No, just smile, nod, and pretend to give a rat's ass about X Factor and Elaine's IVF treatment or Wendy's boyfriend's latest indiscretion.. all while I die a little inside. Perhaps there would actually turn out to be some mercy in the world and I actually would find myself reprogrammed enough to be able to function in their world.. or maybe just dead.

"So, how's the job going?"

HAHAHAHAHAHAHAHAHAHAHAHAHAHAHA.

"Good, thanks – really great of you to get me in there." No lie there, Kate's intervention had lifted my prospects from desperate midnight black to a mere charcoal grey, so I genuinely *was* grateful.

"Rebecca tells me you're doing good work." she smiled, giving me a playful nudge in the ribs.

Bloody hell, really? Must be nice to be so easily impressed – she should probably never go to Disneyland though, her head would just completely explode.

"That's good to hear – I think I'm starting to get the hang of it now."
Left-click. Right-click. Repeat. Die a little inside. "So what brings you down here?"

"Oh, you know.. sometimes it's nice to have a few minutes to yourself, away from everything."

"Kate, I've seen your everything – it's a palace! What's the park got that your place hasn't?"

"Pigeons", she zinged right back at me. "And.. well, it sounds horrible, but a bit of peace and quiet"

"Yeah?" *I can get on board with that.*

"Yeah, you know – the office is always pushing for more and more, wanting results yesterday, and then you get home and it's *Mummy mummy, what's for tea, can you do this, can we do that, I want chips....* I mean, I love them and everything but there are times you just need to get off the treadmill for a little bit, just calm down and be me. Even if it's just for a few minutes."

So this is what I've got to look forward to. This is life from now on. Stealing a few minutes of calm and then having to lie about it to avoid screaming rows and domestic meltdowns. Fan-fucking-tastic.

"What about Martin?" - *yes, what* about *Martin, does that poor sod have any idea what you've been playing at?* - "I mean, surely he must help out a bit?"

She backpedalled a little.

"Oh, yes, of course, I mean he's great, but I just... you know..." she tailed off.

Yeah. Actually yes, yes I think I do know.

"...I suppose I just want to forget sometimes that I'm someone's wife, and someone else's mum and just be me for a bit."

"Yeah, I get that."

We sat in silence for a moment, both contemplating lives that had spiralled out of control. One jammed full of people and possessions and money, a success by every possible measure, and one that had – let's be honest - never really got started. And yet both had led us to find ourselves sitting on a park bench on a Wednesday evening wondering what the hell had happened to us.

She turned to me, the familiar twinkly smile looking perhaps slightly more brittle than it had done before? Or was that just me?

"So how are things with you? We never did have a proper catch up after you had that freak out at my place the other week."

Ah, yes, the freak out where I found Louise was pregnant, just after you'd attempted – none too subtly – to seduce me on your kitchen floor. But I guess that's not something we're going to talk about now.

"Good thanks," - *Really? What's good, exactly? Are we just making reassuring noises now?* - "yeah, that was quite a big day... that whole thing.."

I cleared my throat.

"Well, as it turns out, Louise was- is, in fact – pregnant."

Kate seemed genuinely taken aback by this. Well, nothing strange there - fuck knows I'd been.

"Wow. Well.. um.. congratulations?"

Smile nicely now, Daniel. There's always a chance she's not taking the piss.

"Thanks"

"So- I mean I'm just guessing here- I get the impression this may not have been entirely planned?"

I smiled thinly.

"Whatever gave you that idea, Ms Gardener?"

"Female intuition, Dan!" she tapped the side of her nose.

I groped around blindly for a witty comeback, but they were all floating way out of my reach. Thankfully Kate broke the silence.

"It's okay, you know. People do it."

I almost didn't know what she meant for a moment. Then it hit me – it was the same thing I'd been trying to tell myself months ago when I first found out. *People do it. All the time.* And a hell of a lot of them are not even as well placed as Louise and I.

I leaned back, exhaling. There was so, *so* much I wanted to ask her.

"How did you... you know, when you first had your daughter – it was your daughter, right?"

She nodded. There was a half-smile on her face and sympathy in her eyes.
"Becca, yeah. I was twenty-six."

"How did you know..." *What am I asking here?* "how did you know it was right? How did you know what to do?"

"Who says I did?"

Who indeed. Frankly, it had never occurred to me that someone as apparently poised and successful as Kate could ever have been as ravaged by self-doubt and worry as I was.

"Well, I just sort of..."

"Assumed?"

"Yeah."

"Well, I didn't. I didn't have a clue. I was terrified

beyond belief. I'd literally just turned twenty-six, I was just a kid myself, I hadn't planned any of this. Neither had Martin. We were just trying to get ourselves sorted in the house, I was trying to start a business.. none of it was planned. We nearly split up over it. It was a horrible, horrible time."

This was a revelation.

"Wow.. so how did you get past it all? All the fear, the uncertainty.."

She sighed.

"I don't know, Dan. I don't know that we ever really did. We just took it one day at a time. Some days were hard, I mean *really* hard.. But you know, you adapt. It's amazing what you get used too. I can't imagine life without them now."

She paused, immaculately manicured hands smoothing immaculately coiffeured blonde hair.

Okay, I was going to have to address this. The elephant in the room was basically ramming it's arse into my face.

Deep breath.

"Look, Kate, I don't really.. I mean, I don't want to.. But the other week, in your kitchen.. What was that all about?"

She looked away. "Nothing."

I recognised this behaviour. Deny the tricky, embarrassing stuff and maybe it'll just all go away. This was classic Louise, I knew it all too well. *Was it really worth pushing this?*

As it happens, I didn't need to.

"Alright, I'm not happy. I mean I *am*, of course I am, but there are.. days. Days when I just feel lost. There's so much I haven't done."

"Kate, come on, look at everything you *have* done, I mean your business, all those places you've been.."

"That's not what I mean. I just..."

She sighed.

"I just don't feel I got my chance. I was someone's wife and someone else's mother before I was even *someone*."

I could see her point. Me, on the other hand – I'd failed spectacularly at being "someone", and now by a one-in-a-hundred-thousand chance was going to be someone's dad. Strange, how two such divergent paths through life could have led us both to the same point – sat on a park bench, hiding from our lives.

We'd gone for the first scan last week. Sat in the unnaturally cold ultrasound room, holding Louise's hand while the nurse moved the scanner across Louise's stomach. Then I saw it – well, him or her. A vague, fuzzy shape at first. The nurse's finger outlined the shape, making sense of the alien uterine landscape while I squeezed Louise's hand and smiled and tried to force back the tendrils of ice cold terror that gripped my insides.

Smile. If you smile hard enough, maybe this will turn into a good thing.

Maybe you'll stop shaking.

You ever get that thing where you see an ant, and then all of a sudden realise there's a thousand of the bastards all over your floor? That's pretty much what was going on here. I recognised a head, then a leg – didn't take a genius to recognise that connecting those things together was a torso, and look at that, a teeny teeny tiny arm...

We made that. That's so cool.

SHIIIIIIIIIIIIIIIIIIIT.

Quite a tricky thing, to process two completely contradictory emotions at once. On the one hand – tiny tiny teeny weeny little person, my son or daughter. Wow. Just – *wow*.

On the other hand, of course – my old friend, absolute bowel-clenching terror. Tiny tiny teeny weeny little person that I'd put in Louise completely by accident who was now going to be utterly dependent on me **forever** and was going to be my responsibility **forever**.

What to do, what to do. Well, there weren't many immediate options. I smiled at Louise, a little manically perhaps and squeezed her hand until she politely asked me not to as I was starting to cut off the blood supply.

We bought copies of the picture on the way out and mine was currently stashed in my wallet, folded up neatly next to the Tesco Clubcard .

"You'll be OK".

Snap back to the present. Kate smiled sadly at me, sympathy in her eyes.

"You will be. It's amazing how adaptable people are. Trust me, a year from now you'll wonder why you were ever so scared, and how you ever lived without her. Or him."

We hugged.

Thank you. It's probably just bullshit, but thank you.

Chapter 18

"Dan."

"Dan."

Sorry, wasn't paying attention. Where were we again? Oh, right.

One thing that no one had ever told me about was the quite drastic effects that pregnancy hormones have on a female psyche. Mood swings, for one. *Lots* of mood swings. And bear in mind that these were something of a hobby for Louise even before I, with my incredible odds-beating SAS ninja sperm, got her pregnant. It would seem that pregnancy hormones have the same effect as two bottles of Chardonnay on her emotional stability. This can make for some pretty strained domestic situations, such as the one I find myself in right now.

"So who's this then?"

For fuck's sake woman, it's 4am. What is this shit now?

"Who's what?" Muzzily, I went into autopilot, retreading a route taken a thousand (or so it seemed) times before.

"This Paula bitch. What's she doing sending you kisses?

You think you're something special, getting text kisses from some whore?"

> *Just to clarify, Paula is the woman who works in the cubicle next to mine. She's married, 41, with three kids and occasionally we swap shifts (which is the context of the text). She's an extremely pleasant person who I have next to nothing in common with, and likes to put kisses on the end of her texts regardless of who they're to.*
>
> *Now we've established that, let's move on.*

"She's just a friend from work.." I mumbled, muzzily. *Which is where I have to be in about a little over four hours time, so can we cut the bullshit and just let me get some sleep?*

"Oh, yeah, some friend, putting bloody kisses on the end of a text! Who does that?"

Well, all your mates, for one. But this wasn't an argument in the sense of a rational exchange of ideas where one side goes away at least willing to contemplate the ideas of the other and both parties are enriched by the experience. This was Louise, full of hormones and spritzer and paranioa, doing her Godzilla impression.

Again.

She'd been like this for weeks. The pregnancy books and websites – and the girls at work – had all said the same, cut her some slack, her hormones and emotions are all over the place, she doesn't mean any of the things she's saying... but you know what? None of that helps at 4am for the fourth night on the trot. I am utterly exhausted, utterly sick of my job, my life, and of her constant paranoia. This is torment, pure and simple.

Louise's voice shifted up a couple more octaves.

"So what is she, then, your secretary? You think you're some big shot businessman fucking your secretary over the desk while I'm at home carrying your baby? You think you're all that? You're not, you're nothing, you hear me? NOTHING!"

Actually, believe it or not, I was starting to get used to this. The tantrums. The tears. The screaming. There comes a point when you just lose the ability to care.

Unfortunately, that's when your tongue occasionally slips.

"So why don't you fuck off out of it then?" I asked, as I found myself doing more and more in these situations.

This particular time though, it seems I actually asked out loud.

Yep, that'll do it. Must remember the distinction between thinking things and saying them out loud in future.

I briefly experienced what it must be like to be an atom at the heart of the Sun.

Off she went. Fists flying, grabbing my hair and trying to yank it out by the roots.

This is it, Daniel-san. The final humiliation. You're actually being beaten up by a pregnant girl.

The thing is, it's all very well and funny *ha-ha-Dan-you-got-beat-up-by-a-girl-you-gaylord,* but it actually quite fucking hurts, and I'm pretty sure I'm not allowed to hit back. So what to do?

I tried grabbing her hands to restrain her, but all that resulted in was a swift and unceremonious kick in the bollocks. Pregnant girl or not, that fucking *hurt.*

"Jesus *FUCK!*" I crumpled up into -oh, irony of ironies – a foetal position, gingerly cupping my vulnerable knackers.

"Get up! Get UP, you bastard, you did this to me!"

An alarm bell went off in my head. Fuck this, I need OUT. Before Louise got a hold of the frying pan, be it a literal or proverbial one. I ducked a wobbly swung fist, grabbed my keys and coat and hopefully trousers, and dove out the door, hearing glass break as I did so.

Now what? This isn't in any if the books.

I wandered lonely as a cloud that's just had it's ass kicked by it's girlfriend – *sans* purpse, *sans* answers, *sans....* well anything much, really. A thin grey early morning sun wanly tried to shed some light onto my predicament.

5am. Not, as I'm sure you'll understand, my normal haunt. The world looks very different at this hour. There's an ethereal, almost otherwordly calm that accompanies the morning mists.

It's bloody cold though.

Autopilot had led me to the vicinity of the park and the Red Lion. Well, you know – old habits and everything. Thankfully there's a small transport cafe nearby, and I'd managed to grab my wallet with some change before being run out of the house by Ms Rocky Balboa. So you find me once again in the corner, shaking just-ever-so-slightly, pouring yet another sugar into a cardboard pint mug of coffee.

Trying to work out just what the fuck had happened.

First things first. Had I hit her back? I replayed the events for the umpteenth time in the past couple of hours. No. I hadn't, thank Christ.

She'd sure as all holy fucking hell hit me though. I could feel an unpeasant lump on my cheekbone and another one starting to swell up under my lip. Dabbing at it with a tissue , it came away faintly bloody and very tender. This would take some explaining at work.

Work. Oh, Christ. The adrenaline was wearing off and I could feel the fatigue washing over me. I yawned, rubbing the balls of my hands into my eyes. Not only that, but Jesus wept, would you look at me. What in the *fuck* was I wearing - office trousers containing keys and wallet and *hopefully* phone, yesterday's socks, office jacket and sweat-and-sleep stained Dukes Of Hazzard T-shirt. Oh, and in place of office shoes, battered two year old Converse with the soles coming off.

Hmm. If I still had my old life, this little ensemble would probably represent some kooky indie kid schtick that would serve simply to enhance the old places' credibility. But that life was gone, irrecoverable. I couldn't see the icily professional Ms Parsons' HR outfit going for this. Some sort of explanation was in order. And Kate, oh fucking hell, Kate.. she'd gone out on a limb to get me this job, I couldn't let her down.

And, oh yeah, I have a teeny tiny little poential son or daughter waiting in the wings to be provided for somehow. Lucky me. Lucky them – *follow your daddy's example, kids, he's proved to be the roaring success of his epoch. Life – don't talk to me about life* (not mine - Marvin The Paranoid Android,1982 I think).

Right. Time to strike while the caffeine was still hot. I availed myself of the less-than-five-star toilet facilities to scrub myself to a hygiene level equivalent to that of "tramp-signing-on-after-bath-with-garden-hose", bought myself a second "cup" of "coffee" and started trying to salvage the day.

First on the list – Kate. I decided to text her, as I wasn't sure what time small children got you up (*although you're going to find out pretty fucking soon, Danny-boy*). Happily, my phone had survived the confrontation intact, although – boy oh boy, would you look at this. I'd left it on silent and wow, would you just look at all these texts from a certain overly hands-on young lady.

I'm so sorry. Please let me know you're ok.

WheRE the FUCK are you you cowardly CUNT

I'll fucking KILL YOU GET BACK HERE

Please dont leave me I love you

And so on. A good couple of dozen, all told. Difficult to really know what to make of the situation. I made the mistake of rubbing my jawline – ow, *bollocks*, that hurt.

Hmm. I felt an involuntary scowl brewing. *Fuck that bitch*. Right, we'll leave her for now. I'm not really in any mood to be charitable. Or confrontational. Or anything. Christ, I just wanted somewhere quiet to sleep, to be honest.

I sent Kate a text message explaining – in the broadest, most diplomatic terms available to man – the situation I found myself in. I checked my watch, which was made a good deal harder by the fact it was back in the flat (and probably smashed into a squillion tiny pieces by now). Still, judging by the old Nokia, there was about an hour before I needed to be at work.

Right, here's the plan. Go in to work. Explain to Rebecca the circumstances, clean yourself up as best you can, get through the day without breathing on people and keeping your armpits to yourself. Nip out at lunchtime and treat yourself to a spare shirt, pants and socks. There's a Travelodge in the town centre, see if they've got a room for a couple of nights. Bit soulless, but they're cheap and above all *quiet*. Rest. Sleep. Get your head together. Don't think about Louise until all the emotions have subsided, because more fireworks and drama are going to do *no good whatsoever*. The last few nights building up to this particular blow-out had left me exhausted and I desperately needed a decent night's kip to get myself thinking straight again before walking back into the dragon's lair.

I finished the rest of the coffee, took a couple of mobile phone pictures of the more colourful bruises and strode off purposefully to attack the day.

Mid-morning. Ugh. Head crammed full of stimulants, feeling sticky and sweaty and distinctly unpleasant. Stale coffee and staler adrenaline mixed with fatigue and fear.

One positive though, Rebecca had been a great deal more sympathetic than I'd expected – she'd even asked me if I was sure I was ok to be here and didn't want to go home.

Home. Do I even have one anymore?

I explained about a "domestic altercation", feeling more than slightly ridiculous as I did so. It also occurred to me that everyone in the office would assume that *I* was the one on the dishing out end of the "altercation" - to be brutally honest, before the previous night's events, I would have done too.

Thankfully I'd had the good sense to leave a charger at the office, so my mobile was a damn sight more awake and alert than I was. The texts from Louise were coming through less frequently, but they still oscillated between "I love you, I'm so sorry, I'm going to kill myself" and "I hate you, you bastard, I'm going to kill you".

I mean, a passionate relationship is one thing, but come on.

The truth was though, I was more than a little scared. This was not a situation I'd ever encountered and it seemed to be beyond any kind of training, or upbringing or experience I'd had. It also seemed to be beyond anyone else's experience. Talk of "domestics" was rustling its way through the office, and just as I'd feared, everyone had got the roles reversed. The odd looks coming my way were due to more than just breath, armpits, and clothing choice.

This was a problem. How exactly was I supposed to explain that a pregnant girl beat me up and expect to be taken even remotely seriously? I mean, the reactions were going to be a mixture of hilarity, incredulity, and more than likely suspicion – *what did he do to deserve it?*

Thankfully I was able to avoid the lunchtime inquisition by diving out into town to buy new pants (amongst other things). Waves of tiredness assaulted me as I hacked my way through the long grass of the afternoon, but by 5.30 I was able to stuff my various belongings in a couple of purloined carrier bags and wound my weary way to the local hotspot for suicides and adultery.

The receptionist eyed me suspiciously as I signed in – frankly, I must have resembled a tramp who'd won on a lottery scratchcard.

Frankly, by this point I couldn't have cared less. I flopped down on the bed in a state of sheer exhaustion, savouring the lack of anyone shouting at me. I lay there for a moment or two, revelling in the glorious, glorious silence. I found myself dozing, adrift in the netherworld between true sleep and consciousness. Visions of Louise with shark's teeth and dragon's claws flashed through mind, and I woke to the sound of a baby's cries. Real or imagined- I've no idea.

I checked the clock – 7pm. The old Nokia flashed with "Message Received" in blocky 8-bit graphics across it's screen. Nothing surprising there, the poor old thing was bursting at the seams with Louise's bipolar outbursts. I wondered if it was the turn of threats or cajolery. *She loves me, she loves me not.*

Neither, as it turned out. It was Kate.

Hi Dan, sorry it's taken me so long to reply – crazy day. What's happened are you ok? I'm here if you need a place to stay. Kate xx

I mulled this one over. Despite the attendant risks, it was awfully tempting – apart from anything else, the simple financial considerations meant I wasn't going to be able to spend more than a couple of nights here, and trying to think about what was waiting for me at home was like trying to imagine what was at the centre of a black hole. The normal laws of logic just didn't apply.

The torrent of text messages had at last started to abate. I had no idea how to go about engaging with any of them – Louise didn't seem to have any kind of neutral emotional ground and I was damned if I was going to let myself in for a repeat of the previous night. Giving her some space – giving myself some space – seemed to be if not the best, then the only practicable idea. And lord knew I needed some sleep before plunging myself back into the maelstrom.

I sent Kate a rather wan thank-you text and decided to treat myself to a shower before hunting down something to eat that wasn't sugar coated or a Pro-Plus tablet.

Stepping out into the car park, I surveyed the plethora of fine haute cuisine options open to the Thursday night diner on a budget. McDonalds, Burger King, greasy fish & chip shop, kebab, Pizza Hut.... but for true olde-world charm and the personal touch, you just can't beat the local pub. And before I knew it, I was in the Red Lion ordering a burger.

I recognised the staff.

They didn't recognise me.

Tottering back to the hotel, full of burger and a couple of swift ales, I was almost able to convince myself that life was normal and there was no sword of Damocles hanging over my head.

Just get through today. Just breathe.

I collapsed onto the bed and let sleep overwhelm me.

Next morning found me in a surprisingly good mood. The Travelodge had the benefit of being a good deal closer to work, giving me fifteen extra minutes to put my feet up and slurp tea while psyching myself up for the day. I treated myself to a much-needed shower, after a couple of false starts with the controls, and made sure to use every single towel I could find on sheer principle (the principle of being a cheapskate bastard being the dominant one), removed my new officewear from their hermetically sealed cellophane and cardboard enclosures and tarted myself up. I caught a glimpse of myself in the mirror – *heyyy....... not too shabby.*

Well, apart from the bruises. Don't get me wrong, it didn't look like I'd gone ten rounds with Mike Tyson or anything, but there were a few unpleasant looking bumps and lumps. Bloody sore to the touch too, like spots ready to burst. No point worrying about them – not exactly anything much I could do about it – but a nasty black wedge was beginning to force its way into my previously sunny demeanour. Everything was most definitely **not** alright.

I checked the Nokia. No new messages. Was that good? Was it bad? *Fuck, how am I supposed to know?*

Well, one thing was for definite, it was telling me the time. And I needed to get to work.

Fewer stares. Well, that's a plus. I filled up on office coffee and sidled to my cubicle to get on with some serious business.... well, low-level admin busywork. Keep your head down and just get on with the job in hand. The world can right itself in it's own time.

The day passed in steady rhythm of mouse clicks, photocopying and filing.In a moment of recklessness, though, I took the opportunity to check my bank balance on the office internet. *Balls.*I wasn't going to be able to keep up the Travelodge "holiday" for too much longer without landing myself in some serious financial shit.

Time to go home?

I stroked my jawline. Bruises still present and correct.Maybe not.

You know what ? Fuck that. I really don't feel like I want to deal with the sequel tonight. A friend is offering me some hospitality and I think I'll take her up on that.

A few minutes of thumb-grinding and swearing under my breath and I'd managed to compose a proper text message to Kate.

Hi Kate, sorry to sound cheeky but is the offer of a

place to crash stll open? Not to go into details but it's been a difficult few days. Don't worry if not though :-) Cheers, Dan

Send, you bastard. SEND – ah, off we go.

Surprisingly, I got an answer almost instantaneously.

Hi Dan, yeah, of course! Come over tonight if you want, be glad to have you xox

Briefly I wondered where Martin and the kids were. Hmm. I've got my own can of worms right now. Can't go home, can't afford to stay in a hotel.. not a lot of choice. I'd seen Kate's soft furnishings as well, and was willing to bet that her sofa probably had not just a "massage" function, but also an open bar and a "therapist"function. I could just stay there until a toddler or a husband turfed me off, and eat delicious expensive Waitrose snack foods. *Live the dream, Dan, live it hard.*

Thank you so much Kate, you're a star. About half 6 ok for you? Xx

Half 6 is fine, be nice to have the company! See you later, I'll sort the plonk xox

O...Kay. There was, I admit, something vaguely unsettling about this situation but I couldn't quite put my finger on what it was. But I wasn't exactly flush with alternatives, and you know what? I *liked* Kate. I knew there was a dark underbelly to this situation that I was probably leaving myself open to, but my major concern was ensuring a roof over my head that didn't also harbour a woman who seemed to want to kill me.The fact that this roof came free with a pretty blonde who I got on like a house on fire with was just gravy.

With my laundry nestling in a wrinkled carrier bag under the desk, I made it through the remainder of the day fielding no more than the odd slightly suspicious glance. Thankfully, with it being Friday, no one in the office gave a flying arse about anything other than getting out of said office as soon as was humanly possible. Myself included.

Clutching my rather pathetic set of possessions, I trotted off towards Kate's house.

I must have cut a rather incongruous figure as I wound my way through an increasingly well heeled series of estates- battered rucksack, scrunched up Primark carrier bag, £40 suit and £9 shoes, sweating like an.... like an out-of-shape 30 year old carrying his earthly possessions in a variety of carrier bags.

There it was, the immaculate lawn, the shiny Mercedes. I strolled up the path with a nonchalance I didn't entirely feel. Despite the rational part of my mind pointing out *you haven't really got much of a choice here, pal*, I couldn't shake the feeling that this was a *bad idea*. A *very bad idea*. Despite the intervening months and the huge change in my situation, the memories of the awkward moment on her kitchen floor loomed large. Best steer clear of a repeat performance – life was complicated enough now as things were.

I exhaled before ringing the bell. *Relax*. Sure enough, Kate answered in a second, welcoming me with a glass of wine and a beaming smile. Briefly, I was transported to the opening credit sequence of *I Dream Of Jeannie*.

This is how I should be met at the door when I get home

from work. Not by accusations of infidelity and a punch in the face.

Kate hostessed me expertly into the kitchen and demanded I strip off.

"Seriously, Dan – you reek like God-knows-what, you're covered in stains.. do you even know how to use a tea mug? Get 'em off, it's all going in the laundry."

I.... *Err.....* I cast about myself in some confusion.

"Oh, go on then, spoilsport – have a robe. It's an old one of Martin's."

She tossed me an old black towelling dressing gown. Embarrassingly, it hung almost to the ground. My hands disappeared inside the sleeves and the hood came most of the way over my face.

I couldn't resist it.

"*Now, young Skywalker*" I croaked, shakily raising both hands, "*you will die*"

She giggled, hunched on a stool nursing a glass of Chardonnay.

"So where are Martin and the kids this weekend?" I asked.

"He's taken them to stay with his mother, she's got a place in London, near the Thames. The kids love it, there's loads for them to see and do down there."

"You don't go down with them?"

"No, not any more, we.. there's.." she tailed off, before shaking herself and reinstating the trademark light-up-the-skies beaming grin."They're having a great time, that's the important thing."

"Anyway," she continued "-look at us- house to ourselves, enough wine to float a battleship, I've got Netflix and you sure as hell need a break – I suggest we pick a film, get good and pissed and forget about the world for a day or so."

We clinked glasses. "Hell yes, girl, that sounds like a plan"

I checked my phone. Nothing. Right. Let the holidays begin.

Cut to a couple of hous later on. So there we were. Feet up, wine in hand, reclining on a big soft comfy leather sofa, working our way through a clutch of 80s classics... *Gremlins, Ghostbusters*, all the classics. Pretty much the perfect evening. And then the Chinese takeaway arrived. Fuck, this is *awesome*.

An hour later, the Stay Puft Marshmallow Man had been banished, Bill Murray and Sigourney Weaver were united, and both our stomachs were groaning under the strain of a gallon of wine and a hundredweight of Peking duck.

"When there's something strange" warbled Kate.

"In your WAAAAAARRRP" I responded, as a personal

best belch escaped me, reverberating around the living and rattling the furniture.

Kate looked at me with a mixture of shock and awe, before collapsing into giggles.

"You've still got the moves, Dan!"

"You know it- all the nice girls love a musician"

"I wasn't always a nice girl", she smiled crookedly.

Deep in the recesses of my chow mein and booze sodden brain an alarm klaxon started sounding. *There were going to be consequences...*

Oh, you know what, fuck it – there were all manner of consequences waiting for me at home. Trying to do the right thing had got me a smack in the mouth and fuck all else. Just for tonight, I was going to blow off some steam. Tomorrow, we'll hit reset.

Yeah- nothing that could go wrong with **that** plan, surely.

Still, to be fair, nothing past mild flirtatiousness had really happened yet, and I was quite happy for things to stay that way. Louise was still in the back of my mind, but every time I tried to try and understand her point of view I just could not wrap my head around what in God's name she thought she was doing. I'd tried *so fucking hard* to get everything together to raise this kid, to get my life in order, get stable, and the harder I tried the worse she'd got. And the other night had just been the straw that broke the camel's back. This was **not** the way thigs were supposed to be.

I checked my phone surreptitiously. Or rather, what I thought was surreptitiously- Kate, despite being a bottle and a half of Chardonnay to the good, twigged.

"Hey- " She put her hand on my wrist and looked into my eyes, speaking quietly -"leave her for a while, ok? You need some space."

"Yeah, it's... I just.." a thousand thoughts tried to force their way out of me at once. Result – traffic jam. Mouth flailing wildly, no sound.

"Come on" she took the ancient handset, flipped it to silent, and eased herself up onto the arm before sliding across to me (it was a *big* sofa) and lay down resting on my now extremely full belly."Talk to me"

I tried, I really did. I tried to tell her everything I'd tried to do, taking a job I hated, moving her into my flat and watching her take it over, enduring sleepless night after sleepless night while she screamed at me for being unfaithful when I hadn't been, for getting her pregnant, for being less than the man she wanted, for just being who I was.. I tried to package it all into something she could make sense of... but there was no chance. I could barely make sense of it myself. It all just seemed so.. ridiculous, from a distance.

"I just don't know what to *do anymore* "I heard myself say, voice cracking in embarrassing prepubescent manner. "Whatever I do or don't do is wrong, she gets worse every day.. God almighty, is this *it*? Is this all there is to look forward to?"

Kate wrapped her arms around me.

"It will get better. Honestly. I was a nightmare when I ws first pregnant, I was so scared. She'll be the same. Look, tomorrow, walk back in there like nothing's happened. She wants to test you, wants to see if you'll stay. Just stay calm, don't let her get to you, ok?"

I nodded. She made sense – well, sort of, anyway. The idea that Louise was trying to test our relationship to destruction to see if it would survice seemed utterly ludicrous.... and yet. Think about it. We'd split up, by a million-to-one chance the condom involved in our goodbye bonk had failed to do it's job properly... it wasn't exactly the fairytale, was it? No wonder she was worried. No wonder she was acting out.

So tomorrow, I was going to have to walk back in there, head held high, and take whatever she threw at me on the chin and just act like everything was as normal as it was possible to be. Whew. Well, no one said it was going to be easy... whatever "it" was.

"You look like you need another drink". Perceptive girl, Kate.

We clinked glasses. *Eat, drink and be merry – tomorrow we die.*

Soon enough, another bottle was emptied, and we were lying on the sofa with legs entwined.

"So how did you wind up at that weird little shop?"

God, all that seems so long ago.

"I don't know really, I just sort of.. backed in there, I guess, while I was waiting for something proper to come along, and it just... never did, I guess."

"But you're a clever guy, you've got A-levels, got a degree.."

"Tell that to all the interviewers who turned me down" I smiled ruefully.

"Yeah, but you must have had some plans..."

"Plans? Oh, yes, had lots of plans... just life has a way of.. I don't know, not caring about them. I guess eventually you just sort of get used to where you are, what you are... you make the best of your circumstances."

She looked at me curiously.

"You say that a lot, don't you?"

"Say what?"

"I don't know. You say it a lot."

Uhm, ok.

"Well, I suppose... I'd not really thought about it."

"Don't get me wrong, it's not a criticism, it's just.. I think you *react* to life, don't you?"

"Well... I..."

"*That's* what I mean."

"What?"

She looked at me almost pityingly.

"I mean you react. You don't *act*. Let me ask you – did you mean to wind up working at a record shop?"

"Well... no, but.."

"And did you mean to get Louise pregnant?"

"No. But it's happened and-"

"That's what I mean! Look, Dan, you're such a sweet guy, and I can see you're trying to do the right thing.. and you're hoping somehow that life is going to reward you by giving you a break but it *won't*. It just won't – life doesn't work like that."

She clasped my hand and looked deep into my eyes (have you ever had anyone do that? It's really, *really* disconcerting).

"If you're going to change things, Dan, then *you* have to change them. Figure out what you want and go for it, and the hell with what other people want. Other people can take care of themselves. The only person who sort your life out is *you*."

Wine + lack of sleep + undeniable atmosphere of sexual tension = massive potential for an equally massive mistake.

Thing is – she's kind of got a point. Go back to the me of ten years ago and you'd have found someone brimming over with positivity, energy and direction, someone who was convinced he could make things happen for him and take his life in whatever direction he wanted. Someone - not coincidentally - who'd had exactly zero experience of the real world. So yeah, maybe I do react to life, and maybe it hasn't exactly brought me wealth, success.. but fuck it, you want to show me what the options were? I don't recall turning down the offer to head up Google or Apple. I played the cards I was dealt as best I could.

And it worked out brilliantly, snarked my inner monologue.

She was close to me now. Very close. Head on my shoulder, hair brushing my cheek.

I thought of Louise, and everything she'd put me through these last weeks. Everything she'd accused me of. The last, fatal evening, when a text with a kiss on it had led directly to me lying curled up on the floor nursing bollocks that had just had an intimate introduction to Louise's knee.

Her lips were so close to mine. So achingly, tantalisingly close.

Fuck it. *Fuck it.*

As it happened, I barely had to do anything. Whatever the hell this was, Kate was just as involved as I was. We tumbled off the sofa, kissing deeply and urgently. Fingers pulled at catches and and straps, zips and belts.

This is wrong, this is wrong, this is wrong......

And being right got you WHAT, exactly?

Kate breathed hot and hard in my ear .

"Not here. Bedroom. Upstairs. First on the left"

Five minutes later. We collapsed onto the bed, lips locked together. Hands ran through each other's hair, skin pressed against skin. I couldn't remember ever feeling anything like this before. She was intoxicating. *Sixteen years of wanting her. Sixteen years of..* Her body writhed against mine.

And then the phone bleeped.

Chapter 19

I stared at the screen in pure, undulterated shock.

I'm at the hospital. I think the baby's gone. I'm sorry for everything.

What. The. Fuck.

I'm ashamed to say it, but my first thoughts were along the lines of *oh fucking hell, not again.* Louise hadn't been above telling me she'd lost the baby before now – a good (*hah!*) three or four times by my reckoning. Usually blaming me for it, in a teary, fearful torrent of hormone induced rage. But the messageswere usually accompanied by a good deal more "bastard", "fucker", "heartless selfish cunt" type terms of endearment. This.. oh, God. I had a bad feeling about this.

All of a sudden reality snapped itself back into focus. Christ almighty, what was I doing here? On a bed with someone else's wife while my girlfriend was in hospital? No.No fucking way. This wasn't right. I had to get out of here. I had to get to Louise.

I lurched upright, practically falling off the bed in the process. Kate was understandably confused.

"What is it? Dan, what's the matter?"

There was a lump in my throat the size of a football.

"I – Louise.. she..." I gave up and showed her the phone.

"Oh no. Oh Dan, I'm so..."

"I need to call a cab, do you.."

"I'll drive you." Kate busied herself getting upright and dressed.

"Kate, that's really sweet of you but we've both had way too much for that." I wrestled myself into trousers, hopping from foot to foot while trying to thumb numbers into the ancient Nokia's keypad.

"Hi, yes, I need a taxi, as soon as you can, to the hospital please.... 12 Kingfisher Avenue, just as soon as you can, please, I'll be waiting"

I caught Kate's eye. "I'm sorry. I have to go"

She smiled weakly and nodded. "Yeah, it's fine, it's fine.."

It was anything but fucking fine.

Ten minutes til the taxi got here. Ten minutes trying not to make too much eye contact while pacing figure eights across the floor. Ten minutes asking myself what in God's name I thought I was doing here. Thankfully Kate didn't try and force small talk, pouring herself a very large glass of wine and retreating to the kitchen under mumbled pretense of having some urgent laundry to take care of.

I bade her the most awkward farewell possible – a hug, a peck on the cheek seemed somehow ridiculously inappropriate. We settled on a handshake. Seriously, a handshake.

No one tells you what you're supposed to do in these situations. Books and movies – they just cut to the next scene with a car chase in it.

The situation was made even more surreal by the most unbelievably chirpy taxi driver I'd ever met. I've met plenty that thought they should be doing stand up, thought they were the font of all mirth. This guy.. he actually was. Any other day, literally *any other day*, I would have been in stitches.

"'Avin' a good night mate?" he asked me, all chewing gum and lopsided smile as I scurried into the passenger seat.

Oh yeah. Just fucking fantastic.

Not to be deterred, he tried again as we got underway. "Hospital then? Is it family then?"

Umm, well... kind of both.

"It's... it's difficult." was about the best I could come up with.

From there, twenty-seven minutes and fourteen seconds (oh yes, believe me I was counting) of anecdotes about mothers-in-law, girlfriends current and former..while all I could do was chew fingernails and eye the meter. *Come on, come fucking **on**.*

I ground my thumb down to the bone trying to get Louise's mobile, but you guessed it, straight to voicemail. Every time.

Finally, finally we got to the hospital. Twelve quid and a set of fingernails lighter, I made it to reception.

"Hi, I'm trying to reach my.." *Girlfriend? Friend? Nemesis?* "partner, Louise Marshall, I think she's in the maternity ward."

She rustled papers and Shift-Ctrl-F12'd her computer several times over.

"Yes, she's in the maternity unit, the other side of the building."

Of fucking course it is.

Ten minutes later, having performed the requisite number of lefts and rights, I finally found myself somewhere where there were signs to to the Maternity unit.

Hell, as it turns out, is painted a faded grimy shade of mint green. And lit by puttering fluorescent tubes. I desperately sought out anyone in a pastel NHS uniform and was rewarded with an astonishingly tiny and wonderfully calming Filipino nurse.

She'd better be here. Or there again, maybe she'd better not. Oh God, oh God, oh God..

"Louise Marshall?" she pointed down the corridor, before taking my arm. "I'll show you"

A tentative tap on a blank door. The nurse edged her way inside and put on her most comforting voice.

"Louise? How you feeling, darling? I have someone here for you."

"Heyy..." I peeked through, learned responses telling me to expect a smack in the mouth.

There was nothing. The room was dark.

"Come in" said a weak, familiar voice. The last time I heard that voice, it was calling me every name under the sun and accusing me of being an abuser while punching me in the face. All that seemed an awfully long time ago now. Another lifetme, another dimension. Another universe.

Where the hell do you start?

"Are you ok?" I shuffled over to the fold up sofa bed.

It was quite possibly the most banal, pointless, stupid question ever asked by anyone in the entire history of people and questions, and I fully expected to be hauled over the coals for it. Involuntarily, I braced myself for the tongue lashing (or just flat out lashing, depending on what stuff Louise had brought with her).

"Yeah, I'm ok I guess, I just.."

And then she crumpled, collapsing onto my shoulder.

"She's gone, Dan, our baby's gone, I lost her" she sobbed. I gathered her to me, pulling her head to me as my own tears welled up.

"It's okay, it's okay.. it's not your fault" I tried desperately to reassure her. Her tears soaked into my T-shirt as mine did into her hair.

I don't know how long we stood there, sobbing into each other. Time seemed to stand still. I think we actually managed to cry ourselves dry.

After an eternity, the sobs began to slow and we detached. I set on the bed next to her, holding her hand. I had to know.

"So what - I mean, how... what happened?"

She looked away, over her shoulder to the pastel painting of a yacht on an open sea. Eyes red and raw from tears, and with a voice that seemd to be at once ten and ten thousand years old, she tried to explain to me. Like I'd ever be able to understand.

"After that night... after you left.. I started getting pains. I didn't think anything of them at first, I thought it might be the stress of the row."

Which you created, I couldn't help but add silently. I nodded and stroked her hand.

"I went into work and tried to forget about them, and I

did, for most of the day.. you know, the familiarity helped, talking to the girls and pretending like there's nothing wrong, you almost come to believe it yourself."

Sounds familiar. How many times had I done the exact same thing?

"And then last night, I was asleep, and got woken up by these horrible, awful stabbing pains, like cramps... I thought I was going to give birth there and then, it was agony, and Jesus Dan, I was so scared, I just didn't know what to do... I couldn't even get up off the bed, I was in so much pain."

She paused, gulping water from a flimsy plastic cup.

"Then I looked down and I was bleeding, and that was it, I just panicked, freaked out... I called 999, it was the only thing I could think to do.."

She sipped at her water again. I noticed a small tear starting to make it's way from the corner of her eye. I had the sensation of my heart actually starting to break for her.

"So I was in the ambulance- " her voice smaller now, throat tightening and frightened - "and the pain came, it was just unbelievable, everything started going grey, I couldn't see... the medics were trying to hold my hand and calm me down, but I knew what was happening, I was going into labour.."

She squeezed my hand. I squeezed back. *Oh God, why, why why..*

Her voice was barely even a whisper now.

"She came out and I couldn't even hold her, I couldn't even look at her. By the time we got to the hospital she was already dead. They told me she was born dead but I swear I saw her breathe, I saw her move.."

It was too much. She crumpled. I tried to stay strong, to comfort her – that lasted all of ten seconds before I crumpled with her.

"She was so *small*.."

An age passed while we sat in that room. Silence stifled our attempts to connect to each other, to try and share the awful pain. As those dreadful, frozen, shellshocked hours passed an invisible wall came down between us. Our baby – our *daughter*, Christ, that had barely registered - From this moment, Louise would always be the woman who lost our baby. And me... I would always be the guy who was eating Doritos and watching Ghostbusters with his old high school crush on the other side of town while it happened, completely oblivious. Jesus fucking wept.

All of this was so wrong. *All* of it.
I don't know how long we were there. It felt like forever. When they finally let us go, walking down that corridor dimly lit by flickering fluorescent tubes that seem to illuminate the grimy miserable squalor that both our lives had descended into.

I tried – awkwardly – to comfort her. Pulling phrases and motions from books and weepy movies.. ridiculous, really, but I had nothing else to go on. I wanted so badly to "be there for her", but I had absolutely no idea how. Nothing I could say or do would take away the agonising pain she was feeling. Clumsily, I tried to hold her hand, to ull her to me – but I was met with a shake of the head as Louise pulled away from me, her eyes firmly fixed on the floor.

We left the hospital two entirely different people. Hollow. Numb.

Another taxi. Back to Louise's mum's.

Louise turned to me. "I'm going to stay here for a little while. I think it's best."

I nodded, mute. Moved in to try for a hug but she was already gone.

I looked at my phone. Out of signal. Out of cash. Out of luck. Time to walk home.

As I walked, the rain came. Blending with the tears as I wept quietly. Back at the flat, now silent and unfamiliar, I collapsed onto the sofa and the weeping turned to shuddering sobs.

My daughter was dead. And I never even saw her.

Chapter 20

Blearily, I came to on the sofa as the sun wriggled and burrowed its way through the curtains. It illuminated a pretty depressing scene – centre stage, a somewhat doughy thirty year old man with a line of drool across his chin. Pull back to reveal a dilapidated couch under said equally dilapidated thirty year old man. Pull back slightly further to reveal a carpet of empty wine bottles, consumed in a desperate attempt to reach oblivion.

Thank Christ it was the weekend. For a moment, I woke with a sense of unaccustomed happpiness watching the motes of dust played in the beams of sunlight.

Then it hit. The tears came unbidden, as the world lurched.

I'd tell you what I did with my weekend, but frankly I have no fucking idea. Have you ever seen the bit in the film (there's always this bit) where you see the main character sat stock still, centre of the frame, while around him the world moves in a time-lapse whirlwind of activity? That was me. I don't know how to explain it – I didn't feel depressed, or sad, just... just numb.

I wanted to call Louise, or text her, or.. Christ, I don't

know. I just... sat there. A big numb, grey cloud of "don't know". There was nothing I could do, nothing I could say.. God, I was fucking useless.

Next thing I knew it was Monday. Work. Shit, I'd never thought of that. Do you go back to work after something like this? What happens?

Well... there didn't seem to be anything else much to do. And my internal alarm clock had already got me out of bed. I suppose I may as well.

What happened in my case was, I went to the office as normal. Wandered in in a daze, logged into the work PC and stared blurrily at letters on a screen. Nothing made sense.

I sat. I drank coffee. I entered data – *what* data, exactly, fuck only knows – but outwardly, there was little to suggest anything much was wrong past a hangover. I even managed a little small talk – *Hi Dan, you alright? Yeah, ok thanks? How was your weekend? Yeah, good, thanks.. yours?*

Admittedly not exactly a riveting Wildean discourse, but it was very disconcerting watching my mouth form banal everyday pleasantries basically by itself. I just sort of drifted through the day, watching myself negotiate the office on autopilot and wondering what I was going to do next. But no – no hiccups, no disasters, no breakdowns.

Well, until I got home. Then it hit. *Oh boy, did it hit.* I drifted around the kitchen watching myself make tea, when all of a sudden everything went cold. It was like every drop of blood had turned to ice. I shuddered, losing balance, grabbing the counter for support. My legs had turned to elastic bands, I couldn't stand. Next thing I knew, I was on the floor curled up into a ball, wracked by sobs. My thoughts were nothing but white noise while this panic and fear coursed through me. I'd never known emotions could be as real, as physical as this.

Eventually, the roaring fire inside my head calmed enough for me to be able to think and act. I fumbled my phone out of my pocket and managed to ring Louise.

Voicemail.

Of course.

It didn't matter, I had to reach out and connect with the only other person who could possibly understand how this felt. I had to try and make her realise I now had at least an inkling of what she must be feeling.

The words fell over themselves trying to get out.

"Louise – honey – god, I'm... I'm so sorry babe, so fucking sorry... I get it now, *I get it*. I'm just... please call me when you can. Just tell me you're ok"

Or something like that, anyway.

I shut my eyes and breathed hard and slow, forcing a rhythm to come. *Earth to Dan. Just breathe, mate. Calm it the fuck down. This doesn't solve **anything**.*

I slumped down against the kitchen cupboards, hugging my knees and trying to regain control of limbs that had turned to spaghetti. I could hear an echo of my Dad's voice frm when I was little after falling off my bike and hurt my leg – causing a long bloody scar that went up past my knee and tore my favourite tracksuit bottoms – *come on, son, it's okay. It's okay.*

My reverie was broken by a knock at the door. I hauled myself up, quickly splashing water on my face and wiping it on my sleeve.

Dear God, don't let it be Jehovah's witnesses. The state I'm in, I'd probably convert.

I opened the door. A large, tall, expensive-looking man stood there, seeming more than a little uncomfortable. He looked vaguely familiar, but I couldn't quite place him...

"Hello. Are you Dan Wyman?"

A little cautiously, I answered "Uh huh, yeah... can I help you?"

"Yes. My name is Martin. I think you know my wife."

Oh, FUCK.

Chapter 21

Deep in the bowels of my.. well my bowels – an icy vacuum took firm hold. Fuck, I'd been kissing – Christ, damn near slept with – this guy's *wife*. Not his girlfriend, not his "missus" - the woman he'd bought a house with, had children with, comitted his whole life too.. Jesus, what the fuck had I been *thinking*?

Fuck. OK, I earned this. I tensed my jaw, waiting for the inevitable fist to smash into it.

Martin must have noticed some subtle giveaway in my body language. A remarkable feat, given that I was by now largely hidden behind the sofa.

"Look, Dan.. it's ok, I do just need to talk to you."

Warily, and whilst attempting to maintain a lithe Kung Fu pose at all times, I closed the door behind him and motioned him over to the sofa.

I kept the coffee table between us and visualised escape routes.

"Okay.. so what.. where.. where would you like to

start?"

Martin exhaled hugely. He was one of those men that did everything on a massive scale. Just one of his farts would have blown down a forest of redwoods.

"Right, well.. Dan, you've probably gathered that everything isn't quite.... quite 100% with me and Kate".

Yep, got that pretty much the first time she crammed her tongue down my throat. Figured things might not quite be hunky dory in the maritals department.

I nodded cautiously.

"I think I should probably explain why that is."

I tried and failed to look masterful and in command of the situation.

"The fact is.. well, Kate and I, we've had our ups and downs. But about seven months ago, I did something very stupid. I had an affair."

I knew damn well that if I tried to say anything intelligent, it was just going to come out as an unintelligable squeak. So I kept quiet, relying on the time honoured solemnity of the nod.

"We'd been drifting apart for a long, long time. We both knew it. We'd hoped that relocating, getting new schools for the kids... that it would help us to get a new start, a new perspective.

It didn't. And it was my fault.

The girl from the estate agent.. we just clicked. We swapped numbers, supposedly just about the house, but we both knew there was something else."

There was something about that phrase – *the girl from the estate agent.....*

...it couldn't be.

"I was a fool to get involved, but I did, and we slept together. It was just one night, and we both knew we'd done something really, really terrible. Something irreversible.

Anyway, Kate found out. They always find out, eventually. We fought, we rowed.. I offered to leave but there's the kids to think of.. So we decided to make it work. Well, try to anyway.

I had to pay a penance. Prove I was sorry."

He sighed.

"It sounds ridiculous, but the thing that's always meant most to me has been my record collection. My Dad died when I was very young and he left me his Beatles records.. ever since then music has been something fundamental to me. My collection was like my lifeline.

Kate made me give it up as part of the deal for forgiveness."

...part of the deal..

"The other part of the deal was she got to have a... I guess you'd call it a 'freebie' – she could sleep with someone. Like as a way to balance things out."

Martin ran king-size hands through his hair. A penny wobbled on it's side in my mind. *Hang on.*

I guess Martin got bored of waiting for the wobbling penny to drop.

"You're the freebie, Dan. I can't say I like this situation, and don't go imagining that we're going to hug and be best friends after this, but if you think I'm here to break your nose then I can out your mind at rest."

Never look a gift horse in the mouth, Wyman. But still..

I cleared my throat, awkwardly.

"Look, you should know.. nothing really happened with me and Kate. I knew she was married, I knew something was going on.... I mean we got close, I'll be honest, but nothing irreversible. Nothing more than a couple of kisses."

"You'll understand that doesn't make things any easier for me."

An awkward silence descended.

"I imagine you've got one or two questions for me."

Well yes, just a couple of million. But they were all fighting their way into my mind at once, and the result was a whirl of white noise in my mind accompanied by my now world-famous goldfish impression. I needed, time, distance – space to work this out.

"Yeah, it's just a bit.." I tailed off.   "Look, do you want to sit down?"

"Thanks, yes, I will."

This was something of a miscalculation on my part as Martin proceeded to take over the entire sofa, whilst I made the unfortunate realisation that I had no other furniture. This led to a certain awkwardness as I hovered, waiting for the inevitable storm to break.

Martin, however, seemed to feel right at home, settling down on the sofa and homing in like a laser on the 78s peeking out of a pile of clutter on the coffee table.

"So you're a fan of Sonny Boy Williamson too then?"

"I – sorry, what?" Discussion of obscure early 1930s Delta bluesmen was somehow not how I'd anticipated this conversation going.

"I recognise these discs – very rare. Must have set you back a few quid." He arched an eyebrow in my direction.

Fuck, the 78s. Jesus, I'd completely forgotten those – sat gathering dust on the coffee table under a pile of forms and God-knows-what else.

Martin peered more closely at the serial numbers on the labels.

"These are mine, Dan. Well, they *were* mine, I should say."

Of course. From the last big haul before I got the boot for being overly curious.

Before the dark times. Before the... before everything. All this.

He snorted, bitter and regretful.

"Five grand, she got for all this. Almost paid her Mastercard off.". Another snort. "*Almost.*".

He tossed the record, safe in its waxy white envelope, back into the jungle of the coffee table.

"So how is the record shop business?"

"Wouldn't know". *Fuck it, what's the point in lying?*

"How do you mean?"

"Well, I got fired. Not long after Miles bought this whole haul."

He chuckled. "Right. Perfect. So you're out of work, Kate decides she's going to rescue you, fix you..."

I felt sick. I'd trusted Kate... what a bloody fool.

And yet she *had* helped me. She'd got me the job – which I might not exactly love, but I'd have been well and truly fucked without it. She'd gone out on a limb for me when she really hadn't had too.. what had she stood to gain?

Well, a revenge lay. A way to hurt Martin, to take revenge for his infidelity. I'd been nothing but a tool.

And yet, and yet, and *yet*. There was no getting around the fact that she had helped me when she hadn't needed to, she'd put her reputation on the line for me.. could she really have been doing all that just to hurt Martin? If that was all she wanted to do, weren't there easier ways? Kate (as I may have previously mentioned) was a stunning looking woman, if she wanted to pick up a guy just for sex, all she would have had to do is wander into the Red Lion in a low cut top and sit there for five minutes, and a queue would have formed.

I felt I had to break the silence. "So, what happens now?"

"Well, as I understand things, you've been through a bit of a personal loss recently?"

Yes, you could say that. I felt the savage twist in my guts as he brought it up. *How dare you mention that, fuck you, that is NOT your concern..*

"Yes." I just about managed.

"So I assumed things between you and Kate were on ice at the moment – I felt you should know the truth."

"Okay". I had to ask this. "Just one thing – you mentioned the girl you slept with was from the estate agents.. what was her name?"

"Louise. Her name was Louise. Why?"

Chapter 22

Oh, HELL no. This is not the Star Wars galaxy – there are more than two sexually active adult women in this town. It couldn't be my Louise. Fucking NO FUCKING WAY.

But it was. I got the details from Martin. Louise Marshall. Late twenties, brown hair, same estate agents, same everything.

You've got to be fucking kidding me.

To give him his due, Martin seemed genuinely surprised. I really don't think he'd known there was any connection between us. Why would he? Louise and I had been so on-and-off, such a grey area for so long...

So, details.

When had this whole thing happened? Well, wouldn't you know it – back in early January, just right around the time Louise and I had had the Battle Of The Coffee Table. No wonder she'd been so brittle that night – projection had always been a Louise characteristic. If she had done, or was doing, something that she felt bad about, that usually manifested itself in her accusing me of something similar.

Slowly, painfully, things began to make sense – the blanks slowly began to be filled in. The week when I'd been accumulating The Leaning Tower of Break-Up, she'd been arranging assignations with Martin in the house she'd been showing him. Sex in a sleeping bag in what would become the master bedroom of the house he would share with Kate and their two children. All the while Kate was home packing their lives into cardboard boxes waiting for the removal firm. Those glittery granite kitchen surfaces had seen a hell of a lot more action than just sandwich and vegetable preparation.

So now, I needed to know – had Kate known about me and Louise? Had she decided that because of our connection, I would be the perfect weapon to use to get revenge? And just what the hell had made Martin do such a catastophically, phenomenally, spectacularly FUCKING STUPID thing?

"So why did you do it? I mean seriously, Martin, what the fuck? You two had everything, what were you.. what the hell were you thinking?"

"I know this sounds like a cliché, Dan, but it just happened. I can't explain it, it wasn't a rational choice.. there was just chemistry. We just wanted each other. And like I said, Kate and I had been drifting apart -"

"Then have a fucking wank! Picture Louise's face on Kate's body while you're fucking her! Don't throw your whole fucking family away, create all this mess, this misery.. just to empty your fucking balls!"

I couldn't believe what Martin was saying in his defence, trotting out tired old cliches that would have shamed an Eastenders scriptwriter.

"Just.. how the fuck did you get so rich, Martin, being SO FUCKING STUPID??"

I don't think he was expecting that. I certainly wasn't, anyway.

Martin raised his hands defensively. "I don't have an answer for you, Dan. I don't believe these kind of situations have answers. I just came to tell you the truth."

He raised himself off the sofa, gently brushing the ceiling with his crew cut as he stood.

"I should go."

Just a fucking minute, pal.

"Wait."

I barred the door. Pulled myself up to my full height and looked him straight in the chin.

"Was she mine?"

"What do you mean?"

"*I mean was she mine. My baby.*"

Martin seemed to shrink visibly. He stepped back.

"I don't know, Dan. I truly don't. And that's the truth, I swear to you."

Maybe he was telling the truth, maybe not. I didn't know.. I couldn't know. I never would know. You couldn't DNA test a dead baby – could you? And even if it was a possibility, just the idea made be gag. Whether that tiny, harmless little soul was mine or his, she deserved to be left alone in peace now. I was trapped in a black dark maze, groping blindly for a light switch.

Martin gathered himself. "I should go"

I stared at him, full of a toxic cocktail – anger, loathing, contempt, frustration, pity... milk, two sugars and a healthy slug of Scotch.

"Yeah. Maybe you should."

"You and Kate – it's done now."

"I have questions for her, Martin. I don't appreciate being a fucking pawn. But I have no desire to get sucked any deeper into whatever misery you two have created for yourself."

He nodded.

"Leave." I pulled open the front door – the drama slightly diminished by the amount of fucking around with the handle necessary to open the bloody thing - and held it for him.

He nodded, and as he passed our eyes locked. I saw the shame and regret this big, big man carried with him every day.

To my immense surprise , I actually felt sorry for him.

But no time for that. I needed answers.

Chapter 23

Three days and nothing. Three days spent trying to contact Louise. Texts ignored. Phone to voicemail. Her mum answering the door, awkwardly and apologetically explaining she wasn't able to see me right now. Three days to sit and think and brood.

Louise had slept with Martin. While we were - technically - together. That whole confused, messy period that started the year.. we'd been on again, off again. All that time, she'd been bouncing between me – The Known (if slightly inadequate) Quantity – and Martin, The Bigger Better Deal. And managing, rather niftily, to pass herself off as the injured party. I remembered the flash of righteous anger in her eyes at our "reconciliation" meeting at the Lion a few months and a thousand years ago. Along with all that crap she'd fed me about her friend getting cheated on, and how it had made her feel insecure.. all that time she'd been flitting between his bed and mine, channelling her guilt into aggression and projecting onto the chump who'd been willing to stand there and take it.

Another thought struck me. We'd been in our holding pattern, grey area, whatever you wanted to call it - for six yeas. How many other times had she pulled this shit with me? It wasn't like this was the first time she'd had mood swings and started fights for no apparent reason. How many other times had she started a fight so she could disappear off and try on some other guy for size?

Once again, I realised I would never – could never – know the truth. I certainly wouldn't be able to trust any answer Louise gave me.

Again, I felt the world lurch beneath me. It wasn't just that life wasn't what I thought it was *going to be*. It hadn't even ever been what I thought it was at the time.

Weirdly though, the anger building inside me helped. Whatever the fuck had happened, whatever games had been played around me – I didn't care anymore. I hadn't asked for *any* of this. And I wasn't going to be a part of this bullshit for a moment longer.

I looked around my dusty, clutter strewn flat. Enough. Out came the Hoover, and for the next hour I was a domestic whirlwind. Surfaces were freed of clutter, cups and crockery washed up, books, CDs and magazines back in boxes and on shelves. By the time I came to rest you wouldn't have recognised the place.

I looked around, pleased with my handiwork. And it was still early – ish – and a rather pleasant evening out there. I changed out of the office gear (making a point of putting dirty laundry in thedirty laundry basket, rather than just letting it fall to the floor and have nature take it's course). Back in my natural attire of worn old T-shirt and jeans, I picked up the ancient Nokia, selected a number I hadn't dialled in far too long a time, and thumbed a one word text.

Pint?

Message Sent.

Right – pub.

It's a rum thing, this, but do you know what... as I strode down the well worn path to the Red Lion, I found myself feeling lighter somehow. The stress and frustration and misery of the past few weeks – months, really – had been like a concrete block roped to me, forcing me to drag it everywhere, sapping all my energy and motivation. It made no sense, but I could swear I felt happy.

I eased myself onto a barstool, ordered my pint, and examined this unfamiliar sensation.

Why the fuck are you feeling happy? What do you have to feel happy about?

Reasonable enough question. I'd discovered that I'd been cheated on, used as a pawn in some absurd marital power struggle, and that the baby my entire life had been centred on, and who had been so cruelly robbed of a chance of life, might well not even have been mine after all. Why the hell **was** I feeling happy?

Why not, I suppose. The situation was what it was however I felt about it. Life just *is*, it doesn't give a damn how you feel about it, life just happens. It's not fair, it's not right, it doesn't make sesnse.. it just is.

Before I knew it, I was at the bottom of the glass. Crikey, that hadn't lasted long.I fumbled around in my back pocket for some change when a familiar hand clapped me on the shoulder and an equally familiar voice said "I'll get these."

Ah, my date for the evening had arrived.

"Good to see you mate" Chris beamed at me.

"You too. Been a while.." I tailed off.

"Too bloody long. Come on then, what's been happening?"

Oh boy.

An hour or so later, the glasses are stacked three deep on the bar.

Chris exhaled deeply. "Fuuuuuck. Dude. You've been through the mill with this."

"I've had better summers."

"She really hit you?"

I fiddled with my phone and showed him the pictures of the bruises.

"Chin to God mate. There's got to be some Mike Tyson in her DNA somewhere."

"Speaking of DNA.. I'm so sorry about the baby, Dan."

Tears pricked the back of my eyes. *Danger. Don't lose*

it. Not now. Not here.

"Thanks man. Do me a favour though, let's just.. not, not right now."

He patted my arm. "Okay mate. When you're ready, if you want to talk.."

"Yeah, I know. And thanks. But just - not now." I swallowed, forcing back the feeling of panic and loss that were hazing into view. I finished my drink.

"So what about you? Still at the shop?"

Chris snorted. "Barely. Down to four days a week now so I'm absolutely fucking brassic. He's still faffing about, off god-knows-where half the time."

"Still losing money?"

He smiled wrlyly. "Couldn't tell you mate. He's finally changed the code on the safe... "

"Wow, after only nine years?"

"I know.. my hunch, though? We're pretty fucked. Maybe make it past Christmas, but after that.. I dunno. I'm looking around myself, so if you hear of anything at your office.." He raised his glass and drained it.

"Your round? I'm off for a slash."

I ordered us a couple more and pondered The Situation.I hadn't forgotten the row, the way we'd left things – but to be honest, so much had happened, everything had changed so much that it just didn't seem to matter. I wanted my mate back to have a few beers with and set the world to rights. And you know what, it helped, it really did. It was reassuring to know for all the madness, the fear, the loss.. the world had kept on turning. My friend was still there. Not everything was wrong.

He didn't look great, though. Not that he ever really did, but this was different. He looked ill and drawn, not just unwashed and hungover. I decided to probe him on it, gently, subtlely.

"Jesus, you look like shit."

"Thanks mate, love you too." Chris raised his glass, we clinked and slurped.

"You're right though, I'm not as pretty as I once was.. With work and everything, all the stress, my sugars have been all over the place."

"Been to the doctors?"

He shrugged. "Not much point. It's not like they can cure it, it's just managing it. Crème Egg to pick me up, insulin to bring me down. It's a tricky balancing act."

"Dude, seriously – there's got to be a better way of doing things than that."

He grinned at me. "Look at you , all concern."

"Well – yeah. I've seen.. stuff, mate. Don't go taking things for granted, I worry about you."

"You're breaking my heart". The shit-eating grin now threatening to consume his entire face.

It was infectious.

"Oh, well, bollocks to you then, I was going to suggest we get some lettuces and go jogging together, but let's get pissed instead."

"Now you're talking."

A couple more ales followed, and I began to notice the time.

"Shit, mate, I'm going to have to make a move. School night and all that."

Chris checked his watch a little blearily. "Yeah, I suppose you're right. Could use a decent night's kip myself, it's been a bastard trying to sleep when my sugars have been the way they are."

We yawned, stretched and stumbled our way out into the car park.

"Cheers for tonight mate, I needed this."

"Yeah, it's been too long by half, mate." He grinned again, a little unsteady on his feet. I grabbed his outsretched hand for a the customary shake – and was momentarily disturbed to find it shaking already.

"Dude, are you -"

I was going to finish the sentence with "OK", but Chris took it upon himself to answer the question by collapsing.

Chapter 24

For one horrifying moment I actually thought he was trying to kiss me.

Chris pitched forward limply taking me completely by surprise. Off balance, I tried to catch him but succeeded only in tumbling to the ground with him, although mercifully we managed to avoid heads smashing into the unyielding concrete.

My first instinct was that he'd passed out drunk on me. That had come very close to happening many times before. I reacted accordingly as I struggled out from underneath him.

"The *fuck*, man?? What's wrong with you, you drunken bastard", I spluttered, "Wake up, get the fuck up, come on!"

I tried to haul him over to the wooden benches arrayed as part of a makeshift beer garden. Thing was though, he was fucking heavy. Really, war films where Arnold Schwarzenegger runs around with a wounded comrade on his back don't give a true impression of how difficult moving an unconscious intermediate-sized pisshead is.

Crouched over him, I improvised a torch with my phone and... wow, this was **not** good. He wasn't just drunk, this was... oh, Christ, this must be his diaebetes at work.

I dialled 911. Fuck knows why. I dialled 999.

"Hi- ambulance, ambulance, please", I gabbled, trying to keep down the rising panic from overwhelming me.

The woman on the other end of the phone was the very model of unflappable NHS phlegmatism.

"I need an ambulance, my friend, he's diabetic, he's collapsed, he's collapsed.."

She kept me calm enough to give her the location (beyond "The Red Lion") and promised me an ambulance would be with me "very soon".

Okay. *Breathe*, Dan, calm.

And then Chris started to spasm. This was not in the fucking script. *Come the fuck on, ambulance.* I moved around him to sit behind his head and manouvered us so that his head was resting in my lap, as it occurred to me that lying as he was he might swallow his tongue.

His blood sugar meter. Frantically, I scrabbled inside his ever-present shabby back pack and pulled out a plastic handle with an LCD screen. This should (if I remembered rightly) let me see the last couple of his blood sugar readings. A normal reading should be around 8 or 9. A bad one (deserving of the full Crème Egg) would be around 2 or 3.

Chris' last reading was 1.1.

Fuck, oh god, don't die on me mate, don't fucking die on

me you shitting fucking bastard, don't you dare..

There was a bunch of high sugar foods in his pack – cookies, chocolate and a weird sort of smeary thing. None of these were any real use to me, I realised – Chris wasn't in any condition to swallow anything. And I worried if I stuck my finger in his mouth to smear anything on the inside of his cheek I might choke him.

I checked my watch. Five minutes since I'd dialled 999. *They should be here by now.*

Christ. I gritted my teeth. Checked his pulse. Panicked when I couldn't find one.

You DICK, Dan, you don't even know what you're checking for. Check your own damn pulse, it's at least 60/40 you're not dead yet.

I found my own pulse. Fuckwit, I'd been checking in the wrong place. I found Chris'. It was tenuous, shaky, but still there.

Hang on. His injector. The nuclear option. I checked my watch – eight minutes. *Where the fuck, where the fuck..*

He was fading. Breath becoming more ragged and shallow. Pulse (now I knew what I was searching for) slowing. *Nine minutes.*

Fuck, I can't even hear a siren. I'm going to have to do this.

I got the injector, made hurried sense of the instructions.

The thing was preloaded, all I had to do was jab it in him in the right place.

A memory from an earlier, more innocent time grabbed me. Chris and I slumped half cut in the kebab shop, Chris about to bury himself face first in a chicken doner and me poised to steal said delicacy.. when my plans were foiled by him rearing to life and stabbing hmself in the belly with a an apparently magic needle. Where had he aimed?

I concentrated as hard as I could on the image from my memory. A foot up and a bit to the left of the belly button.

Ten minutes. Still nothing. He was getting worse.

He's going to die. He's really going to die, in a fucking pub car park.

I've got to try.

Please, god. Please. Fuck. Fuck. FUCK.

I screamed. I screamed and rammed the needle in.

Please.

<u>Chapter 25</u>

Sorry Rebecca, I'm not going to be able to get in tomorrow, there's been an emergency here. I'll explain when I see you. Sorry for the inconvenience, Dan.

MESSAGE SENT.

I've spent far more time in this hospital than I should have done these past months.

I checked the clock on the wall. 2.15 am. I swilled cold tea around in a beige plastic cup and contemplated the walls. This was torment. Again. Only days after I'd been in this same building to meet a white-as-a-sheet Louise to find we'd lost our daughter..

Daniel Wyman, you are just bad fucking news, aren't you? Some shity version of the Midas touch.

The adrenaline was a disant memory now, leaving me weak and shaky. A shuffling zombie, fuelled by caffeine. And god, but I wanted a cigarette. Despite not having smoked in six years I felt a familiar pang, craving something to focus on to take away the anxiety. I settled for gnawing my fingernails down to the quick and trying to grow a beard.

"Daniel Wyman?"

I was snapped from introspection by a blue-clad nurse. Fingernail still in my mouth.

"Yes?"

"Your friend is awake."

Relief like you wouldn't believe washed over me. I almost collapsed myself.

"Oh, thank God. Can I see him?"

There he was – the invincible, immovable object. The unchanging rock of the last twelve years of my life. Lying in a hospital bed under harsh fluorescent strip lighting with tubes coming out of him. Despite bollocking him with monotonous regularity about smoking, drinking, never exercising, balancing insulin against chocolate, not being able to play the guitar properly, not washing regularly.. I never, ever though I'd see him like this.

"Alright mate"

"Dan"he grinned weakly. "You better not have eaten my Rolos, you cunt"

I couldn't help it. I started to laugh. I started to cry.

"Fuck you, you bastard, don't you ever try and kiss me again."

We hugged. I scruffed up his greasy hair and pulled his

head to my shoulder.

"Thank Christ you're ok. I thought.. for a moment there I thought you'd gone."

"Mate, for a moment I did – or so they tell me. While I was out, my heart stopped."

I went cold. "Jesus."

"I know. I was amazed too. I have a heart."

I grinned at him, pure relief coursing through my veins.

"Who knew?"

The nurse frowned at us.

"You two should consider yourselves extremely lucky. What you did with the glucagon needle when you've had absolutely no training or experience could have gone hideously wrong. No untrained person should ever try and attempt that unsupervised."

Especially not panicked, shaking and half drunk in a dark pub car park.

"You could have been looking at an assault charge or even worse. And as for *you*-" turning to supine Chris - "*You* have no business even being alive. Type 2 diabetes is a serious condition. Without proper management the consequences can be – well, you saw tonight what the consequences could be. Frankly, without your friend here and a hell of a lot of luck on his side, you wouldn't even be here. We will have a serious talk to review your lifestyle options."

Oh, what I would give to be a fly on the wall for that particular meeting.

We both did our best to look duly chastened. Frankly though, I was just so damned glad to have my mate back again, it was all I could do not to giggle.

"Anyway, we'd like to keep you in under observation for another twenty four hours. If all is well we should be able to discharge you on Saturday morning."

Chris looked over to me. "Can you let Miles know?"

On autopilot, I nodded. "Yeah, no problem, mate."

Oops. Well, this should be interesting.

"In the meantime, Mr. Wyman, it'd be best if Chris could get as much rest as possible."

I took my cue.

"No problem. You have my number, can you let me know if there's any change in his condidtion?"

She smiled at me. "Not a problem."

I decided to text Miles from the waiting room. *Hi Miles – with Chris in hospital. Hypo –* fuck, how do you spell this? I scrubbed it out – *diabetes attack, they're keeping him in tomorrow. Dan.*

I made my way home, weary, but strangely peaceful. Slumped through the door and hauled myself to bed. And for once... there was no surprise waiting for me. No twist. No unexpected caller. No voicemail. No text. Just peace.

I was asleep before I knew it.

Chapter 26

I was flying. Soaring through clouds, across treetops, through walls. With me was a shadow, someone I knew so well, like a brother, but whose face I couldn't make out. And then something hit, something solid but invisible, and we were falling, falling so fast, the ground rushing up to meet us..

I woke with a start. The Nokia burped and gurgled at me, demanding attention like a petulant child.

A multitude of texts awaited me – the poor old girl was probably about at bursting point. I put on the coffee, made some toast and start to munch and slurp my way through the correspondance.

First, Rebecca – *Hi Dan, hope you're OK. Sorry but we won't be able to pay you for today. Thanks, Rebecca.*

I exhaled. Right, well, there's a way to take the shine off the morning. Still, my problems aren't her problems, she's got a business to run. And it could be a lot worse. She might have ended up firing me.

Next up, Miles. - *OK.*

That was it. Huh. I finished the toast.

Finally, a system message. "You have one new voicemail."

I swigged some more coffee and mashed my thumb into the keypad until finally acknowledged my presence.

Five minutes later I was out of the door, running like my life depended on it.

That clinically efficient, ever-so-slightly-peeved sounding NHS voice. "Message for Mr. Daniel Wyman – we're sorry to say your friend Chris Wheeler had a relapse after you left last night and he's unconscious. He's stable but in quite a serious condition."

That was from *four hours ago*. I'd slept right fucking through it.

*Jesus wept, this wasn't fair, this wasn't fucking fair, he was up and **talking to me** only a few hours ago..*

The only good thing I could think of about the events of the last week was that at least I knew my way to the hospital now. I'll hold my hands up to taking a few stops to get my breath back along the way, but a little over half an hour later I was sweatily panting
my way up the steps to the reception.

"Hi, I'm here to see my friend, Chris Wheeler? He was brought in here last night after a hypoglaecemia, er, incident."

"Just a second."

I allowed just one second to go past.

"Do you have any information on his..."

"Just a moment."

Fuck. I don't know how long a moment actually is, so the girl on the reception desk may well technically have been within her rights when she finally told me.. "He's in ICU. Room 9".

I thanked her and swivelled on my heel.

ICU. Think, Dan, come one - you grew up on Casualty episodes. Intensive Care Unit.

Oh, Christ.

The only, only good thing about his situation was that ICU was well signposted. It took only a few minutes before I found Chris' room and burst in in what would I would have described as a ludicrously over-dramatic fashion. Seriously, managed to trip over my feet and everything – almost managing to fall on to the supine Chris as I did so.

Struggling to my feet, I looked around and made immediate contact with a face I hadn't expected to see here.

"Hello Dan." A quiet, measured voice, with an undertone of barely controlled aggression. A voice I hadn't heard since it fired me from my job of nine years.

"Hello, Miles."

He looked pale and drawn. The kind of look that suggested it had been a long, long time since he'd slept properly.

Good, snarled one vengeful little voice in my head.

Chris' words from earlier in the year played in my mind. *Losing money. Close to a grand every month. Been that way for a year and a half.* I guess he hadn't been kidding.

An awkward silence took root. I blinked first.

"So how is he?"

"They don't know."

"He was OK last night, we were talking, he was fine.."

"They don't know."

I lookd him straight in the eye about to give him both barrels. That he'd fired me for nothing more than trying to help him, that the stress caused by *his* mismanagement of the shop had brought on the intial hypoglaecemia attack, that this was *his* fault as much as anyone's..

I looked him straight in the eye and saw the tears forming there. Of course. Chris was his friend too. They went back even further than we did.

You stupid bastard, Dan, how could you have forgotten that?

"I'm sorry, Dan.". Miles spoke in typically sotto voce

fashion. I strained to hear him even over the occasional beeps and pings of the various hospital equipment.

"Sorry?"

"For him. For all of this."

"How are things..."

"Not good. Not good at all. Haven't been good in a long time, to be honest."

"When.. when it all happened, Chris said we'd been losing money. For quite a while. Is that true?"

He nodded. "Things aren't what they were. This business has been getting harder and harder for several years. People just don't buy records anymore."

I sighed. It was hard not to sympathise with the guy. After all, his business was something he'd lovingly built from the ground up and he was having to watch it die a slow, agonising death. Killed by convenience. Smothered by apathy.

On the other hand though, he had fired me.

"Look, Miles.. you know we were just trying to help, right?"

"I don't want to talk about that."

"It's *important.* We were trying to help, me and Chris. We knew something was up."

It was his turn to sigh.

"Yes, ok, I appreciate that Dan. And if I'm honest, I do regret what happened. ***But***. Rules are rules. You knew the score. What's kept in the safe is my concern and mine alone. If I can't trust you to keep that rule, how am I supposed to trust you around the till or with the stock?"

I was about to respond with a healthy "fuck you then" - but the memory of the 78s gathering dust on my coffee table leapt to mind.

And with it, the seed of an idea.

"Look, I worked for you for nine years. Honestly, in all that time, did I ever give you any reason *not* to trust me?"

He looked down, clearly uncomfortable.

"No, that's true enough. But - "

"What?"

Miles pointed to the bed. "I just saw him twitch. I think he's waking up."

"Seriously? I -"

I saw it too, a vague stirring of head and shoulders on the pillow.

"I'll get the nurse."

As it turned out, I didn't need to. They were already on it, doctor and nurse striding purposefully through the door even as I turned.

"Would you two mind stepping back, we just need to run a few tests."

Miles and I huddled in the corner while they fussed over him, checking sugar levels and.. things.

"He seems to be stable now."

This time my relief was tinged with scepticism.

"Not to be rude, but he seemed to be stable last night, what happened?"

"His blood sugar levels nosedived early this morning. It's not unknown, the body can sometimes struggle to regulate itself and your friend here has been doing himself no favours managing his condition. We're going to keep him in over the weekend on a drip, give the body time to even itself out without any spikes or dips in the blood sugar levels and make sure there's been no permanent damage."

Miles and I glanced at each other anxiously.

"Permanent damage?"

"Yes. It's rare, but not unknown for prolonged, severe hypoglaecemic episodes to result in brain injury."

"Jesus, brain damage?"

"It is a possibility. Basically the brain can be starved of fuel resulting in neurological damage. I should stress though, it is *not* something we are anticipating in this case, it's just a possibility we are looking to rule out."

You know that old, cliché that people drag out about "making your blood run cold"? That. Totally that. I almost froze.

That stupid, idiotic drunken bastard, I KNEW this was going to happen one day if he didn't get his fucking act together.. I bet him ten quid he wouldn't make forty, as a joke, but now there's a real chance he won't. Oh God, not him, not Chris...

The doctor cleared his throat. "Look, I know it's hard to take in, but let's be realistic about this, the odds are very much on your friends side on this. Most people pull through and they tend to view the experience as something to learn from. Your friend - "

"Chris"

"Your friend Chris.. from what you two have told me about his lifestyle, he seems to be remarkably robust in order to have lived his life the way he has for so long. When he comes back to us he's going to have to make some serious changes to his lifestyle, and he'll be needing support from you two."

He turned his attention back to Chris' recumbent form and checked a few things, made a couple of notes on a pad before turning back to us.

"You're free to stay as long as you want, but we will

contact you in the event of any change in his condition."

He gave a curt, professional-looking nod and walked out.

Silence descended like a blanket on the three of us.

How far we'd come these past months. Memories played in my mind of a thousand happy evenings in the Lion. All those times belonged to a different life now. This was a life of hospitals, regret, fear and "permanent damage". How the hell had it come to this?

And yet, in hindsight, it all seemed pretty simple and obvious. Louise and I.. we couldn't have stayed in our holding pattern or whatever you wanted to call it. Eventually, something would have happened to break the cycle – if we hadn't got any further than we had in the past six years, we weren't going to in the next six. And nor should we. We weren't right for each other, we were both just too damn lazy to break the habit.

The shop? Our industry was dying on its arse. People don't buy records and CDs anymore. We were obsolescent already, it was only a matter of time before we became entirely obsolete. Frankly, it was amazing we'd lasted as long as we had. The old place had given me nine good years that I could remember fondly – perhaps I should be happy with that.

And Chris.. well, how many times had I told him he should be dead by rights, that he was going to wind up drinking himself into a fucking coma or worse. And yeah, look where we were.

Nothing lasts forever.

"We're down twelve grand. I don't think Chris is going to have a job to come back to."

Miles startled me out of my reverie.

"Twelve grand? *Twelve thousand pounds*? Jesus.. how are you going to make that back?"

Miles looked resolutely at the floor. Leaning back against the wall, legs outsretched – clearly on a quest to form an isosceles triangle.

"We're not. I've been trying to find a way around it, but business just seems to get worse and worse. I can't pay Chris sick pay and hire someone else to cover him, and I can't do everything there myself. It's just going to get worse now, much worse. " He exhaled, a long slow breath of defeat.

"Time to fold."

I felt completely, totally empty. "Shit, I'm so sorry mate."

Miles gestured toward Chris' inert form. "Thanks, but.. he kind of puts things into perspective. I'll auction off as much as I can and I can at least give the poor sod some sort of payoff."

The news settled over me like a dark, portentous cloud.

Hang on.

The idea that had briefly flickered into being earlier was back.

"Just.. what happened if you got twelve grand?"

"What do you mean?"

"Just that. What would happen if you got twelve K, now – or soon, at least – would that mean that you could keep things above ground? Hypothetically, I mean."

He shook his head. "It's.. no Dan, no. It's not that simple. There's other outstanding expenses, other debts... to get things back up and as they were, we'd need closer to twenty. And that's just not going to happen, not with the way things are now."

It might, you know. We're not beaten yet.

Chapter 27

He wasn't pleased to see me. But then again, why should he be, after everything that had happened between us.. between me and his wife.

Shall I back up a step? OK.

I still had a couple of Kate's cards in my wallet. Those crads listed her contact details, personal and business mobile, email.. and website. The Nokia banged on the door of the World Wide Web, demanding to be let in, and crept arthritically onto Kate's business site. Painstakingly it began to load the page, pixel by torturous pixel.

Finally, after the best part of a decade, all the information was there. Buried in the small print was an additional "secondary" contact number. I had a hunch this was Martin.

The response I got when I dialled confirmed it.

"Hello?"

"Hi, can I speak to Martin Edwards, please."

I recognised the large scale sigh, a mixture of self-pity

and world-weary contempt.

"Who is this?"

Oh, right. People often sound different on the phone.

"Dan. Dan Wyman."

A pause.

"What do you *want*, Dan?"

"I want to make a deal with you. Is there somewhere we can talk?"

"What do you mean, make a deal? Are you trying to blackmail me or something? Is this to do with Kate?"

"No, no, nothing like that. Some friends of mine are in a bad situation, I think you can help, and I've got something I think you might want in return for that help."

"If this is anything to do with drugs, or anything illegal, you can count me out right now."

"No, look, Martin, this is all above board - " *Probably* - "it's just a bit complex to explain on the phone. It's nothing to do with Kate and I'm not trying to set myself up as one of the Sopranos, ok? Look, do you know the Red Lion?"

"I think..."

"It's a pub. Obviously, sorry – it's on Station Road, opposite the park?"

"Oh, yes, I know the one."

"Give me.. " I checked my watch. Just gone eleven. Half hour to get back to the flat.."Half past two, I'll meet you there"

I poked my head back around the door to Chris' room. He was still out cold, Miles apparently dozing in the chari next to him. I nudged him awake.

"Mmmh? Oh, Dan – are you off?"

"Yes mate, got to see a man about a dog." I grinned.

"What are you up to?"

"Probably nothing – I've had an idea, that's all. Call me as soon as you know anything more about Chris, would you?"

He nodded. "Yeah, of course."

"Cheers mate. See you."

"See you."

It's amazing what having a sense of purpose does for you. Arriving back at the flat – by now a little sweaty – I put the kettle on while rooting through the debris of my coffee table for the 78s. Under the seven year old copy of Classic Rock magazine, left at the abandoned TV remote, over the clutch of no-longer-working biros and HAH! I'd hit the motherlode.

I checked over the four vinyl discs, gingerly removing them from the envelopes and scrutinising them minutely for dust in the grooves, scuffs, anything that might have caused them damage and reduce their value.

All were pretty much in mint condition, all crackled into life beautifully when the stylus hit them. I realised as I tested them that since the day I'd walked out of the shop with these in my pocket I'd never actually listened to them. Robert Johnson, Son House, Charley Patton and Leadbelly joined me in my living room, their plaintive voices singing of loss, loneliness and drowning their sorrows.

Now I got it.

"She's a kind hearted woman, she studies evil all the time" croaked Mr Johnson, as his slide guitar echoed his pain and confusion. *Louise. Kate.*

According to every vintage record website I'd been able to check, these were the real deal. Original pre war recordings from the original Delta blues pioneers, men who had lived their music and for the audiences who heard them represented the opportunity to forget their woes and drudgery for just a few hours. These discs were older than me or my dad, they were a link to another time and place but where people loved and hurt just as badly. I wondered about all the hands that had touched these discs on their journey from the Deep South across the Atlantic to here, and thanked all the gods I could think of that I had managed not to break them on my watch.

These were the discs that Kate had made Martin get rid of as part of his penance for cheating on her with Louise. Now they were going to get my friends their lives back.

I liked to think Mr Johnson and his brothers would have approved.

I made a few notes – most of what I'd researched had been on American sites, so the values were on dollars, but I had enough ammunition to make Martin an offer he couldn't refuse. Lastly, I arranged the discs on the coffee table and snapped pictures of each one with the Nokia.

Last swig of tea. Deep breath. Let's *do* this. Keys, wallet, notes, discs. Out the door and off we go.

There he was. Sat at the bar hunched over a cup of coffee that was far too small for him. I could practically see him seething even from ten feet away. Still, no point pussying out now.

I heaved myself up onto the stool next to him and ordered a pint. I turned to Martin enough to catch his eye, and raised my glass.

"Alright."

"Hello Dan. What is it that you want?"

"Nice to see you too, Martin."

"Once again – what is it you want, Dan?"

I turned to face him.

"You know what, between you and Louise, and Kate with her little revenge fantasy, you two have done a great deal to fuck my life up these past few months. You may not have meant to, but you did. I've wound up caught in the crossfire, taking shit from literally all sides, and I've had it."

He eyed me, unimpressed. "Don't play the victim, Dan, you almost slept with my wife - "

"Which would never have happened if she hadn't instigated it, and *that* would never have happened if you hadn't fucked my girlfriend and quite possibly got her pregnant."

His eyes dropped. He shrugged. "And, what now? That's the past and it -"

"You can help me. And you fucking *will*, because you owe me. When I left the shop, I took a couple of items in lieu of a redundancy payment. I think they'll interest you."

I showed the screen on the old Nokia and flicked through the photos I'd taken. Even through the grimy screen and the blocky low resolution camera, it was enough for him to recognise.

"So they were mine. I thought as much."

"They were, and now they belong to Miles."

"Who?"

"The guy who runs the shop. He's my friend, and his business is in trouble, so you're going to save it. You're going to buy those discs back at five thousand pounds each."

He snorted derisively. "I am, am I? And what makes

you think I have twenty grand sloshing around waiting to be thrown away on trivia like this?"

"Oh come off it, Martin, I've been to your house, I've seen your lifestyle. To someone like you that's pocket change. Maybe you keep the Range Rover for an extra year this year. Maybe you wait till next Christmas before you get the new big screen 3DTV. I know damn well you can rustle up twenty grand if you want to."

Martin sipped his coffee. "Alright, just suppose I *could* lay my hands on that kind of money. Why would I want to?"

"Because of what you and Louise did. Because I'll never know if it's my baby they buried or yours."

"I paid my debt for that – "

"To Kate. NOT to me. I've been a fucking pawn for you two to thrash out your petty power struggles, and that fucking stops now."

I think I surprised him. I'd certainly surprised myself. *Keep your nerve, Dan. Nearly there.*

"And besides which, Martin – I'm not waltzing in saying *give me twenty grand or else*, I'm saying *buy these records which are incredibly precious to you for roughly their market value*. It's *is* not exactly extortion, for fuck's sake."

There it was the familiar exhalation of breath. "I suppose when you put it like that.."

"It *is* like that. Look, you win, I win, everyone's happy,

end of story."

He me straight in the eye. "If – *if* – we do this.. I don't want you to have any more contact with me or Kate or any of my family."

"Deal. I'll block your number and hers, same with emails, same with Facebook. We do this and we never have to speak again. Trust me, I have *no* interest in entangling myself with your lives any more than you do with mine."

"Do you have the discs with you?"

"One". I held up the Leadbelly recording of "Where Did You Sleep Last Night". "I'll drop the other three round when we've sorted the money out."

"So what's my guarantee of getting them?"

"That you know where I live and would beat the crap out of me if I try and diddle you, I imagine."

He smiled, in spite of himself. "Alright. Alright, you've got a deal. How do you want to do this? Small bills, unmarked... "

"No – no, Martin.. Bank transfer will be fine. Here are the details." I passed him a slip of paper with shop's account details. He scrutinised it.

"Is that a five?"

I peered at the number. "Three."

"Right... just let me check this." He recited the sort code, account number and name to me.

"Yep, all good."

He opened up the banking app on his smartphone and tapped in a few digits. I must admit, I was impressed. Maybe I should think about retiring the old Nokia.

Although maybe I should have been more impressed by the fact that this guy could lay hands on more than my annual salary in one fell swoop.

Martin turned a very swanky touch screen toward me. There it was, in black and white (or iPhone equivalent) - £20,000 transferred from his savings account to the shop.

"It should show up on Monday. Here - " Martin scribbled down a few notes on the slip of paper I'd given him and handed it back to me, "- this is the transaction reference number, if there's any problems. If it hasn't hit by Tuesday, call the Lloyds bank and quote this, they'll be able to track it."

I nodded, cautiously optimistic. *Have I really just done this?*
"Okay, well, I guess you've earned this." I fished into my pocket and gave him the Leadbelly disc. "I'll text you when the money arrives and sort out handing over the other three."

"Do that." He finished his coffee, eased himself off the barstool and left. No goodbye, no pleasantries, just done.

Still, who the fuck cared. *I think... I think something good just happened.*

The Nokia burped and fuzzed at me. Text message – Miles. Briefly my heart leapt into my throat, and then the letters rearranged themselves in front of my eyes.

He's awake.

Chapter 28

By now the hospital felt like a second home. This time I found my way to Chris' room without a hitch. There he was, looking a little pale and wan, but unmistakeably Chris.

Don't get too excited. He's already had one relapse. If they haven't found what caused that, there's every chance he could have another one.

I resolved not to mention anything about the deal with Martin until absolutely everything had gone through without a hitch – no transfer problems, no lost funds, everything confirmed. There was just too much at stake to jinx things by taking anything for granted now. I could wait an extra few days.

This time, there was no banter. This time we just grinned and hugged each other. I found myself wiping away a tear.

"Are you okay now?" I asked, quietly- almost scared to hear the answer.

He smiled and shook his head. "No, mate, no – I'm a pretty long way from OK. There's a lot wrong in there."

He leaned back onto the bed. "But there's nothing they can't fix, and there's a lot of things I'm going to have to do myself."

"Off the booze?"

He nodded grimly. "There's going to be a lot of brewery workers looking for new jobs out there."

The doctor coughed discreetly.

"We will be consulting with Mr Wheeler about the alterations we'll need him to make to his lifestyle, but of course as his close friends you two will be essential to him making the necessary changes and not letting him fall back into bad old habits."

"No more booze, eat healthy, exercise.. that sort of thing?"

"Wipe that smirk of your faces, you bastards" Chris laughed.

The doctor allowed a half smile to play across his face. I suppose it was that sort of a moment.

"Yes, all those things are important. We'll be checking in with Mr Wheeler quite regularly over the next few months to ensure that these new habits are sticking.. I'd like to think that an incident like this has opened your eyes to the realities of your condition, Mr Wheeler, and I hope we will not be seeing you back here."

Miles spoke up. "Don't worry doc, we'll make sure he sticks to the rules."

"Okay, well, there are a few forms to fill in, but all the examinations we've done are positive, so you're pretty much free to go."

An hour later we were helping him in to Miles' battered old Volvo estate.

I'm pretty sure he could walk fine, but Chris being Chris, he was going to milk the ever-loving shit out of it... it was good to have the malingering old sod back.

We dropped him off at his flat and made him promise to do nothing more than that doze in bed and watch only the softest of porn. I fluffed his pillows, trying not to notice their somewhat.. *brittle..* texture.

"Right, I'll be round tomorrow morning to check in on you, ok? No booze, no Crème Eggs, light wanking only, alright?"

"Yes, matron, whatever you say.. Listen, did you have any luck asking about jobs at your place? Because I really think the old place is on its last legs. I don't want to wind up in the shit when the inevitable happens."

"I – you know what, just don't worry about it. Get yourself a decent nights kip, yeah? We'll chat about it tomorrow."

"Alright mate. Listen, how are things ith you and Louise now, you seemed - "

"Not – not now mate. Just get some rest, ok? I'll see you tomorrow."

As I locked his front door, Miles' car was still there.

"You want a lift back?"

I dithered. But actually, I was kind of knackered afer rushing around like a blue-arsed fly all day.

"Yeah, go on."

There was an uncomfortable silence in the old Volvo. Without Chris to focus on, neither of us really knew where we stood with one another.

We both tried to break the tension. Unfortunately we both tried to do it at once.

"Look - "

"I - "

We engaged in an ogy of apologising. Eventually I persuaded Miles to go first.

"I'm sorry for firing you, Dan. It was a mistake, and I'd undo it if I could. But I think now is the time to wind things up while I've stll got a chance of paying off our creditors."

It was all I could do not pump my fist with glee. *Yes.* This was exactly what I wanted to hear.

"I'm sorry too – look, I did what I did with the best of intentions, but I suppose I did break the rules.. Look, just do me a favour, would you?"

"What?"

"Go in Monday and open the shop."

"There's no point, Dan, it's over. I hate to say it, but that's the truth."

"No, please – just do this for me, Miles. You won't regret it, I promise."

Sunday. I awoke feeling like a little kid on Christmas Eve, oscillating between euphoria at the idea that the shop might be saved, that *everything might be alright again* – and nerve-jangling, fingernail-gnawing tension at the idea that *something*, some gremlin, some inexplicable banking error might have held things up or just buggered the whole deal completely. This was Real Life, after all – not nice, clean, logical fiction but messy, pointlessly complicated and resolutely unco-operative Real Life. Something was going to go wrong, it had to.

Patience, Dan. Santa won't come if he knows you're waiting up for him.

Right. I occupied myself with coffee and toast and then busied myself straightening out the flat. There were some of Louise's things which got boxed up and stuck in the cupboard.

And then there was the baby stuff.

Deep breaths. Let's just get this done.

I packed nappies, baby clothes and cot away in boxes in the corner of the spare room, doing my best to ignore the prickling sensation on the back of my eyelids.

Whether she was mine or Martin's, it wasn't her fault.

Try as I might, the tears came.

Oddly enough, when they'd passed and I picked myself up off the floor about half an hour later, I felt.. lighter. Like a pressure valve had been released and something inside me had gone *No. No more today. Come on, get yourself up.*

I called Louise – no answer. No surprise. If she knew I'd found out about Martin, on top of losing the baby.. well, she was most likely with her mum trying her best to hide from the world. Wouldn't you be?

I both did and didn't blame her. Yes, she had slept with another man when we were (sort of) together.. yes, she had let me believe the baby was mine – but there again she could have been.

The simple truth was - I was never going to know. And I was never going to be able to trust what she told me.

Either way, I wasn't interested in having a reckoning. It wasn't going to solve anything for either of us. I sent her a text, keeping things neutral.

Hi Louise, hope yr OK. What do you want to do with baby things? Dan x

I just couldn't think of anything else to say.

Time to leave. It was a nice, crisp, early autumn day, and it was nearly lunchtime. Chris would be getting up any minute.

I let myself in to his flat and draped my jacket on a strategically placed tower of adult entertainment. A weak, pathetic voice came from the bedroom.

"Nurse... nurse.." followed by a bell tinkling.

I grinned to myself and poked my head round the door.

"Get up, you bone idle fuck."

The helpless invalid tapped his watch.

"What sort of time do you call this? I've been waiting for my breakfast in bed and it's nearly one!"

I tried arching an eyebrow, but I've never really got the hang of doing that.

"Never mind" he continued "you can redeem yourself by giving me a spongebath."

"Right, get up, and go and have a wash."

Chris looked at me with a flannel and a bucket and big sad pleading eyes.

"Under no fucking circumstances, you malingering git."

An hour later we were sat in his kitchen, munching cheese sandwiches. Quite possibly the healthiest, most balanced meal ever to have been prepared within these four walls.

"So have you had a chance to ask about jobs at your new place?" Chris asked between cheddary swallows.

"Not yet- I wouldn't worry about it though, just focus on getting yourself sorted out for the next few days."

A grimace crossed his chomping face. "Bit bloody difficult to focus though, when I don't know whether I'm going to have a job to go back to."

I *so* wanted to tell him. But I couldn't, not until I knew that the transfer was safely done and dusted. If anything went wrong, I really didn't have a back up plan.

"Look, just.. just sit on it mate, I'll ask around when I go in on Monday, we'll sort something out."

"Cheers mate, appreciate that... you know what, it's been a while – do you want to grab the guitars? Have a bit of a jam?"

I couldn't think of anything better.

"As long as you can keep the damn thing in tune mate, you bet."

It was a glorious afternoon – if it hadn't been for the fact that we were drinking tea instead of lager, it would have been just like the old days.

I left in a good natured haze of nostalgia around about eight and headed home. Coming back in to the flat, I was struck by the silence. The stillness. After so many months with Louise, so many rows, the tension, the fear.. the quietness enveloped me and wrapped itself around me like a warm velvet cloak. My flat was *mine* again.

I treated myself to a beer from the fridge, popped my feet up and let relaxation flow into each and every one of my extremeties. For the first time in a long time, life felt like something that just might be worth living.

I passed a quiet evening, getting my things in order for the next week at work.. it was difficult to remember there was still the drudgery of a low level data entry job waiting for me on the morrow, but life continued regardless. A couple of beers and a bit of TV accompanied by idle guitar strumming and I was ready for bed.

Big day tomorrow.

Chapter 29

I slept fitfully. There was *so much* riding on today, and none of it was in my hands. Waking an hour before my alarm, I finally gave up on sleep and decided on caffeine as a substitute.

> 6.30 am. There was no way the banks would be open yet. Stay calm.

I busied myself with toast and coffee and ironing (yes, things were that desperate). It was impossible to relax. I decided on a scenic route into work – better to be moving than sitting around with this knot of tension embedded deep in my belly.

Plus, said belly could probably use the exercise.

I clocked in at 8.30, a personal record for me. You might even have mistaken me for being enthusisastic at the prospect of *all that lovely data to enter, yum yum delicious.* Frankly I just wanted something to do while I was waiting to see if it all had worked.

I got myself a coffee and settled in behind the PC. However, I got no further than logging in before Rebecca stuck her head round the door to the open plan cubicle-drone-worker-bee area.

"Dan, can I have a word with you for a minute?"

"Hmm? Oh, hi Rebecca – yeah, sure."

I trotted off obligingly, following her into her office. Very impressive – sleek leather chairs, frosted glass, expensive-looking desk.

"Take a seat."

I sat. And forced back the terrible old joke about bringing the seat back when I'd finished with it. *Wow, I think I may have overdone the coffee this morning, its -*

"I'm sorry, Dan, but I'm going to have to let you go."

What?

"What?" This wasn't in my script.

"I said I'm going to have to let you go, Dan, I'm sorry."

"Wh-but – why?"

"Well, you've proven to be a little.. erratic.. these past few weeks. I mean there's coming in to the office in an absolute state, covered with bruises.. then this last week you've just not been with it at all, your work has just been full of mistakes – we run a tight ship here, Dan, we can't have people coasting."

"I'm.. I'm sorry, Rebecca, I've been having a difficult time of late, a few.. personal problems."

"I'm sure, Dan, we all have problems. But this is work, we leave personal problems where they belong, at home."

I stayed silent, eyeing her. I wanted to tell her I understood, that I would have *loved* to have left my personal problems at home, *it just wasn't that fucking simple.*

"And the truth is, this was only ever a temporary post. We needed a couple of extra people to get us through a bottleneck and clear some administrative backlogs, and we've done that. Look, we'll pay you for the week as a goodwill gesture, but it might be best if you pack your things and go today."

I nodded dumbly. "Is there anything.. anything I can say or do to change your mind?"

She smiled sadly and shook her head. "Look, Dan, you're not a bad guy, but it's obvious this place isn't for you. I know a little bit about what's been going on in your life recently, and believe me I do sympathise, but we just can't have people here who aren't a hundred percent involved. Like I say, we'll pay you for the week, but if I were you I'd take that time to fix yourself up with another job."

"Ok, well, if that's the way it is..."

I stood. Rebecca moved around me and opened the office door.

"Good luck, Dan"

"Thanks"

Well, that had just put a great big smoking hole in an otherwise promising day. It didn't take long to clear my desk and field the odd query from my co-workers. *Are you off, Dan? Yes, looks like I'm surplus to requirements now.. Oh well, good luck then, nice knowing you.. you too, you too.*

As I finished my goodbyes and headed out into the corridor, the phone rang.

The shop. It must be Miles.

I answered. "Hello?"

"Dan? Dan, what the hell have you done? Where the the hell has this twenty grand come from?? DAN???"

I probably left some of my colleagues with a slightly misleading impression as my fist pumped the air. *YES!!*

"Miles, I'll explain everything in just a little bit, ok? I promise. Get the kettle on, I've got something to do first but I'll be over in about an hour."

"Alright, but you'd better have a good explanation – this is all legitimate, all legal?"

"Skipper, you have my word on it."

Next up, a quick text message.

Hi Martin, I thumbed laboriously, *all OK w transfer, where u want to meet to get discs?*

Almost immediately, he responded.

Red Lion again. See you in half an hour.

Thankfully, I'd brought the discs with me – safely in my backpack, swaddled in layers of old T-shirts and boxers to keep them from being damaged.

I checked my watch. Almost 10am. Right - to the pub.

Thankfully, the Lion was experimenting with attracting the truly committed drinker and were therefore willing and able to serve me a mid-morning beer, which I attacked with a delicious sense of decadence. Between slurps I obsessively checked the discs in their protective nest of underwear – it may not have won any prizes for elegance, but in terms of functionality it got a gold star. Not a scratch on disc or envelope.

I was just coming to the end of my pint as Martin entered, radiating frosty businesslike .resentment. He made no greeting as he pulled up a stool next to me, simply sat down and pointed at the records.

"I'll have those. You can keep the pants."

Fair enough. He'd kept up his end of the bargain – and neither of us were here to make friends. Twenty grand had been deposited in the shops account and Chris and Miles were safe.. for a while, anyway. I passed over the discs, and watched as Martin ran a practiced eye over each, checking the grooves of the vinyl for scuffs and damage.

"Ok, these are fine. Now, I expect you to hold up your end of the deal, Dan. I don't want you to contact myself, Kate, or any of the family again, do you understand me?"

"Martin, you and Kate have brought me nothing but grief. I have no desire to involve myself with you ever again."

I finished the dregs of my pint, gathered my things and nodded him a curt goodbye, and stalked out. *Goodbye and good fucking riddance.*

Ten minutes later I was back on achingly familiar territory. The shop was more or less how I remembered it, albeit a good deal more cluttered. Miles' latent hoarding instincts had clearly been left to run wild in the last few months. Still, the old place felt like home. I almost felt like it was giving me a "welcome back" hug.

Miles bustled out of the back with two steaming coffees. I briefly wondered if the mugs had been washed at any point since my departure. *Probably best not to think about that too much.*

We exchanged some brief pleasantries, and I was able to reassure him that Chris seemed fine, there had been no relapses on the Sunday.

"Thank Christ for that. Maybe this will finally getting him looking after himself properly."

I was surprised – I'd always figured Miles to have been just as suckered by Chris' apparent invulnerability to any aspect of medical logic as I was.

"I think so. Keeping him off the booze is going to be tough though."

"He'll manage. One day at a time, that's the way to think of it."

"I guess, yeah."

The conversation staggered and stalled. We pushed it into a nearby layby and got down to business.

"Ok, well, Dan, could you tell me why the shop has twenty thousand pounds in the account that we didn't have at close of business on Friday?"

I cleared my throat.

"Yes. I can explain, although, it's not entirely.. you might not like the answer."

Miles stood and eyed me with arms crossed. "Go on."

"Ok, well, it all started the day you fired me. I was upset, particularly by the implication that I was a thief - "

"I didn't say that."

"You did kind of imply it, saying you couldn't trust me. So I thought, fuck it, if I'm going to be tried as a thief, I may as well *be* one. So I grabbed some of the 78s that were in that five grand house clearance bundle that me and Chris were cataloguing as I got my jacket, and left with them.

"So you stole from me." His voice hardened – understandably, really.

Deep breath. "Yes, yes I did. And I'm sorry about that. Anyway, as it turns out, the guy you bought them from was – is- the husband of an old school friend of mine, that blonde you saw me with months back.

That wasn't a house clearance you were picking up. It was a penance. He'd been unfaithful – with Louise, as it happens."

Miles' mouth fell open. "What, *your* Louise? When you were together?"

"Well, just around the time we had that break up. Right around my birthday, remember?"

"Yeah.. so that week you didn't hear from her.."

"Right, she was basically bouncing between us both."

"Wow. Jesus.. I'm.. sorry, Dan, that must have been hard to hear."

I half-smiled. "There's more. Basically, his penance was to get rid of the thing he loved most, which was his record collection.. and his wife got to have a free... fling, I suppse you'd call it."

"And you were the fling?"

"Yep."

"Did she know you and Louise... "

"No. At least I don't think so, I don't really know. I

think it was more the fact that she knew me from school, that was the connection. I think she just wanted to revisit her past a bit, have some fun. Be the girl she used to be for a bit." I thought of some of the things Kate had said to me.

"...I suppose I just want to forget sometimes that I'm someone's wife, and someone else's mum and just be me for a bit."

Even just telling Miles the story was helping.

"Anyway, Louise had told me that she was pregnant and I just assumed it was mine, so we'd moved in together. Things were.. well, they weren't always great." *Understatement of the fucking century.*

"I didn't know anything about Martin at this point, just that Kate was coming on awfully strong and I really didn't know why. One night we had a huge fight, me and Louise.. next thing I know she'd lost the baby."

"Oh, shit, Dan, I'm so sorry."

I had to pause for a moment. Despite everything I'd discovered since, I couldn't ignore the fact that *she might have been my daughter. And I would never know.* And that **hurt.**

"Anyway, not long after that, Martin shows up. I thought he was there to beat the shit out of me, but instead he sits down and tells me about the whole thing. Including the records. I guess with the baby and everything their whole weird arrangement was off. I needed someone to unload on, so I called Chris, and we went for a drink to patch things up. That's when he had his first hypoglaecemia attack."

Miles nodded, as the pieces of the puzzle seemed to come together.

"And then you told me about being twelve grand down, and it suddenly hit me how I could help – I rang him and persuaded him to buy them back. I had four 78s, I checked their value online and came up with the figure of five grand each. He did a transfer on Saturday, and I just met up with him in the Lion to hand them over."

Miles reached down to pick up his jaw. "Well.. Jesus, Dan.. that's... that's quite a story. I can't work out whether I should be angry with you or not."

I shifted uncomfortably. "Well, technically, I *did* steal from you.."

"Yes, yes you did, and if you ever do that again I will have you charged and done for shoplifting.. you never, *ever* steal from me." He sighed. "But on the other hand, if you hadn't.. I don't know if we'd have sold them, I certainly don't know if we'd have got a twenty grand lump sum....."

He extended his hand. "Shall we just call it quits?"

I smiled and shook it warmly. "Quits".

Chapter 30

Three pint glasses clinked together on a cold January evening in a corner table in the Red Lion.

"Cheers!" "Cheers!" "Cheers!"

"And a very happy birthday to you, young Daniel-san.. thirty-one, who'd believe it. You still can't grow a beard, can you?"

Thus spake Chris.

"Yes, yes, at least I'm not forty and drinking shandy like a gay" I grinned at him.

Miles eyed us from across the table. "Why don't you two just fuck and get it over with?"

"Who says we didn't while you were having a piss?" retorted Chris, gleefully.

"If you're taking ten quid off me, I'm damn well going to get something in return" I protested.

I know what you're thinking. That nothing's changed, the status quo has returned and *everything's alright again, happily ever after*. And in a lot of ways you'd be right. But not everything has stayed the same.

Kate, Martin and co – they kept their promise, and I kept mine. Done.

I never did hear from Louise. Her mum emailed me to say yes, she was ok – she'd had something of a breakdown after losing the baby though. Facing me was simply too much. She'd come round and picked up the baby things... it somehow seemed more appropriate than eBay. Over a cup of tea, she also explained that after the breakdown, Louise had been diagnosed with a mild mental illness. Borderline Personality Disorder, they called it.

"Her dad.. he always had his demons. Drink, terrible mood swings.. he died when she was only two. She doesn't remember any of that, but she's.. I see him in her when she has these moments. I think the baby pushed her over the edge. At least she's getting help now."

I could only feel sympathy for her. I'd never really got to know Louise's mum, but the more she talked, the more she described a life of struggle and compromise as she tried desperately to protect her daughter from the demons she carried. It was impossible not to admire that.

"She's getting a transfer from her office down to London. It's a fresh start for her, what she needs, really. So I really do think it's best for everyone if you leave her alone, Dan."

I agreed.

Chris – well, he hasn't quite managed to quit the booze. But he's drinking a damn sight less than he was, and couple that with eating healthier (avoiding the deep-fried and chocolicious food groups), he hasn't had a repeat incident in four months and counting. I'd swear blind I even saw him out jogging a few days ago, although he vehemently denies all knowledge of this.

Miles paid off the creditors and mercifully listened to Chris' advice. So let me show you around our new merchandise section. *T-shirts, posters, DVDs - that sort of stuff.* We're doing rather nicely, thank you very much. So nicely, in fact, that Miles decided he was going to need a full three-man squad to man the pumps. And you know what they say, better the devil you know..

As for me – well, it's the same old flat , but I've spruced things up a little. And now we're pulling in a good chunk more custom and profit, Chris and I have managed to chisel a pay rise out of Miles. I've been saving up, and got myself almost enough squirreled away for – guess what? - a car. Small – yes. Old – yes. But a car.

Getting back to the present - with Chris' new healthy (ish) living lifestyle, drinking ourselves unconscious and allowing the fates to guide us home like stumbling drunken homing pigeons was no longer an option. So as the evening drew to a close, we bade each other slightly slurred farewells and parted ways.

Flopping down on my sofa, I checked my messages. An email icon had appeared on the phone's touchscreen – oh, yes, dear reader, this is a brave new era, the old Nokia is discharged from active duty and enjoying a relaxing retirement at the bottom of my sock draw. I prodded it and felt my stomach lurch.

Inbox (1)

From: Louise Marshall

Subj: Hi Dan, how have you been?

I mulled this one over.

No. One thing the last year had taught me - some chapters in life close for a reason. And they should stay closed.

I pressed "Delete", and felt something – a weight, maybe a promise- leave my life forever.

Let it go, Dan.

My guitar (with shiny new strings) was propped up against the edge of the sofa. I leaned over, picked it up, and gave it a tentative strum. And as I did, I felt an unbidden smile cross my face.

Time for a new song.

Printed in April 2023
by Rotomail Italia S.p.A., Vignate (MI) - Italy